C000150181

OVID METAMORPHOSED

OVID METAMORPHOSED

edited by Philip Terry

Chatto & Windus

LONDON

Published by Chatto & Windus 2000

2 4 6 8 10 9 7 5 3 1

First published in Great Britain in 2000 by Chatto & Windus
Random House, 20 Vauxhall Bridge Road,
London SW1V 2SA

Random House Australia (Pty) Limited
20 Alfred Street, Milsons Point, Sydney,
New South Wales 2061, Australia

Random House New Zealand Limited
18 Poland Road, Glenfield,
Auckland 10, New Zealand

Random House (Pty) Limited
Endulini, 5A Jubilee Road, Parktown 2193, South Africa

The Random House Group Limited Reg. No. 954009
www.randomhouse.co.uk

A CIP catalogue record for this book
is available from the British Library

ISBN 0 7011 6941 9

Papers used by Random House are natural,
recyclable products made from wood grown in sustainable forests;
the manufacturing processes conform to the environmental
regulations of the country of origin

Typeset by Deltatype Ltd, Birkenhead, Merseyside
Printed and bound in Great Britain by
Biddles Ltd, Guildford

Contents

In memory of Kathy Acker

Introduction

T his book grew indirectly out of a rather different interest, in the fables of Aesop. Writers have always been drawn to fables, and reading them in turn led me to Ovid: John Dryden, for example, in his collections of fables from antiquity, includes a number of tales taken from Ovid's *Metamorphoses*. The first time I came across Ovid was when a classmate at school wrote an essay on his tale of Salmacis and Hermaphroditus and the rock band Genesis, an exercise that I considered sad and pretentious – I was listening to The Sex Pistols, The Slits, Siouxsie and the Banshees, Wire. More recently however I read Ovid from cover to cover, and was immediately won over by these rich and strange stories of seduction and metamorphosis. For a while I thought of reworking Ovid's stories, but quickly abandoned this idea in favour of an anthology. The range of stories and the variety of tone in Ovid is too much for any single writer – even Ted Hughes in his celebrated *Tales from Ovid* failed to capture the sheer variety of voices.

So I asked a number of writers if they would like to contribute to a collection: they could write whatever they liked, so long as there was some connection to the work of Ovid. As they responded and I started to receive stories through the post, for the first time in my life I began to get excited about looking in my pigeonhole at work. There were ups and downs in finding a publisher – one major publishing house liked the contributors, but not the theme, and suggested a book of football stories instead. Eventually, however, the collection went to Alison Samuel and Jenny Uglow at Chatto & Windus, who greeted it with enthusiasm.

Ovid (Publius Ovidius Naso) was born at Sulmo in central Italy in 43 BC and ended his life in exile at Tomis (present-day Constanza in Romania), where he died in AD 17 or 18. The body of work that he left on his death, including the *Amores (Loves)*, the *Ars Amatoria (The Art of Love)* and the *Metamorphoses*, has had a lasting – even unparalleled – impact on subsequent literature. The *Metamorphoses*, in particular, has inspired a vast and varied range of writers, including Dante, Chaucer, Marlowe, Shakespeare, Milton, Pope, Mary Shelley, T.S. Eliot and, more recently, Jorge Luis Borges, Italo Calvino, Emma Tennant, Roberto Calasso, Seamus Heaney and Ted Hughes.

In the visual arts, Ovid's impact has been no less pronounced. This is in part because Ovid is a supremely visual writer, both in his detailed description of setting and in his treatment of the pleasures of looking – whether voyeuristic (Actaeon) or narcissistic (Narcissus). Yet, above all, the belief that the nature of a person was revealed in his or her physical shape through metamorphosis – Lycaon, in Book I, becomes a wolf because he is rapacious and wolf-like from the start – has made Ovid attractive to artists. Stroll through any gallery and at every turn you will find re-inventions of Ovid's work. We meet the beautiful sea nymph Galatea in a Raphael; Jupiter and his lover Europa in a Veronese; the faithful old couple Philemon and Baucis in a Rembrandt. The minotaur stares at us menacingly from a Picasso; we see the fall of Icarus in a Chagall and in the frescos at Pompeii; and there are countless Ovidian tales in the paintings of Titian.

It should come as no surprise, then, that a supremely visual contemporary writer, A.S. Byatt, should not only be drawn to this material, but should take her inspiration, in part, from a painting, Velázquez's *Las Hilanderas (The Spinners)*, which represents the story of Arachne, told in *Metamorphoses*, Book VI. This is one of a number of Ovidian tales concerning the misfortunes of artists, where Arachne, through an ill-timed boast, becomes involved in a tapestry-making contest with the goddess Athene. Byatt's mixed-genre narrative, weaving together elements of autobiography, essay, art history and sheer story-telling, makes its own tapestry of interconnected tales. These include the story of Velázquez's painting and of Ovid's Arachne, and other tales involving spiders (both real and literary), forming a kaleidoscopic narrative that is both improvisatory and densely patterned, meticulous and de-centred; it no more resembles the tired shape of the traditional story than a spider's web does a piece of 'transfer' embroidery.

In the *Metamorphoses* Ovid himself stitches together some 250 stories from classical antiquity into one continuous narrative, beginning with the Creation and ending with the foundation of Rome and the apotheosis of Julius Caesar. Each of the stories is linked by the theme of metamorphosis, an idea that was not original to Ovid – a Greek poem, the *Ornithogonia*, had dealt with transformations into birds – but which, with characteristic zeal, he pushes to its absolute limits. Here, to give only a few examples, there are transformations of men into women and of women into men; of gods into animals; and of men and women into gods, trees, rivers, birds, animals, fish, amphibians, insects and flowers.

Ovid's ingenuity is also seen in his approach to the epic. In Sara Mack's translation, the poem begins:

My spirit is moved to sing of shapes changed into new bodies.
Gods, inspire my undertaking (for you have changed it too).

Ovid's poem, then, begins in ostensibly traditional manner, by
stating its theme – metamorphosis – and by invol ng the gods,
but this opening also contains the suggestion that th form of the
poem altered as it was being written. This in itself s subversive.
Traditional epic, like Virgil's *Aeneid*, is concerned above all with
stability, with the foundation of states and empires – so Aeneas
must avoid the metamorphic island of the enchantress Circe,
who changes men into beasts, in order to fulfil his epic quest.
And, in formal terms, epic displays a loyalty to genre, a fidelity
to the stability of traditional literary form. The *Metamorphoses*,
however, while it is written in epic's characteristic metre
(dactylic hexameter), is decidedly heterogeneous: it tells many
disparate stories, rather than pursuing one central narrative, and
it contains other genres besides epic, such as pastoral, didactic
and elegy, while often eroding and confusing the boundaries
between them. And it is not on the whole *serious*, but high
comedy.

When Ovid does deal with epic subject matter, he treats it in
the spirit of parody. Nestor's account of the battle of the Lapiths
and Centaurs in Book VI is essentially a parody of *The Iliad*,
where the aged Nestor recounts with inappropriately gloating
precision the means and manner of death of the warriors,
undermining any sense of the heroic. The result is a kind of
mock-epic, which anticipates Alexander Pope's *The Rape of the
Lock* and *The Dunciad* by some 1,700 years:

                                                    In that din
    Aphidas lay with every vein relaxed
    In endless sleep, unwoken, undisturbed,

4

Sprawled on a shaggy bearskin from Mount Ossa,
His wine-filled cup in his unconscious hand,
Out of the fight – in vain! Observing him
Lying apart there, Phorbas fingered firm
His lance's thong: 'You'd better mix', he cried,
'Your wine with Styx's water!' There and then
He hurled his lance and through Aphidas' neck,
As he lay sprawled face-up, the iron-tipped ash
Drove deep. Death came unfelt. Over the couch –
Into the cup – blood gushed from his full throat.★

The black comedy here is in part the result of an incongruity between form and content, the gravity of epic being undermined by the close-up detail, which proceeds like a film in slow motion. Elsewhere, as Italo Calvino has noted in *The Uses of Literature*, the *Metamorphoses* is a poem of rapidity, and here it is the high speed of narration that enables some of the poem's most gruesome moments to pass before our eyes so quickly that we barely register their terror, and even experience it as comic.

Of the stories collected in this volume, the majority take their inspiration directly from the *Metamorphoses*, and the variety of approaches and moods is a tribute to the heterogeneity of Ovid's poem.

Cees Nooteboom's 'Lessons' retells the story of Phaethon (*Metamorphoses* I and II), in which Tethys' grandson, with fatal consequences, asks his father Apollo, the sun god, to let him drive the chariot of the sun. Nooteboom's tale is nested in a contemporary story of betrayal and love in a Dutch *lycée*, which both reflects and enlarges upon this core. His conception of character is at once 'postmodern' and profoundly Ovidian: 'We

★ Ovid, *Metamorphoses*, trans. A.D. Melville (1986).

act as if it is fixed and unchangeable, but it changes all the time, until it is discarded.'

Nicole Ward Jouve's 'Narcissus and Echo' (*Metamorphoses* III) is set at an academic conference, where there are a number of psychotherapists, and no shortage of narcissists – chief among whom is the celebrated author, Miranda. The story not only re-works and echoes the Ovidian source – in which Narcissus, who ends up falling in love with his own image, is fruitlessly pursued by the nymph Echo, who is only able to communicate by repeating his words – but engages with the psychoanalytic tradition which, in the work of Freud and Lacan, has related the concept of narcissism to a whole nexus of psychological states, from jealousy to megalomania, and from depression to aggressiveness.

The story of Leda's rape by Jupiter disguised as a swan – best known to modern readers through W.B. Yeats's poem of 1923, 'Leda and the Swan', and retold here by Paul Griffiths – is not one described at length in the *Metamorphoses*, but it is illustrated in Arachne's tapestry in Book VI. Griffiths's version is the clearest illustration in this collection of Ovidian disjunctive style, the raw brutality of rape dissolved by an image-filled surface with the serenity of pastoral. And Griffiths artfully builds metamorphosis into the very texture of the writing, as different letters (marked in italics) progressively disappear from the story's vocabulary.

Two further stories take their subject matter from *Metamorphoses* VI: M.J. Fitzgerald's 'Antiquity's Lust' and Marina Warner's 'Leto's Flight'. The grotesque story of lust, mutilation, infanticide and cannibalism involving Tereus, king of Thrace, and Pandion's daughters, Procne and Philomela – retold here by M.J. Fitzgerald – has been one of the most frequently adapted tales: in drama, from Shakespeare's *Titus Andronicus* to Timberlake Wertenbaker's recent *The Love of the Nightingale*, and in stories like Emma Tennant's 'Philomela', which re-interprets it from a feminist perspective. M.J. Fitzgerald's version at first seems closer to a direct translation, and yet there are significant additions and differences of emphasis. Here, for example, Procne boasts of the beauty of her son Itys (which she does not in Ovid) and this boast threatens to attract the anger of the gods. In this way, Fitzgerald's story comes to resemble that of Ovid's Arachne (and, for example, Niobe), and in so doing suggests that translation, however close, is always a departure from the original: an interpretation, involving both repetition and inevitable difference.

Marina Warner's 'Leto's Flight', in contrast, freely adapts its source, deliberately confusing it with other stories. This kind of strategy was by no means unknown to Ovid, who in his own story of Narcissus and Echo combined two previously distinct tales for the first time. Ovid's Leto, pregnant by the king of the gods, Jupiter, flees the wrath of Jupiter's wife, Juno. In Warner's story Leto's flight is from the court of Cunmar – a character nowhere to be found in Ovid, but, as Warner explains in her study of myths *From the Beast to the Blonde*, a ruler of Brittany in the mid-sixth century, reputed to kill his wives as soon as they became pregnant. In a word, a precursor of Bluebeard. There are echoes of other stories here, too: Leto *hatches* her divine children, Apollo and Diana, confusing the stories of Leto and Leda. The two stories had already been identified in various re-tellings, and the name Leto is, indeed, a variation on Lada (Lycian for lady). There are also echoes of the stories of Romulus and Remus, and of Oedipus. Warner's narrative is itself metamorphic, a reminder of how stories can proliferate and change from one telling to the next, even as they are being told.

Ovid was as aware as any writer of the need to alter pace and style. One of the longest, as well as most touching, of the stories in the *Metamorphoses* is that of Ceyx and Alcyone in Book XI.

Ceyx, disturbed by the death of his brother, decides to consult the oracle at Claros, which is best reached by sea. His wife Alcyone, knowing how dangerous the winds can be to even the most sturdy ship, begs him not to go, but he insists. As Gabriel Josipovici reminds us in 'Heart's Wings', a meditation on the death of his mother, the distinguished translator Sacha Rabinovitch, Ovid's story is ultimately about the anxiety associated with departures, loss and death.

The story of Ceyx and Alcyone is, among other things, one of fidelity and, though not an isolated example in the *Metamorphoses*, it is vastly outnumbered by stories involving violent – often perverse – passions, especially tales in which the predatory gods rape their mortal victims: all in Arachne's tapestry are of this latter kind. Like the tapestry, Ovid's poem drains the dignity from the pantheon of Olympian gods, and almost certainly this is one reason why the book would have offended the Emperor Augustus. And while Ovid ends with verses in praise of Augustan Rome, as the culmination of historical destiny, his general message is that no state lasts for long, that change and disintegration are the hallmarks of human endeavour. This, of course, undermines the poem's overtly Augustan message. It was in AD 8 – the year when Ovid substantially completed the *Metamorphoses* – that he was exiled to Tomis, on the Black Sea, at the very margins of the Roman empire. Strictly speaking, Ovid was 'relegated', not exiled, and as such was allowed to keep possession of his property in Rome. To be sent to Tomis, however, was an especially harsh form of relegation.

In the poems of exile – the *Tristia (Poems of Sadness)* and the *Epistulae ex Ponto (Black Sea Letters)* – Ovid indicates that the reasons for his exile involved a poem and an error. The poem, most critics agree, was not the *Metamorphoses*, but almost certainly the *Ars Amatoria*; the error, less certain, might have been anything from a political indiscretion to the witnessing of some scandal, perhaps involving Augustus' adulterous granddaughter Julia, who was also exiled the same year, or her mother, Augustus' daughter (also named Julia).

Although the *Ars Amatoria* was published some fifteen years before Ovid's banishment, it is not difficult to see why it would have angered Augustus. It is a mock-didactic poem, essentially a handbook for adulterers, and as such it pokes fun at Augustan reforms, in particular his attempts to legislate morality by promoting marriage and making adultery a capital offence. In addition, many of the pick-up spots Ovid recommends are public buildings of particular importance to Augustus, such as the temple of Apollo on the Palatine. While the regime of Augustus – through the initiation of moral reform, civic building projects and the like – was trying to promote itself as ushering in a new Golden Age, Ovid ceaselessly undermined and punctured its hollow rhetoric: 'Today,' he writes, 'is truly the Golden/Age: gold buys honours, gold/Procures love.'*

Considered in context, then, the *Ars Amatoria* may be seen as demythologising political satire, and this, without doubt, was one reason for Ovid's exile. Paul West's story, 'Nightfall on the Romanian Coast', narrated from beyond the grave by a high-spirited and unrepentant Ovid, comes to much the same conclusion. As West puts it:

My own view . . . is that I was sent packing for being unfaithful to poetry, for not writing the wholesome stuff the Emperor wanted; as the Boss, he owned all that was thought, said or done. To put it in Soviet terms, I had refused to come up with tractor poems, paeans to hydroelectric stations, to the

---

* Ovid, *The Erotic Poems*, trans. Peter Green (1994).

founders of the party, to the rustic rabble and the proles of Rome.

Rosalind Belben's 'Disjecta Membra' and my own story, 'Void', have their roots in Ovid's *Ars Amatoria* itself. In Book I of the *Ars Amatoria* Ovid advises the adulterer to become acquainted with his quarry's maid, but only as a means to an end. In 'Disjecta Membra' Ovid ironically ignores his own advice as he becomes entranced by an African slave-girl. The slave-girl, in her meanderings from the margins of the empire, has happened to visit the real island of Circia, home of the mythological enchantress Circe. The island – described by Homer in *The Odyssey*, by Virgil in *The Aeneid* and in turn by Ovid in his *Metamorphoses* (also hinted at in Belben's story) – was traditionally described as heavily wooded, with oaks and rivers and herb-clad hills. Belben's slave-girl, though, tells of an island that is *flat*, and 'not wooded, no hills, not so many herbs'. Ovid is dumbfounded, and tries to account for her story by suggesting climatic change – 'I went beyond her understanding,' he says smugly – and there follow a series of further questions: has she seen Venus pass over the island in her swan-drawn chariot, and is the white flower moly (given by Mercury to Ulysses to counter Circe's spells) to be found there? Eventually, Ovid has to face the uncomfortable fact that the literary tradition might be wrong. Densely allusive and full of wit, Belben's story (like contemporary post-colonial writings) gives a voice to the barbarian, reminding us that the Roman empire was sustained by slave labour, and undermining the claims of knowledge and power that underpin the whole classical tradition.

My own story, 'Void', is essentially a free translation of passages from Ovid's *Ars Amatoria*, but framed in a way that suggests a parody of contemporary men's magazines, such as *FHM*. That such a juxtaposition might be possible brings us inescapably to the question of Ovid and feminism. The case against Ovid was clearly stated as long ago as the fifteenth century by Christine de Pisan in *The Book of the City of Ladies*, in which Christine speaks with the lady Reason. The passage is a gem, so I make no apology for quoting it at length:

'My lady, how does it happen that Ovid, who is thought to be one of the best poets . . . attacks women so much and so frequently, as in the book he calls *Ars amatoria*, as well as in the *Remedia amoris* and other of his volumes?'

She replied, 'Ovid was a man skilled in the learned craft of poetry, and he possessed great wit and understanding in his work. However, he dissipated his body in every vanity and pleasure of the flesh, not just in one romance, but he abandoned himself to all the women he could, nor did he show restraint or loyalty, and so he stayed with no single woman. In his youth he led this kind of life as much as he could, for which in the end he received the fitting reward – dishonour and loss of possessions and limbs – for so much did he advise others through his own acts and words to lead a life like the one he led that he was finally exiled for his excessive promiscuity. Similarly, when afterwards, thanks to the influence of several young, powerful Romans who were his supporters, he was called back from exile and failed to refrain from the misdeeds for which his guilt had already punished him, he was castrated and disfigured because of his faults. This is precisely the point I was telling you about before, for when he saw that he could no longer lead the life in which he was used to taking his pleasure, he began to attack women with his powerful reasonings, and through this effort he tried to make women unattractive to others.'★

★ Christine de Pisan, *The Book of the City of Ladies*, trans. Earl Jeffrey Richards, with a foreword by Marina Warner (1983).

If this is a protest against defamatory representations, it is also, in its picture of Ovid, a spectacular example of defamatory literature itself. In the *Tristia* Ovid warns his readers not to confuse the poetic persona with the author of the poem: 'My morals, believe me, are quite distinct from my verses – /a respectable lifestyle, a flirtatious muse –'* There is little reason to disbelieve him, for his work is full of experiments in the use of differing narrators. And de Pisan's account of Ovid's exile, return, castration and subsequent literary revenge on women – in a poem written some fourteen years *before* his exile – is not only confused, but entirely fanciful. Indeed, in an argument that aims to refute male assertions that women are faithless, Rectitude offers Christine examples of women who are notable for their fidelity; two of her examples, Thisbe and Hero, are drawn from Ovid.

Nonetheless, representations of Ovid as rake or as defamer of women, or both, have had considerable currency: we meet the defamatory Ovid in Chaucer, where Ovid's *Ars Amatoria* is one of the texts contained in the 'book of wikked wyves' owned by the Wife of Bath's fifth husband, and which she makes him burn; and Ovid the rake reappears in this very collection in Paul West's 'Nightfall on the Romanian Coast'.

From a woman's perspective, Sara Mack gave what is perhaps a more balanced, though sometimes contentious, view of the *Ars Amatoria* when she wrote in her *Ovid*:

Older women will probably be impressed with his perception that they often make better lovers than the young . . . all women will be pleased with his insistence that the pleasures of love be shared by both partners . . . On the other hand, any woman is sure to be infuriated by his claim that women

* Ovid, *The Poems of Exile*, trans. Peter Green (1994).

actually like to be raped . . . and nearly everyone today will be put off by the lack of sincerity advocated throughout.

Again, it is an oversimplification to attribute *any* of these views to Ovid himself: they are expressed through a literary persona, and a transparently obnoxious one at that.

Yet another of his poems, the *Heroides (Heroines)*, is itself a proto-feminist work, anticipating in its strategies much recent feminist fiction, from Jean Rhys's *Wide Sargasso Sea* to Michèle Roberts's *Impossible Saints*. Here, in verse letters from women in Greek mythology to their lovers, by whom they have more often than not been used and abandoned – Dido to Aeneas, Ariadne to Theseus, and so on – Ovid tells, from a woman's perspective, the stories of 'heroism' that the epic tradition had invariably seen from the man's point of view. In 'Hypsipyle to Jason' Michèle Roberts rewrites one of these letters. In Ovid, Hypsipyle – queen of the women of Lemnos, who have sought their freedom by slaughtering their menfolk – has been abandoned by Jason, who is now seeking the Golden Fleece with the help of Medea. Roberts recasts the story in a contemporary setting – 'You've gone. You left four days ago, at nine in the morning, speeding off in the little blue MG.' However, by making the sought-for Golden Fleece Hypsipyle's sex, she cleverly folds the masculine epic back on itself, feminising it by bringing the female body into the heart of the narrative.

Four more stories approach Ovid's work from a broadly feminist perspective: Patricia Duncker's 'Sophia Walters Shaw', Margaret Atwood's 'The Elysium Lifestyle Mansions', Joyce Carol Oates's 'The Sons of Angus MacElster' and Suniti Namjoshi's 'Eurydice's Answer'. Patricia Duncker's terrifying and gripping story is a feminist dystopian fable, reminiscent both of works like Margaret Atwood's *The Handmaid's Tale* and recent experiments in cyberpunk. 'For us,' says its heroine, Sophia, 'pornography was like religion used to be, a condition of being, the way we thought, the way we earned our livings. And rape can't exist if all women, women everywhere, all of them, always say yes, yes, yes.' The story rings the changes on Ovid's tale of the rape of Proserpine by Pluto, god of the underworld, who here presides over an underworld of sex shows and grotesque sexual services. The heroine, Sophia, is a reimagining of the nymph who attempts to prevent Proserpine's abduction, and is transformed into a pool of water for her pains. This Ovidian metamorphosis is in turn transformed by Duncker into the fluid, three-in-one identity that develops between the story's main characters.

Margaret Atwood's 'The Elysium Lifestyle Mansions' retells in spirited fashion the story of the Cumaean Sibyl. In *Metamorphoses* XIV, Apollo tries to seduce the Sibyl by offering her immortality – she accepts, but, as Apollo points out, makes the mistake of not asking for eternal youth as well. Nonetheless, she refuses to give in to Apollo's advances, even though he offers her this second wish if she does so. As such, the Sibyl stands as an icon of woman refusing male domination. Atwood turns her into a wry and spunky character, who, though shrivelled in size – 'I'm pretty conspicuous . . . carried around as I am in a three-foot-tall decanter – I can't eat out' – runs a successful business empire and thrives in the metamorphic capital-dominated world of the late twentieth century.

Another powerful female figure appears in Joyce Carol Oates's tale, which reinvents the story of Actaeon, who accidentally catches sight of the goddess Diana bathing, when he is out hunting, and as punishment is turned into a stag, subsequently to be savaged by his own hounds. Classicists have often been puzzled by the disproportion between the crime and the punishment; Oates's reworking, which lets us see the violence of the male gaze from the woman's point of view, provides an incisive answer.

Finally, Suniti Namjoshi's 'Eurydice's Answer', which, in Ovidian fashion, intertwines two stories usually kept apart (those of Orpheus and Eurydice and of Proserpine), boldly offers a woman's perspective on a story normally seen to be controlled by men.

Introducing their anthology of new poetic translations, *After Ovid: New Metamorphoses* – a book in some ways complementary to this one – Michael Hofmann and James Lasdun wrote that 'Ovid is once again enjoying a boom'. Since this was written in 1994 the 'boom' has continued, and in 1997 Ovid became a best-seller, in Ted Hughes's *Tales from Ovid*. In his short but suggestive preface, Hughes notes that the *Metamorphoses* is contemporaneous with the birth of Christ, and suggests that at this period belief in the Roman pantheon had collapsed, while Christianity was still some way off. For Hughes, Ovid's poem gives 'a rough register of what it feels like to live in the psychological gulf that opens at the end of an era'. It is this that makes Ovid relevant to our own times, our own *fin de siècle*.

Cultural critics writing on 'postmodernity' have suggested that we live in an era of incredulity, an idea that echoes Hughes's point and suggests that the notion of the postmodern might be relevant. Indeed, two landmark studies of postmodern aesthetics and fiction take their titles from Ovid: Ihab Hassan's *The Dismemberment of Orpheus* and Linda Hutcheon's *Narcissistic Narrative*. For Ovid, *post modo* meant 'the hereafter', not 'after modernism', but this ancient meaning seems apt in the way that his ghostly presence has made intrusions into contemporary culture. Critics have described 'postmodern fiction' as being characterised by play, irony, parody, heterogeneity, disjunctive style and difference, a list that uncannily resembles Ovid's strategies. The French philosopher Jacques Derrida argued that meaning in language is always deferred, never finally settled, always differs from itself. The *Metamorphoses*, in which one story sheds new light on and alters the signification of the one before, is a perfect illustration of this: it is not only the constant metamorphosis of bodies, but of meaning, that characterises the poem. This aspect of Ovid's work is picked up by Italo Calvino in his novels *If on a Winter's Night a Traveller* and *The Castle of Crossed Destinies*, both of which are encyclopaedic collections of different kinds of stories and have, in turn, influenced many writers, from Julian Barnes to Milorad Pavić.

Ovid ties together the disparate strands of his *Metamorphoses* with an extended speech from the philosopher Pythagoras, preaching the doctrine of metempsychosis. If Ovid were writing today, he might well have given this role of honour to Derrida.

A central modern insight is that a 'sign' has no inherent meaning, but is given one by its complex relationship to other signs that surround it. The point is beautifully illustrated by Roger Moss's story 'Hick, Hack, Hock', which opens this collection:

In the playground, the hand turns to paper. The other hand, two fingers opening and closing, turns to scissors. They cut the flat hand of paper. The scissors win.

The hands go behind backs. When they appear again, the hand that was paper has turned to stone. The one that was scissors is now paper. According to the rules, paper wins against stone. In life, it is not clear that paper wins against anything. But in the game, the open hand of paper wraps itself around the closed fist of stone, and the same hand wins again. When they appear for the third time, the first hand, with its fingers snipping the air, has turned to scissors. The second hand blunts the scissors with a curled-up fist of stone, and wins yet again.

Here, scissors, paper, stone carry different values, depending on the second term that enters the equation. The uncertainty and instability that result from such a perception infect the rest of Moss's story, which is in fact several stories, juxtaposed so that they alter – and are altered by – each other. Among these is the story of the young Ovid, dreaming of writing a book of metamorphoses that collects together the tales he has heard in his youth, and the story of the modern translator of the Penguin *Metamorphoses*: each fails in different ways. For each, the dream is transformed, just as the trees are felled and mashed into paper to make the book – a process of death in life, life in death, transformation after transformation.

Metamorphosis is inevitably connected with loss and death: points echoed in Gabriel Josipovici's 'Heart's Wings'. This anthology, which has gathered its contributors along the way, and lost them too, for one reason or another, has inescapably changed in the process of composition. The most irrevocable loss was undoubtedly the death of one of the book's leading contributors, Kathy Acker, in 1997: it is to her memory that the anthology is dedicated.

The order of the stories roughly follows Ovid's order of composition. Apart from Moss's story, three further pieces falling outside this schema have been placed either at the beginning or at the end: Ken Smith's 'The Shell Game', Victoria Nelson's 'A Bestiary of My Heart' and Catherine Axelrad's 'Report on the Eradication and Resurgence of Metamorphic Illness in the West, 1880–1998'. All three are metamorphic stories, but only loosely rooted in Ovid. The *Metamorphoses* itself contains a number of tales that celebrate pure invention, so it is appropriate that there should be a handful of newly invented stories here.

The riches of Ovid should be transformed to reshape the present, waking us up to the fact that nothing in our world is ever as solid as it seems, that our dreams of shopping schemes, luxury apartments, holidays in the sun, sex shows and success are no more substantial than the cloud-capped towers, the gorgeous palaces and the solemn temples of myth.

PHILIP TERRY

Hick, Hack, Hock

Roger Moss

I n the playground, the hand turns to paper. The other hand, two fingers opening and closing, turns to scissors. It cuts the flat hand of paper. The scissors win.

The hands go behind backs. When they appear again, the hand that was paper has turned to stone. The one that was scissors is now paper. According to the rules, paper wins against stone. In life, it is not clear that paper wins against anything. But in the game, the open hand of paper wraps itself around the closed fist of stone, and the same hand wins again. When they appear for the third time, the first hand, with its fingers in the air, has turned to scissors. The second hand blunts the scissors with a curled-up fist of stone, and wins yet again.

Each time the hands change, the voices say, *Hick, hack, hock.* This too is part of the game. It is as if the horrid lists of Latin words from the classroom can be turned to nonsense in the playground. *Hick, hack, hock.* This, that, and the other. Scissors, paper, stone. Until the bell rings, and it is time for both of them to go inside.

On stony ground, at the mouth of a cave, the woman picks up the leaves that have fallen from the trees. Some women have the gift of being able to hold your hand in their hand, and to read the future there. This woman reads the future in the veins and creases of the leaves that drop from trees. Softly she whispers to herself in gentle Latin phrases the messages she finds there. Patiently she gathers the most important messages into piles, and keeps them in a special place at the back of her cave.

Carefully the woman copies the messages from the yellowing leaves on to clean sheets of paper. She stitches the sheets together into volumes, until she has twelve. The knowledge that has fallen from the trees turns into twelve books, which she takes to the king.

The woman from the cave arrives at the king's palace with her twelve volumes in a parcel. She offers them to the king for a fabulous price. The king laughs at her, and tells her to go away. Quietly the woman goes away, and on the hard ground at the mouth of her cave she cuts six of the twelve volumes into kindling, and lights a fire. Calmly she watches as the leaves turn to light and dust. Stone, scissors, paper. *Hick, hack, hock.*

The woman goes back to the king's palace with the six remaining volumes in a parcel, and offers them to the king for the same price as before. The king dismisses her impatiently, and the woman goes away. At the mouth of her cave, she adds three of the six volumes to the fire, and watches impassively as the future contained in them is burned up and lost.

When she returns to the king's palace for a third time, still asking the same fabulous price for the three volumes that are left, the king does not dismiss her immediately. He turns to his advisers. He tells her to wait in another room. When he calls the woman back, it is to buy the three remaining volumes for the price that had first been asked for twelve.

Once the woman has returned to her cave, the king and his advisers look into the volumes they have bought. They begin to realise the wonderful knowledge that the books contain. A special place is built inside the palace to house the books. From that time on, whenever the king or his kingdom faces a dangerous crisis or a difficult decision, he and his advisers turn to the books in the palace, and are guided by the wisdom that they find there.

The boy in the classroom listens to the story of the woman's books with the same pleasure that he listens to all the stories he is told. He likes what happens in the story, and the way things change. He likes the way it makes him look with different eyes at all the leaves lying on the ground, unnoticed by nearly everyone. He likes the verses of the story, and the way the words are made to end in changing ways in his subtle Latin tongue.

When he walks past the ancient palace, where the three volumes still lie in their special room, he feels the same surge of pride that the other boys feel at all the stories they have heard of the times that Rome has owed its safety to the knowledge contained in the books from the cave. But he feels a separate satisfaction as well, not at what the story says about the wonderful knowledge that has survived, but at the solemn wisdom the story contains concerning the much larger quantity of knowledge that has been destroyed and lost, and from which no ruler and no country can ever hope to learn a thing.

At night, in his bedroom, the boy thinks about how, when he is older, he will make up for this loss. I shall become a poet, he says to himself, and I will put the wonderful stories I have heard, and the delightful variety of our Latin tongue, not into three, nor into six, nor even into twelve, but into fifteen books of wisdom and beauty. But the most beautiful and the wisest part of my poem will be in the way that it shows how everything changes and nothing lasts for ever. Beyond everything that men know and remember, there is always far more that is swallowed up and lost, and that finally turns to nothing. Even my own books, when I have written them, will not survive for ever. Pages from them will be torn into fragments to burn on fires, or cut into shreds and used to stuff shoes or to cover jars.

Eventually all of them will turn to dust. Paper, scissors, stone, *hick, hack, hock.* And this knowledge will be contained in my books, even as I am writing them.

In another classroom, the boy who was winning in the playground is failing in front of the pages of his Latin Primer. The stiff dead lists of words in front of his eyes turn to nothing in his brain. The terrifying voice of the master booms above him.

Monstrum horribilis, the master loves saying, turning the booming phrase around in the great cavern of his mouth. *Monstrum horribilis*, he says, telling the terrified boys the story of the monster in the cave. *Monstrum horribilis*, he says again, reminding them that *horribilis* means covered with hair.

Stiff with the certainty of failure, and aching in head and stomach with the impossible effort of getting the horrid hard lists to lodge in his brain, the boy glances up at the master looming over him. The master is a giant standing over him. Mouth, nostrils and ears are the entrances to dark cavernous pits where monsters live. Whiskers and hairs sprout from the nostrils and ears, like the dying dried-out shrubs that stand at the mouths of sulphurous caves. Yellow smoke-stained teeth are the gravestones of earlier victims, that show in a jumbled row whenever the rasping monstrous voice booms from the cavern of the mouth.

The boy looks at the pale inert hand lying on the desk, keeping the book open at the page of word-endings that has to be learned. The page, like his brain, turns to dead, hard stone. If I had scissors, the boy thinks in his hatred, I would put out the eyes of the monster, and all of us would be free. Paper, stone, scissors, *hick, hack, hock.* But there are no scissors. There is only his useless hand, and, in his useless brain, the hopeless knowledge of failure.

At night, the boy tries to turn his mind away from the words that have to be learned for the morning. By half-closing his eyes, he can change the darkness in the bedroom into a shower of turning varied shapes, so that there are a thousand falling things like leaves, filling the emptiness. When he opens his eyes, by squeezing the muscles that are in his brain, he can make the window at the foot of the bed into the tiniest, farthest window; or he can make it so large that it fills the whole of his vision, swallowing up the rest of the bedroom, the bed, the boy in his bed, and everything. Or he can take his mind off the pages of his Primer by turning to face the wallpaper beside the bed. In the half-light, the patterns on the paper turn into faces, houses, letters, creatures, trees.

One night, he puts his hand out to touch a loose flap of wallpaper he has never noticed before. As soon as he touches it, the flap of paper uncurls its wings and flies across him in the darkness. All the monstrous horrid shapes that fear takes come screaming in on the boy immediately, and swallow him up. He lies under the covers, hands stiff by his sides, eyes shut tight, unable to sleep another moment until the morning.

Early in the morning, in the back room of her cottage, the retired classics mistress rises to her task. Nobody knows the pleasure it gives her, the secret satisfaction that will not let her rest. All her life, she has tried to give her girls an idea of the exciting precision and variety of the Latin tongue, and of the satisfaction of putting it into something workably precise in English. She knows how rarely she has succeeded, and that for every one girl who came to share her pleasure, there were a dozen or two dozen others for whom Latin would always remain the dullest, hardest thing imaginable.

Now she has been given the chance to pursue this pleasure without having to give a thought to anyone else. She has been asked to do it so that, in the end, thousands of people, far more than all the girls she has ever taught, may be able to share her delight. She has been asked to turn the fifteen books of Ovid's Latin poem, the *Metamorphoses*, into English prose. At the end of my life, she says to herself, I have the good fortune to turn all that dancing variety of language and of stories into something of my own, a book that may outlive me. To metamorphose the *Metamorphoses*, she laughs to herself in her glee. Even if there is only one reader who is brought close to sharing my excitement, she thinks to herself, the work will not have been for nothing.

When the work is hard, and the straight lines of English prose are too stiff for the subtle variations of Ovid's verse, she goes for a walk in the wood near her cottage, and turns her mind to the restless diversity of leaves on the trees to refresh herself. Softly she whispers phrases as she walks, turning various versions over in her mind, until she settles on the one that works best. Even when she is certain of failure, and her brain seems frozen in front of the charms of Ovid's pages, still she persists, patiently searching for the best words, carefully making changes in what she has already written. And then there are days when she is king, and everything goes smoothly. Quietly smiling to herself, the retired teacher secretly becomes a succession of sensual, agile, elegant Romans, lounging on divans, circling the hall of a palace in an intricate dance, bringing cups of wine to her lips in between the witty well-turned phrases that come from her mouth.

In the wood, trees are already growing that will become her book. The flesh will be cut and crushed and soaked and mashed. The mash will be bleached and strained and pressed and dried and cut again, process after process, transformation after transformation, until trees have been turned into paper. Ink will be pressed on to folded sheets, and folded sheets will be stitched and trimmed, stone, paper, scissors, *hick, hack, hock,* until in the end the trees will have changed into thousands of copies of the woman's book.

The day will come when a package arrives at the cottage door, containing half a dozen fresh copies of the woman's translation, sent by her publisher. Opening the package, she is torn between pride and anxiety, with the pages of the finished volume in her hand. She thinks of all the failures contained in what she has written, all the beauty and subtlety that has been lost. And she thinks with satisfaction that at least it is done, and that now it is there for others to read.

Walking in the woods, she finds herself looking at the trees with different eyes. Thank you, she says to the unknown trees that have made her book. Thank you for allowing yourselves to become my book.

One of the copies is bought by Robin, Robin who knows no Latin, but whose pleasure in the stories he reads is real and lasting. Robin can, if anyone can, read between the stiff lines of the translation, to find the dancing beauty in the stories themselves. Robin can, if anyone can, see beyond the knowledge that the stories contain, to the knowledge behind the stories of everything in the world that cannot be contained in books, and of the way that everything, in the end, is swallowed up by change, and does not last.

But Robin dies. Robin's own life does not last. All the fears and horrors of life, beyond anything that can be contained in books, come screaming in on Robin in the night, swallowing him up, and Robin dies. His life is cut short. He is buried in the hard ground. Only his books remain. Scissors, stone, paper, *hick, hack, hock*. The books are packed away into boxes, and given to Robin's friends. The friends plant a cherry tree in the ground where Robin used to walk. Nothing is left of Robin but the boxes of his books and a tree.

Some of the boxes are given to a friend who used to be the boy lying awake at night, trying not to be afraid of Latin, or of his Latin master, or of the other monsters in the dark. He opens the boxes, including the one containing a copy of the *Metamorphoses* of Ovid, and arranges the books. He thinks to himself that perhaps now he will try to overcome his old fears, and read the book he has always turned away from. And this is how the trees in the wood, which became the copy of the Latin poem that was turned into English by the woman in her cottage, and was bought by the young man who became a tree, came into the hands of the friend who was the boy who hated Latin.

All this is a long time ago, the bedroom, the classroom, the playground, the cottage, the palace, the cave. The book remains. But the book remains unread. However hard he tries, however old he gets, the friend never quite escapes the monster at his shoulder, looming over him whenever he thinks of Latin, or of Latin books, freezing his heart, and turning his mind to stone.

There are several occasions when he starts, thinking that this time perhaps he will succeed. Each time he reads through several books, but he never finishes. He reads three, six, perhaps as far as twelve of the fifteen books. But he never gets much beyond Orpheus. Something in him has stayed unchanged, as if a part of him was long ago turned to stone by the nightmares of school. He can never get beyond his old hatred of Latin, or the deadness it has left in his brain. He can never get beyond the flatness of the English prose to the pleasure and the elegance that he is willing to believe the poem contains. Too many times, the book falls unfinished from his hand. Too many times, with moving and with rearranging things, it is put back into boxes, or placed on out-of-reach shelves, and forgotten.

Time passes. Everything changes. Age comes. The leaves on the trees turn yellow and fall to the ground. The teeth in the mouth stain and loosen in the jaw. The hand that was a boy's hand mottles with liver-spots. The fingers stain with nicotine.

The thinning skin turns to paper and lifts away from the bone. Everywhere, ageing is a yellowing and loosening of things. The pages of the unread book turn yellow with age. The glue that binds them hardens and cracks. If he picks the book up now, it sheds yellow leaves, and the loose pages drift to the hard floor. Scissors, paper, stone. *Hick, hack, hock.* The woman who comes to clean gathers the forgotten sheets of Ovid's book and adds them to the fire, where they become a moment's burst of light, and turn to a tiny quantity of dust.

The Shell Game

Ken Smith

A pproaching over the long flatness of the lagoon, the city rose out of the water in hazy afternoon sunlight, its domes and towers no more than clouds on the sea. It was a dream everyone should have. They pulled up at the Riva, and he stepped out alone into the city, checked into his hotel, took the air of the evening, ate, drank a little red wine, returned early to bed and slept deeply, aware through his sleep of the rain on the red tile roofs beneath his window. In his dream he met a dark woman with dark eyes and flashing black hair who explained to him in the dialect of that district that *Venezia* meant simply *the place to come to*. And then she was gone.

In the days that followed he walked, randomly, exploring the city at his own pace, content to be without map or guidebook in streets and alleys where water lay at the end of everything, the flat slow movement of the inner sea rippled by its commerce. He did not seek conversation and fled from those he heard speaking his own language, content to let it go, to rest from it and let the babble of unknown tongues wash over him. One slow afternoon as he drank wine in a café in some remoter *campo* he became slowly struck by the silence of the city's afternoon nap, a few pigeons shuffling and dozing in the dust, sparrows squabbling over crumbs. Across the far end of the square a thin trail of tourists passed purposefully to and fro, and suddenly in English a child's voice broke the silence: *But these are wild birds.* And with that siesta came to an end, and the square woke slowly as a bell struck the fourth hour, and the magazine stand that had been till then a cabinet of shadows opened again for business. At windows shutters opened an inch or two, curtains twitched, and at one a hand emerged holding a blue enamel jug and began watering the geraniums in the window box. From their high perches canaries dropped their small thin notes, a radio burst briefly into dance music and was turned low, someone yawned loudly, and in a doorway one of two old men made the next move in their long slow game, a piano ran back and forth across a practice piece of Chopin. The city woke, as if a wind had stirred it, and the tide began churning at the timbers. Suddenly the pigeons gathered into a flock and flew up on to a church roof, and everywhere there were echoes, voices calling just offstage, an air of events about to happen, news about to break.

He wandered the alleys of the honeycomb, peering into empty tombs and glass boxes in side chapels where the waxy flesh of dead saints slowly rotted through the centuries. The city was ancient, alien, old loot stacked everywhere. The movements of the citizens and their speech seemed to him, northern puritan that he was, dramatic and exaggerated. Those two men across a street, loudly discussing some weighty matter, their faces animated, their arms waving, seemed about to come to blows. And then they laughed, embraced, and went their different ways, briefly calling back to each other. It was speech always on the edge of song, gesture always on the edge of dancing.

At night, standing on a bridge, he saw the approaching shadow of a gondolier on the further wall, and then the shadow of the boat's prow, like the clef of coming music, but boat and boatman never appeared. From another bridge a stout woman in a ball gown sang an impromptu aria in high soprano. All seemed strange, and not strange. He felt the oddness of being outside his language, in a place he knew no one. Sometimes the faces and figures of strangers approaching or receding would suggest people he knew, and he would turn to look, about to call a familiar name, only on closer inspection to see his error. He confused left and right, cold and hot, high and low, up with down, and he was forever hearing Italian as if it were his own tongue, making instant meaningless translations. It was a habit he had hoped to leave behind, this persistent listening for meaning, but he found he couldn't stop, just as on a long ocean voyage the eye, starved of the familiar, seizes habitually on the chaos of the waves and resolves them momentarily into the known images of horses, bushes, trees and rocks. It is a persistent need, this urge to make sense, though it makes no sense of itself. One afternoon waking from a siesta, the radio by his ear began delivering the hour's rapid news but in his head the words formed into meaningless meaning: *And let me tell you who else is a boxer.* And then: *So what are you gonna do with a Marks and Spencer's cotton bra?* He rubbed his eyes, realising he had misheard, sat up, turned off the radio, put his hand beneath his pillow for his watch, and found there a round sea-shell, its spiral writ small the spiral of the galaxy, in the same progression. He turned it about, a curl of faint brown shades centred round a blue eye, the coil of shell called baby's eye in the coil of his fingers. He had picked it up somewhere, and was sure he'd last night put it on the nightstand, to watch his sleep. Puzzled, he didn't recall putting it under the pillow, and put it back on the nightstand. He showered and left.

Towers that leaned in the soft footings of the city slowly sinking back into the sea from which it had risen. Along the north shore he sighted down the perspective of the Fondamente Novo, and gazed across at the walled tree-shadowed Isle of the Dead. He took a boat there, where he sought in the Evangelical cemetery among the dead who were not turned out of their graves every fifteen years for the grave of Ezra Pound, finding only a hand-lettered board nailed to a tree, pointing at an angle to a bright ring of flowers. Two men standing to row a boat seemed in the distance to be walking on water. The timbers of the wharfs stood in the water like upright men. Every step was a new revelation. At the Lido he paused to sit in the sand, and took off his shoes, and discovered movement beneath his bare feet: flat white grubs wriggling upwards that seemed interested in the soles of his feet. In sudden panic he ran off, fearing the infested sand beneath his feet. In the grass round white stones, like tiny eggs. Walking in the gardens he picked up a fallen cone, flinging it away when he found inside its opened fins a baby snake, hissing. In the museums masks, armour, a helmet like a horned wolf's head, crossbow arrows in their flèche like a box of lethal pencils. In the churches chalk-white effigies of saints posed in mid-miracle, their wire haloes rusty. And on the wall of an alley into Campo San Marco a faint image from another time, white paint fading into the wall: an arrow and the word *Kommandatur*. Everywhere carved stones, images and reliefs pillaged from Constantinople and other unnamed unknown cities to the East.

The place was unfathomable, bizarre. Perhaps, he wondered, the secret of the Serenissima was that they did not know, and lived with the daily miracle of their survival on the sand banks, their empire the domain of secrecy, the dominion of not knowing. They had stumbled on the thought that God did not know either, and used men to think with, like pieces in a game. The rules were simple: when the city was at peace, the winged lion gazing out to sea, the high casements of the watchtowers sighting every angle of approach, the book was open. When the book was closed, the city was at war.

Night fell. He came back to his room, slightly drunk, to find the bed turned down and the baby's eye shell again beneath his pillow. He put it back on the nightstand. He slept, dreaming again of the dark woman of his first night's dream. She was far off, treading the water to her waist, her dress floating about her on the flat sluggish surface, a great open flower. In some other life he dreamed they were lovers, working in the long shallow armpit of the lagoon among the kelp beds harvesting shellfish, living on the long slow sea-swell. It was a dream that seemed to have nothing to do with him, someone else's dream leaking into his. They waded in the tides that were barely tides, sifting the sand banks, their rakes and shovels scraping up the blue mussels, open and iridescent for a moment in the sudden air. Through the watery haze she drew closer, and closer still he saw she wore a necklace of the round baby's eye shells.

On his last day he examined the palace. The Room of the Inquisitors was any courtroom of varnished wood, benches and tables, but a floor of black and white marble tiles that trumped the eye and confused the feet. On the wall a Bosch painting of souls in torment. And in the corner, through what appeared to be merely a cupboard, the door that opened into the Chamber of Torment, where a rope hung innocently above a block, and the light from the high window streamed down into the place of agony. Steps led up to the cells of the prison sweltering in the heat beneath the roof. Here it was enough to be accused to be guilty, stretched, imprisoned without length of sentence, without charge, sent to the galleys or hung on a gibbet or discovered at dawn buried feet in air in the *campo* as a warning to others.

And behind all this the Segretto: the palace behind the palace, housing the government behind the government. Behind the opulence and ceremony of the palace, plain quarters without fuss or decoration where the real business was conducted in small bare offices up back corridors and stairways. Behind every Doge, a shadow Doge; behind every official an unknown double in a government of shadows.

In the afternoon he slept again, woke again, and found the shell again under his pillow.

There was only the maid, one of several who cleaned the rooms and made up the beds. This was some game she played, the shell game. It was a silent game, played in secret, with only two moves, hers as she put the shell beneath his pillow, his as he moved it back to the nightstand. In both they acknowledged the presence of the other. He would never work out which of the maids she was, or whether it was a game they all played, or whether it was played on all the guests. And if he left it there, would this indicate some sort of invitation? Beyond the one move he could make – or not make – there were no other moves. He was involved in a secret, a moving back and forth like the tides, like the corner game in chess, not knowing who his partner was.

Whoever she was, he was already in love with her.

Void

Philip Terry

 fter the takeover by the Aphrodite conglomerate all articles had to be on sex. In the old days we'd done articles on pottery, fishing, tennis, cars, more or less everything in a word. Now we only did sex. We were still able to cover topics like cars, certainly, yet we had to do it from a sexy *angle*. Vintage cars were no go, leggy blondes on bonnets were in.

Tesco's

If in search of a partner, don't despair. Remember: there are plenty of available women at large, and tracking them down won't be hard. It can be enjoyable too. The aisles at Tesco's are as good a place as any to begin talent-spotting: normally there's always something very tasty on display. A man in search of a lover can look nowhere better. Rich rewards are certain. As swarming bees fill parks and playing fields, hovering over the clover, bobbing from dandelion to dandelion, so girls swarm to Tesco's in crowds.

As redactor of the poetry section I was a bit miffed at first. How was I to do *poetry* from a sexy angle? *N'importe!* Then I had one of my brainwaves, fairly predictable, perhaps, yet it felt like a brainwave at the time: I'd do a weekly selection of *love* poetry. What simpler! I sat down excitedly at my PC and concocted a list of likely candidates, from Sappho to Tony Harrison, shook the lot into alphabetical order (no problem for the Whipp-IT) and *voilà*! There it was: my next six months' work completed in seconds. I was feeling rather pleased with myself, zesty, so I resolved to nip over to the Café Sélavy for a light snack. I gave Di a bell to see if she'd come along – she wasn't interested for some reason or other. Afterwards, a little heady, I called in to speak with the new editor, Gross.

Image

People say that dress is very important here, and in a way they're right. Yet try not to be one of those who spend a lot of time in front of the mirror or who stick pots of gel in their hair. A nice pair of jeans and a good shirt is all that's needed. Nothing too fancy. There's no harm in getting one's hair done at a good salon, yet don't waste time with hair-spray or wax. Leave that to the ladies. Yet keep the nostrils free of bristles, and watch those hairs in the ears. Above all a man needs to keep himself clean. Wash the back and face properly to avoid spots – and don't forget the genitals.

When I left the editor's office I was cross. Very cross. I was *fâché*. In brief, his lordship wasn't interested in my project – he had plans of his own he said. Poetry was to be axed – it had no mass-market appeal – and he wanted me to deliver a new weekly slot, anything I liked so long as it was sexy. Like some latter-day Gradgrind he wanted facts, not fiction, and he wanted them fast: dismissing me, he gave me till the end of the week to present my draft. I was indignant, for I'd taken a certain pride in the poetry section, had even, I felt, commanded an appreciable readership. What was happening to the world, I wondered? I'd hand in my notice and decamp.

E-mail

Too mannered a style is likely to repel the girls, so take care. Write in an everyday manner, with familiar yet well-chosen words. If she rejects the message, files it as trash, press on – she may look at it later. In time intractable oxen take the yoke, schoolboys learn to do homework. There is nothing as soft as water, nothing as hard as stone: yet the constant dripping of water hollows the hardest granite. Keep sending messages – in the end, with perseverance, she'll be won over. To begin with she might send back angry notes, protesting 'Lay off, for God's sake!' Yet what she wants, what she really really wants, is for the messages to keep coming. Be a pest, at the end of the day that's the only way to win.

On reflection I decided not to give in so easily. I didn't want Gross to have too facile a victory. I'd take him on. I'd write his sordid slot if it was the last thing I did. I sat myself in front of the Whipp-IT, took hold of my pipe and waited for inspiration to come. After a short while my pipe lay dormant and I'd made no progress. My mind was a blank, as was the screen of the Whipp-IT. *Anything I liked so long as it was sexy.* I didn't see myself as an Agony Alec, nor did I wish to mastermind an interminable series of confessional-style interviews with men on their bedroom habits. Ben Bishop, thirty-five. Head of Foreign Exchange at P.K. Marks. Has slept with more than ninety-five women. I'd have been interested in a piece on changing libidinal mores in the West, starting with the Greeks. Yet this might take a lot of work and Gross still find it lacking. Then I had a better idea.

Skill

In love as in all else, skill is indispensable. The skill-less man won't get anywhere. Whether one is in search of a steady relationship or simply a good night on the town, skill will be needed. As the saying goes, skill and confidence are a winning team. Skill can control love itself. Many people, when they're in the mood, simply dive in and don't think twice. And, certainly, there's a lot to be said for spontaneity. Yet if a man has skill on his side, there'll be a proportionately greater chance of reaping the greatest rewards from the occasion when it arises.

I'd been wrestling with Ovid's *Ars Amatoria* in the evenings. On and off I'd been working on a translation, yet it wasn't really coming together as I'd have wished. What if I were to redirect this project and present it – in prose – as my slot? I'd have to take a few liberties with the original, certainly, even stray into the realms of *free-translation* if I were to get away with it, yet despite my reservations on these matters the project had an irresistible appeal. Firstly, it kept me in work – it gave me a theme. Secondly, it acted as my secret revenge on Gross. He'd never spot the trick, so the joke was going to be on him. In this way the project kept a roof over my head and threatened the stability of the roof over his. What better?

Dogs

Go to the dogs: the broad arena offers loads of openings. Here there's no need of secret finger-talk, private signals, nods and winks: stand right next to the woman who's most attractive, breathe down her neck, give her a winning smile. Then invent some reason to start a conversation – anything will do. Ask who owns those dogs trotting by: discover her preferred canine, then back it later on. If some lager spills on her dress, wipe it off. If her coat's trailing, grab it, make a great to-do of saving it from the dirt. If she permits it, reward is instant: a licensed peep at perfect thighs.

On my way home from the office I dived into a little second-hand bookshop I knew to grab any versions of the Ovid they might have – they were very obliging, had three. Took me for a postgrad – at my age! I set to work that evening, preferring not to commence the project in the office in case my constant looting of Ovid's *Ars* seemed odd. To start with I reread the poem from start to finish, to refresh my sense of its overall design. I decided rapidly that I'd have to concentrate on Books 1 and 2, which gave advice to men on where and how to catch a mate. Book 3, with its advice to women, was inappropriate for a men's magazine. Having in this way narrowed down my target, I looked more closely at the first two Books, jotting down any ideas in the margin as I went. So as to avoid anachronism I allowed myself to change the locale when necessary: there was no point sending my readers to the woodland shrine of Diana near Aricia. Similarly, I saw few prospects for javelins and chariots. And I let myself play with the order of the poem whenever necessary.

Season

It's a mistake to imagine that only ferry companies and farmers need pay attention to the season. Grain cannot always be committed to the disloyal soil, nor bow doors to the ball-shrinking sea. Similarly it's not always wise to chase girls; the occasion will often condition the victory. Times to avoid are:

BIRTHDAYS

BREAKDOWNS

DIETS

DRIVING TESTS

EXAMS

LOTTERY WINS

PERIODS

PERMS

There are certainly others too – it will pay to keep a list, adding to it when occasion arises. Never make a move at these times. Best sit tight: those who set sail at the wrong moment hobble home with a dismembered vesicle.

Pretty soon I'd arranged my data by heading, and I set to work translating this information into blocks of prose. The voice which emerged was neither Ovid's – even if it shared his cynicism at times – nor my own, yet rather that of a different persona altogether: a species of lecher-come-man-of-the-world for the most part, yet not entirely. The whole enterprise was very T-in-C, yet I tried to work at the tone till this wasn't too transparent. Finally, when I felt I'd hit the mark, I showed these early drafts to Gross.

Timing

Timing might be seen as part of skill, yet I give it a separate entry since it has a bearing on more aspects of love than performance alone. Timing is as important when dating as in the sack. Even in those first moments of a nascent relationship, when a man doesn't know whether it's game on or game off, timing is of the essence. In order to break into a conversation with the object of desire, it doesn't really matter what's said, it's more important to say it at the right time, so as to get heard. Keep an eye on her, while ogling the competition, wait till her friend's gone to the toilets. That's the moment to make a move: sitting on her own she'll have her defences down. Taking the seat next to her, pay attention to bearing — she'll be more interested in looks than anything else at this stage. And where opening lines are concerned remember the importance of first impressions. Don't say anything too corny.

This time, it seemed, I'd got it right. Not only did Gross approve the project, he positively gave it his benison. He even praised its modernity! *La vache!* We agreed SEX-TIPS as an apposite title, and he allowed me to present the pieces beneath the *aegis* of a pen-name. VOID'S SEX-TIPS was destined to start the following week. It was all stations go.

Exercise

The importance of exercise can't be stressed too strongly. Exercise of the whole body. Try going jogging twice a week. And go swimming too if at all possible. The swimming pool is an ideal place for talent-spotting as well, a chance to get a good look at what's on offer in the area. If swimming doesn't appeal, there are plenty of alternatives which will do: archery, tennis, allball, golf, anything at all. In the case of golf, don't neglect the nineteenth hole. Like the swimming pool, it's a good place for talent-spotting, especially if older women appeal. Avoid snooker, however, darts too, and above all avoid going to the gym. It won't help to be smelling of smoke and beer, nor is there any point spending time somewhere that doesn't allow mingling. Many gyms now hold women-only sessions, so be warned. Whatever one's personal preference, however, it's exercise which is the key.

Take-off went well and my slot seemed to go from strength to strength over the first few weeks. Gross was very pleased with the general response. Men all over were pleased, he said, it was the sort of thing they'd been wanting to hear for a long time. It was so fresh. We even had some letters asking VOID's advice on specific sex-related problems. How important was length? What was to be done with smelly feet? There was, indeed, little on the down side, only one acescent and incognito fax: F★★★ VOID.

Complexion

Lovers need to be pale: this is the proper complexion for love. Only an anaemic look will do the trick. Try TOTAL BLOCK *— don't be tempted by parasols.*

After the keenness of the initial response, to stop things from flagging, Gross had some T-shirts printed, which were given away to selected readers. FOLLOW THE VOID. VOID IS LOVE. My slot became widely talked over in many circles, even if the T-shirts didn't make the front page of *Paris Match*, yet I kept wondering when someone was going to blow my cover. This, after all, had been my initial plan – so as to embarrass Gross – yet as week followed week, and soon weeks slipped into months, nobody seemed to notice the deceit. VOID became the talk of the town, while Ovid rolled over in his grave.

Drink

A word of warning is called for on the matter of drink. Keep the mind clear and the feet steady. Above all avoid drinkers' brawls, never get involved in a scrap when it can be avoided. Drink of an evening was intended to promote high spirits and games. Yet while excess can be damaging, to act pissed can help. Stammer words and roll eyeballs, then however sex-laden the speech, it'll be blamed on the booze. This way she can get to know what the man within really thinks of her. And if it backfires — booze is to blame.

One day I met Di for a bite at the Café Sélavy. I remember the occasion distinctly, for the place was teeming with workmen. Almost immediately she mentioned VOID. I was certain she was going to mention Ovid too, and blow my cover. After all, she had a degree in Classical Civilisation, albeit from a Polyversity. Yet I was mistaken. With *acharnement*, she went into an endless diatribe on sexism and sexploitation, charging my magazine with being reactionary, spoke of complicity with the backlash against feminism. I said nothing. It was clear that Di, and many other women in her office, if she were to be believed, reckoned VOID's SEX-TIPS extremely OFFENSIVE. She finished off by asking me if I'd do something to stop it. Told me it was my obligation, as a NEW MAN. I was deeply embarrassed, yet said I'd do anything in my power.

Feet

No girl I have ever met has been attracted by smelly feet. Yet this is no reason for a man to be ashamed if he's the sweaty type — he can see this as part of his maleness. As long as it never gets beyond control. There are plenty of good deodorants on the market which can solve the general problem. Personally, I stick to 'Thor', it has a strong male image and not too potent a smell; however, there are plenty of other brands to choose from which are as good. Where looks are concerned, don't neglect footwear. Many women maintain that one can tell a man by his shoes. Yet don't be misled by this: it doesn't pay to be too showy. It's best to avoid extremes, like cowboy boots and sandals. Slip-ons are a safe bet.

The following day at work I revised the forthcoming SEX-TIPS on the Whipp-IT, toning them down if anything, with deference to Di. For example, I remember deleting a passage on the flabby stomachs and backsides of older women. Later, I took the machine on at chess, beginners' level. People had the impression I was working, while in reality I was playing chess; or being beaten at chess, it came to the same thing between myself and the Whipp-IT.

Presents

Don't be too lavish with presents – anyone can win over a lover that way, yet they'll soon have their pockets emptied. As every gambler knows, a prize held back breeds hope: if one can contrive to catch her present-free, she'll keep on giving lest she give in vain. Every girl knows a thousand ways to fleece an ardent swain. When she's in a mood for spending she'll take him to the sales, ask him to inspect the merchandise – it's so cheap! – give his expert opinion. She'll slip into something sexy and give him a snog, then insist he pay for it, swear it'll really satisfy her, insist she have it right now, that she really really needs it. No, tricks like this are to be avoided. A sensible man has to tell her at the beginning he's skint, that he's between jobs, that money can't win love. That way, even if she lets him down, at least he won't be the worse off.

There was an easing off at work for a few days after this, leaving plenty of time for me to get beaten at chess by the Whipp-IT, time and again. In the end, lighting my pipe, I resorted to watching the Whipp-IT play itself, *beat* itself, which gave me a certain sadistic thrill. One day, I was alarmed to find two letters among my correspondence which took VOID to task. One was a complaint from a chap who'd tried to accost a woman in Tesco's and finished with getting ejected by the store detectives

– they had the whole thing on CCTV and were going to press charges. The other was from a woman, and complained that E-MAIL was sexist.

Waterfalls

Waterfalls, whether or not accompanied by the added boon of a nearby mill, are romantic places, and their isolation can be handy. Here a man may chance on a maiden on her own. If she's to his fancy, it's okay to bring force to bear – force like that always goes down a treat with the women. Indeed, what they'd love to give freely, they'd really prefer to have stolen. Coarse love-making drives them wild, the boldness of raw passion excites them – and the woman who was almost forced into sex, yet managed to get away, while she may feign relief, in reality feels disappointed. If things get problematic afterwards, don't worry. Let's face it, only the base gives delight; a man only wants to get his end away, and finds added joy when this comes from another's pain.

It was company policy at this time to ignore complaints, so we did. As Gross said, what was the point in being a writer if nobody ever got offended? We gave both letters the scissors treatment. Regrettably, while we had no way of foreseeing this, these first written complaints were only the thin end of the wedge. As the days went by, to great alarm, the complaints grew and grew and ignoring them became correspondingly harder and harder. Typical complaints relied heavily on the word 'sexist'; others complained of 'macho ethics', the denigration of 'woman-as-object', some bemoaned VOID's 'phallocentrism'.

Older women

If she's no spring chicken and already applying anti-wrinkle creams and tinting her hair, don't ask her date of birth – leave this sort of thing to the Passport Office. Women of this age-bracket and above are well worth it. Moreover, they have experience and know-how on their side, and compensate for their age with art, concealing their years with expensive powders and ointments. Best of all, they have a million positions for the sack, many more than The Joy of Sex *contains. For novices, new bottled wine will do; for me, a fine claret that has ripened over the years. Does anybody disbelieve me? Take me at my word, I promise satisfaction.*

Complaints peaked after the appearance of VOID on WATER-FALLS. The piece was seen – with a certain logic, granted – as an incitement to rape. Recent statistics had shown that rape was on the rise again, and VOID, along with several readily available video nasties, was targeted as an IMPORTANT FACTOR. We received an avalanche of mail, containing several letters from prominent feminists, and another acescent and incognito fax: F★★★ VOID.

Availability

Always remember, every woman can be trapped. Any man can catch a bird if he sets his nets right – once this is mastered the thing's as good as done. Swallows will more readily cease their singing in spring, and crickets lie silent in the corn, than a keen lover's entreaties fall on deaf ears. Why do men not acknowledge that they can win any woman in sight? The girl who responds with a no is rare indeed, and whether or not they're game, an amatory proposal will be cherished by all. And if she doesn't take the bait, rejection carries no shame. Yet how can rejection follow when joys delight? What we don't possess has ever more charm than what we do. The grass is always greener in another man's garden, the cattle over the road have fatter teats.

Before we knew it we were swarmed by libbers. It was like Greenham Common all over again. When we kicked them from the foyer, they took root on the stairs. When we kicked them off the stairs, they camped by the front door, not for an instant ceasing to rail at their attackers: 'Fascist bastards!' 'Alien aggressors!' 'Men!' We were forced to call the police in, to keep the peace, and soon the parking lot was swarming with Panda cars and Black Marias. The women carried banners.

VOID = RAPE

AVOID VOID

Opening gambits

Avoid things like 'Does madam come here often?' or 'Haven't we met somewhere before?' If it's appropriate, ask her if she'd like a drink, or, if she's a smoker, whether she'd like a cigarette. This way, before committing himself, a man can get her talking and form some impression as to her character. A lot can be decided in those first few moments, so it's best to take one's time. And even after the romance is off the mark, when he's been going steady with her for two or three weeks, what a man says is still very important. Is it the moment to give her a French kiss? The time to reach for her breasts? This kind of decision, certainly, is finally in the hands of the party concerned, and is dependent on a lot of criteria. Yet whatever decision is reached, be certain to make the move with the help of an appropriate opening gambit.

Soon the libbers had pitched their tents in the fields opposite. It was going to be a friendly protest, they said. They lit bonfires and toasted tea-cakes, forever playing their cheap banjos, chanting their inane slogans:

> VOID spells RAPE
> to every girl,
> so say Sally, Jane
> and Shirl!

It was not my idea of a *fête champêtre*. It became impossible to concentrate at the office, and there was a bad atmosphere.

Aphrodisiacs

There are plenty of aphrodisiacs on the market these days, from Spanish Fly to Danish Egg, all sold on their bedding-power. My advice is steer clear. Giving aphrodisiacs to women can be a real danger: they can interfere with the brain and promote schizophrenia. Nasty tricks of this kind are to be avoided. To get a lover a man needs to have charm, and this cannot be achieved by good looks alone. If he really wants to try aphrodisiacs, he might go for those which spring from mother earth herself. Eat white onions from Spain, enrich the diet with avocados, honey and the tasty kernels of the pine tree.

While everybody else at the office was negotiating with the police and the libbers, trying to end the protest, I was becoming increasingly concerned that my cover might be blown, that someone might bring Ovid into the debate. In a way my worries were hypocritical, yet at the same time that I wanted my trick to be discovered – in the end – I was enjoying my work in a way I hadn't for years; so I didn't relish the prospect of being laid off, which was inevitable if a revelation came. As it happened, I need not have worried as I did. For while the crisis was receiving ever-increasing media attention, and people started associating themselves with one side or other of the debate, the exiled Roman poet was never mentioned. As Ovid himself said, anticipating one of the moderns by over 1,900 years: 'Poetry, I fear, is held in small esteem.'

Season

Never forget the importance of season. As there are bad times to strike, so there are good. These often fall immediately after positive or negative events, so be alert. Be on the watch for some of these:

BEREAVEMENTS

BIRTHDAYS

DIETS

EXAMS

FESTIVALS

HOLIDAYS

LOTTERY WINS

PERIODS

SEPARATIONS

SHOPPING SPREES

These are only a few ideas to be going along with – it'd be easy to add to the list. These really are the best moments at which to strike. If a man sets sail now, he'll come home to port with swollen nets.

The libbers carried on toasting their tea-cakes and playing their banjos, waving their banners and chanting their slogans. Things at work became tense: nobody was able to concentrate on what they were doing and it became impossible to meet important deadlines. Gross was always in a shitty mood, and while he was adamant that we had to stick to principles, that we weren't going to give an inch to these lesbian vagrants, his temper flew in my direction more often than not. To make matters worse, the media debate was swinging more and more against the magazine, against VOID, and sales, which had soared in the first weeks of the protest, had now dropped to an all-time low. Gross was not happy, and, increasingly, I felt like a pariah.

Poetry

Nobody cares for poetry. Girls aren't interested – they prefer expensive presents. Any ignorant blockhead finds a welcome if he's rich. Today really is the Golden Age: gold gets friends, position and love. If Byron dropped in, accompanied by the Graces, yet short of cash, he'd be shown the door at once. The only time to flatter girls in verse is St Valentine's day – a bawdy declamation, the trashier the better – this will do to win their love. Sophisticated or plain silly, at these times they'll take an ode composed at night time, for them, as a welcome present.

Things had reached the point where something had to give, and the decision had to be in the hands of Gross. Not only was he editor – indirectly, the whole thing was his creation. If he'd let my selection of love poetry see the light of day the libbers might never have batted an eyelid. One afternoon he called me to his office, solemnly told me I was to take a month's leave. That VOID was to stop, following the appearance of those in press, at least till the crisis blew over. He told me that my job was safe, that personally he rated my work, he even gave me an idea for a new slot I might like to take on, on the sex lives of insects. He wanted me to cover something less controversial. I met Di that day at the Café Sélavy. Told her I was going on leave; and of the editor's decision to end the VOID slot. She was delighted – thanked me for my good work, said I was a winner. Evidently, she didn't connect my leave with the VOID affair.

Two-timing

No man can be expected to stick to a single girl. Have a good time by all means, yet act with discretion. Don't boast of affairs simply to boost the ego. If well-hidden liaisons are discovered nonetheless, deny them flatly. Never be slavish, don't resort to excessive flattery – to do so is certain proof of wrong-doing. Go for it in the sack, that's the only way to win her over, with a screw so good it eradicates all misgivings.

I was away for a month, in what felt more like exile than leave. I spent some time in Constantinople – I can't bear to call it by its official appellation – visiting the temples and palaces, then spent a week or so on the Black Sea, a desolate, barely habitable region. I sent a few postcards – one to Di depicting the harem at Topkapi – telling people what a great time I was having, and that I wished they were here; yet in reality I was bored to tears, dying to get back to *terra nostra*. The Ottomans are a dreary race, all kilims and cartomancy.

Variety

Women's characters are all different. To trap twenty hearts calls for twenty different methods. Some soils are best for barley, some for genetically modified oats, and some for rye: they can't all be grown in the same field. Women have as many altering roles as the protean gods. One needs to adapt oneself as occasion demands, to transform oneself, like the shape-changer, into water, then a horse, now a dog, a hog, a headless bear, sometimes a fire. Some fish are got by trawling, some with nets, some with line and hook. Above all, don't attempt the same method on all age-brackets: an old bird will spot the nets from afar.

When I got back things had altered irrevocably, as if by some bizarre sea change. There were no tents opposite the office block, no chanting femos. Traffic was flowing normally. There were no Panda cars, no Black Marias. When I went into the office – *C'est pas possible* – it was no longer there. After the initial shock, one of the porters told me we'd been relocated on to floor eighteen. Here, I was greeted by the new editor, Goodman, who welcomed me back with open arms. I'd find editorial policy somewhat changed, he said, now that the Aphrodite conglomerate had gone into receivership. My desk was new – false mahogany – yet the Whipp-IT was still in place. I switched it on. Lit my pipe. Had a few games of chess. Lost. Then I spotted the NO SMOKING sign.

Ending a relationship

Ending a relationship is never easy, especially if it had some happy moments, yet even the brightest stars fade, and there's always a time when it's best to close shop. An amicable parting is best – don't dash to the bench from the bedroom, and let her hang on to any gifts to avoid litigation. Be pitiless, don't go all soft when she starts to cry – women teach their eyes to sob at will. Silence is strength: the lover who reproaches a girl is inviting her to prove him wrong. Don't give reasons for wanting a separation: foster a grievance, don't give her it in black and white.

The new management regime had a new brief: 'Sexy not Sexist'. And Goodman gave the go-ahead to my long-cherished selection of love poetry. I battled with limbo in the Whipp-IT, emerging the victor in the end, and re-began work on my selection, avoiding Ovid to be on the safe side. I printed some risky pieces, yet the slot proved to be well liked, giving rise to no protest.

In the end things were resolved fairly satisfactorily. Gross got the boot and I'm still in work. Yet the victory seems hollow somehow, for it took place behind my back. Paradoxically, now, I look back on those days beneath Gross with nostalgia. Yet it still irritates me that nobody spotted my scam.

Hypsipyle to Jason

Michèle Roberts

Y ou've gone. You left four days ago, at nine in the morning, speeding off in the little blue MG. A kiss, a wave, a toot on the horn, and you shot away.

I watched you vanish out of sight around the bend in the lane then came back into the empty house which suddenly felt much bigger. It isn't empty of course. But I've had to discover a new relationship to the space which is your absence. I've forgotten what unbroken solitude, day in, day out, is like. I'm no longer used to living on my own. All day long we work in our separate studios, not seeing anyone, not talking, as though we're on two different islands, and then at night we throw rope bridges across; we're together. Last night I was woken by an owl hooting outside, and reached for you, and you weren't there. The bed felt too wide, even though I'd filled it with pillows.

While you're away I listen to the silence. I discover that the silence here is full of sounds. Sitting on the front step, cradling a glass of red wine, I can hear the rasp of invisible crickets, the thrumming of bees sucking at the geraniums, the skitter of lizards dashing from rock to rock. I distinguish the song of different birds, from the cawing of rooks to the cooing of wood pigeons to the squabbles of chaffinches, blackbirds and bluetits over the nuts and bread I've put out for them. Jays and magpies whirr through the orchard. Sparrows zip past my ear, showing off the tight neat circuits of their flight, dart round the pines at the side of the house once or twice, then shave back past my cheek again. The wren nesting just above the doorframe does the same when I go in or out, just to show me who's boss. A dark streaking whistle of wings and she vanishes. Then a moment or two later I spot her hopping along the path under the honeysuckle arch, sidling back towards the door to reclaim her territory.

Aeroplanes dawdle across overhead in the afternoons. A sound of summer I remember from childhood. Lounging outside, sprawled on the grass hearing planes go by, high up. Another constant thread of gentle noise is that of machinery. This time of year the tractors are out till late at night. Sometimes I hear them coming home at nearly dawn. With rain threatened, the harvest must be got in as fast as possible. The rain won't wait and nor must the corn.

In the meadows surrounding the house the cows and bullocks chew grass noisily with slapping jaws. Sometimes they low and bellow at each other across the dividing hedges, suddenly get frisky and thump up and down their pastures. You can hear their hoofs beating the ground. At six o'clock every evening a deep hum rises as the milking machines are switched on in our neighbours' farms. You can't see most of their houses behind the gentle hills enclosing our tiny valley, but you hear their vehicles trundle along the road that joins the bottom of our lane, their dogs bark on the other side of the forest. You hear the women hullooing at the geese, rounding up the turkeys and ducks and chickens at night, driving them into their sheds.

The silence is made up of all these sounds, and it's also a geography which opens up around me and under my feet. A new country which now I must explore.

Your absence means no one telling me ridiculous jokes or clowning to make me laugh, recounting anecdotes about your day in the studio and tales of your childhood and sudden memories of your earlier life which just pop up on to your tongue, no one putting on silly voices, doing imitations, singing exaggerated loud snatches of pop songs or old-time music hall, teasing me, inventing nonsense words and crazy poems which you recite aloud, calling for me in elaborate imitation bird-song, dropping things and cursing, thwacking the axe on to logs of wood, walking around warbling and whistling upstairs as you run your bath while I sit by the fire, playing jazz very loud while I get the supper on. Your voice my music. I listen for you. When you've been out doing the shopping I hear you coming home when you're still a mile away, my ears are attuned to you, there's a slight alteration in the silence which is you changing gear and then five minutes later you arrive, charging up the slope to the house, pull up outside the back door, scattering gravel. Over supper, by candlelight, you tell me your secrets. In the bath, reclining opposite me, you lift your foot and stroke the curly blonde hair on my cunt with your toes. The golden fleece. In the night, in the darkness, you whisper to me words of love as you hold me in your arms. You are my treasure. I want to give you everything.

Now, while you're not here, while you're far away, I hear your voice all the time, whether I'm working indoors or digging the vegetable garden or lounging on the front step watching the evening light go pink on the roof of the farmhouse across the valley.

So don't come back just yet. Stay away just a little while longer.

Let me enjoy delay and lack and have a honeymoon of not having you. Give me the time to miss you more, to relish that, to feel even more lonely. Desperately to long for your return. To wait impatiently by the open door hours before you're due. To walk about in this full, roomy solitude and this resonant silence, to compose this letter, my ship that sails to you, my freight, my spell magically conjuring your presence on paper, imagining what we will do and say on your return, words I shall not need to write down and send to you because you will have come back, you will be here with me and I'll never despatch this letter but tear it up into bits and scatter it, white fragments falling silently like our clothes on to the floor.

Lessons

Cees Nooteboom

hat was it that I always told my class? Purely as *form* Tacitus' *Histories* are annalistic (yes, you oaf, that means in the form of annals and not what you think), but he frequently interrupts his narrative in order to stick with the strict order of events. Perhaps I should do the same: buy a sun hat, get my head together, keep past and present apart, go up the hill, flee the tortuous labyrinth of the Alfama, rest for a while in the cool shade of a *bela sombra* by the Castelo de São Jorge, contemplate the city lying at my feet, survey the state of my life, reverse the order of the clock and make the past run towards me like an obedient dog. I would, as usual, have to do everything myself and I might as well start straight away. But first a sun hat. White, woven straw. It made me considerably taller. 'Hey, guys, Socrates is wearing a poofter's hat on his specs.'

Of all the minds corrupted by the swinging sixties, our headmaster's was the most severely affected. If he'd had his way we would have been getting tuition from the pupils. One of his choicest inventions was that staff could sit in on each other's lessons. The few who sampled my classes did not come back for more, and I myself only tried two. First I joined the optional religious instruction class, which was attended by only three pupils and in the course of which the good Doctor of Divinity was alienated from the Christian love-thy-neighbour principle for once and for all. The other lesson had to be hers, of course.

Why? Because she had never deigned to look at me in the staff room. Why? Because I dreamed of her at night such dreams as I had not dreamed since adolescence, and because Lisa d'India told me what a *fantastic* teacher she was.

And it was true. I had found a seat at the back of the classroom, much to the embarrassment of the gawky teenager next to me, but *she* pretended not to notice my presence. I had asked her if it was all right, and she had said: 'I can't stop you, and who knows, it may do you some good: I'm going to talk about death', and that was curiously inaccurate for someone with scientific aspirations because her lesson was not so much about death as about what comes after, about metamorphosis. And although hers was of a different order than mine, the subject of metamorphosis was familiar to me. It was many years since I had sat in a row of desks, and because of the reversal of the habitual roles I suddenly saw what a peculiar profession teaching really is. Twenty or more people are sitting down, just one stands; and the knowledge of the one on their feet is somehow supposed to be transmitted to the still-empty brains of all the rest.

She looked good, her red hair waving like a flag through the classroom, but my enjoyment of the spectacle was soon cut short by a film screen being unrolled in front of the blackboard and the nondescript beige curtains being drawn. 'Mr Mussert is a lucky man,' she said, 'his very first lesson and right off he gets to see a film!' Jeers all round.

'Keep your hands to yourself, Socrates,' I heard someone say in the dark, and then it grew quiet, and a dead rat appeared on the screen. It wasn't a big rat, but it was tremendously dead – mouth slightly open, some blood on its whiskers, a final glint from a half-closed eye. The broken body lay somewhat arched, in the pose that bears the irreversible mark of death, of arrested motion, of the inability to move ever again. Someone made retching sounds.

'No need for that.' It was her voice, short, almost like the crack of a whip. It was quiet at once. Then a sexton beetle appeared on the screen. Not that I knew that that was what it was, but she said so. A sexton beetle, wearing the flaming colours of a salamander. I saw a noble creature, ebony and deep ochre, with what looked like escutcheons on its cuirass. Or rather, her cuirass.

'This is the female.'

That had to be true, because it was she who said it. I tried to envisage what this meant. Someone else was doing the same, for a voice said: 'Nice bit of stuff!' No one laughed.

The beetle started digging a miniature trench all round the dead rat. A second beetle came along, but it was far less active.

'The male of the species.' It would be.

The female began to push against the stiff, unyielding corpse, shifting it very slightly with each nudge. The dead do not wish to be disturbed, whoever they are. The beetle seemed to want to bend the rat's rigid body: the thick, armoured, gleaming black head battered repeatedly against the cadaver, a sculptor working on an outsize block of marble. The image on the screen jumped from time to time, indicating breaks in continuity.

'The film has been edited, as you can see. The whole actual process was recorded. In all, it takes about eight hours.'

The abbreviated version was pretty long, too. The corpse grew rounder, the legs became tangled, the rat's head was pushed deep into its soft belly, the beetle danced its *danse macabre* around a furry ball.

'This is what we call the carrion pellet.'

Carrion pellet, I tasted the phrase. Never heard it before. I am always grateful for additions to my vocabulary. And it was an interesting one. A furry ball of rat flesh, slowly rolling into the trench.

'Now she is going to mate with the male in the grave.' Someone smacked his lips in the half-light. She switched on the light and turned her gaze on a big, spotty boy in the third row.

'Don't act so shuttered,' she said.

Shuttered. What a word! Said in the flat North Holland way. The light had been turned off again, but I knew then that the vague emotion that she already invoked in me had suddenly been promoted to love. *Don't act so shuttered*. The two beetles scurried around to get on top of each other as though under orders, which of course they were. We are the only species that has strayed from that purpose. The same awkward bungling as ever, odder still because most animals don't tend to lie down for it. The antics on the screen had something of an informal dance with one partner having to shove the other around, all in complete silence. A dance without music (the grating of those carapaces must make a deafening noise). But possibly beetles don't have ears, I forgot to ask her about that. The two tanks fell apart and one started pursuing the other. I had lost track of which was which. She hadn't.

'Now the female is driving the male out of the grave.'

The classroom buzzed, the girls making high-pitched sounds. In the midst of it all I could hear her low, conspiratorial laugh, and I felt insulted.

The female started digging a second trench. 'For the egg chambers.' Again such a novel term. This woman was teaching me new words! There was no doubt about it, I loved her.

'In two days' time she will lay her eggs there. But first she is going to tenderise the carrion.'

Her eggs! I had never seen a beetle vomit before. I was sitting in the classroom with the woman I loved and I watched as the science-fiction head of a beetle, magnified a hundred times, vomited green bile over a pellet of carrion that had resembled a dead rat less than an hour ago.

'Now she is gnawing a hole in the carcass.' And so she was. The excavator, mother, egg-bearer, lover, murderess mamma, chewed a lump out of the ball of rat and regurgitated it into the hole she had extracted it from. 'She's making a food-trough.' Carrion pellet, egg chamber, food-trough. And the acceleration of time: in two days the eggs, five days later the larvae. No, I know time cannot be speeded up. Or can it? The eggs are pale and gleaming, seed-coloured capsules, the larvae more gently ringed, the colour of living ivory. Mother takes a bite of puréed rat, the larvae lick the inside of her mouth. Everything is connected with love. Five hours later they are eating by themselves, the next day they are crawling around in the rolled-up cadaver. *CAro DAta VERmibus:* flesh given to worms. Latin scholar's little joke, sorry. The light was turned on again, the curtains opened, but what was really turned on was her hair. Outside the sun was shining, the branches of the chestnut tree swayed in the wind. It was spring, but the notion of death had slipped into the classroom, the link between killing, mating, eating, changing the voracious, serrated chain that is life. The class melted out of the room, leaving the pair of us standing rather awkwardly face to face.

'Next week, mites and maggots.'

She said it provocatively, as if she could tell that I was a bit taken aback. Everything I had seen seemed in some way or other to have to do with rage. Rage, or volition. Those grinding mandibles, the medieval stamping of those mating carapaces, the gleaming, blind masks of the larvae licking food out of the armoured mouth of their mother – life in the raw.

'The never-ending story,' I said. Well done, Socrates, any other great ideas lately?

She puffed up her cheeks. She did that when she was

thinking. 'I don't know about that. There's sure to be an end at some point. There has to be a beginning, too.' Again that provocative look, as if she had just invented the notion of transience and now wanted to try it out on a scholar. But I was not going to be driven out of the grave that easily.

'Do you want to be cremated?' I asked. That question works wonders in any company. The addressee is reduced to a mere physical encumbrance which must at some point be disposed of. That has a certain piquancy, especially in erotic situations.

'How do you mean?' she said.

'A forensic pathologist once told me that it hurts.'

'Nonsense. Well, I suppose there's the possibility of some local sensation.'

'Local?'

'Well, when you burn a whole match it curls up, which obviously creates enormous tension in the material.'

'I saw a public cremation in Nepal once, on a river bank.' I was lying, I had only read about it, but I could envisage the pyre.

'Oh. And what happened?'

'The skull exploded. An insane sound. As if they were roasting a huge chestnut.'

She laughed, and then she stiffened. Outside in the play-ground – do they still call it that? – Arend Herfst and Lisa d'India strolled by, wearing tracksuits. That was legitimate, he was the team coach. Herfst was on his best behaviour. With his set grin the poet took on something of the larvae I had just seen.

'Is she a pupil of yours?' Maria Zeinstra asked.

'Yes.'

'What do you think of her?'

'She is the joy of my old age.' I was over thirty, and said this without any irony. Neither of us looked at him, we just watched how the woman beside him redefined the space outside, how the centre of the playground shifted as she walked.

'Have you fallen for her, too?' It was intended to sound mocking.

'No.' It was the truth. As I have already explained.

'Can I sit in on one of your classes next week?'

'I'm afraid you won't enjoy it.'

'Let me be the judge of that.'

I looked at her. Green eyes half-hidden by her red hair, a bouncy curtain. A galaxy of freckles.

'Why don't you join my Ovid class. I'll be dealing with change, too. Not rats into pellets of carrion, but still . . .'

What should I read that afternoon? About Phaethon and half the globe being consumed by fire? About the dark recesses of the underworld? I tried to imagine how she would sit in my classroom, but I could not.

'Well, see you then,' she said, and off she went. When I entered the staff room some time later I saw that she was in the middle of having an argument with her husband. His fixed grin had taken on something of a sneer now, and for the first time I saw that she was vulnerable.

You ought to change out of your tracksuit before getting into tragic discussions, I wanted to tell him, but I never say what I think.

Life's a bucket of shit that keeps being added to, and we have to drag it around with us till the end. St Augustine is supposed to have enunciated this; unfortunately I never looked up the Latin text. If it is not apocryphal it is sure to be in the *Confessions*. I should have forgotten all about her by now, it is all so long ago. Grief is supposed to be etched into your face, not into your memory. Besides, it is old-fashioned, grief. It is seldom talked about nowadays. Bourgeois, too. Haven't grieved in twenty years.

It is cool up here in the park, I followed a white peacock (why isn't there a special word for *all* white animals?) as if my life depended on it, and now I am sitting on the wall of the castle, looking out over the city, the river, the dish of sea beyond. Oleander, frangipani, laurel, great elm trees. A girl is sitting nearby, writing. The word 'goodbye' is drifting in the air around me and I can't seem to catch hold of it. This entire city is a goodbye. The fringe of Europe, the last shore of the first world, it is there that the corroded continent sinks into the sea, dissolves into the infinite mist which the ocean resembles today. This city does not belong to the present, it is earlier here because it is later. The banal now has not yet arrived, Lisbon is reluctant. That must be the word, this city puts off the moment of parting, this is where Europe says goodbye to itself. Lethargic songs, gentle decay, great beauty. Memory, postponement of metamorphosis. Not one of those things would find its way into Dr Strabo's *Travel Guide*. I send the fools to the *fado* taverns, for their dose of processed *saudade*. Slauerhoff and Pessoa I keep to myself, although I do mention them, I direct the poor sods to the Mouraria and to the Brasileira for a cup of coffee, and for the rest I'd sooner keep my mouth shut. I won't breathe a word about the soul-changes of the alcoholic poet, the liquid, multiformed persona who still roams the streets of Lisbon in all his sombre brilliance, who has insinuated himself invisibly into tobacconists, quaysides, walls, dark cafés where Slauerhoff and he could easily have been together, unknowingly.

The liquid I. The subject had arisen after that first and only time she came to my class. She wasn't having any of it, and I can never explain exactly what I mean. *Regio Solis erat sublimibus alta columnis . . . Metamorphoses*, Book II, that was how I had started my lesson. Maria Zeinstra had sat there watching me, while d'India translated in her high, clear voice: 'The palace of the Sun was a tall building with tall columns . . .' and I had said that I preferred 'lofty' to 'tall', and that it was better anyway not to use the same word twice, and she had bitten her lip hard as if to draw blood and had repeated: 'The palace of the Sun was a lofty building with tall columns . . .' and only afterwards had I got it into my thick Socratic noddle that I was the only one still in the dark about the affair, and that d'India knew that Zeinstra knew and that Zeinstra knew that d'India knew she knew, and all the while I ranted on about the *fastigia summa* and Triton and Proteus, and about Phaethon slowly climbing the steep path to the palace and having to keep his distance from his father because he could not bear the searing light of the Sun God. Oblivious to the third-rate theatricals in the rows in front of me, I was rabbiting on about Phaethon's destiny. Regret? No! None? Any idiot would have seen the fear in d'India's eyes, and of course I can still see her before me, the eyes of a wounded deer, her voice clear as always, but much softer than usual. Only, behind her eyes I saw other eyes, and it was to them that I spoke of the son of the god who sought to encircle the earth in his father's chariot. It is obvious from the start that disaster will befall him, that Apollo's foolish son will come crashing down with his golden chariot and fire-breathing horses. I leaped to and fro in front of the class like a whirling dervish, this was my star performance. The purple gates of Aurora flew open to admit the doomed youth with his horses under their jewel-studded yoke, the misguided progeny headlong to his rendez-vous with death. His downfall would be retold a million times in those hexameters, but I was blind to the live television drama unfolding before my eyes and certainly to the role that *I* might play in it, it was me in that gold and silver chariot sparkling with precious stones, I held the reins of the indomitable double span riding across the five zones of heaven. What had my father the

Sun said? Not too high, or you will set fire to the dome of heaven, not too low or you will scorch the earth . . . but I am off already, I charge through the air ringing with joyful whinnies, I see the hooves kicking up a storm as they slice through the clouds like knives, and then it is all over, the chariot hurtles across the sky, spinning out of its eternal orbit, the light refracting in all directions, horses clawing the air, the heat singeing the hide of the Great Bear. I feel how the darkness draws me downwards, I know I shall crash; countries, mountains, everything shoots past me in a bolt of confusion, my flames set forests ablaze, I see the poisonous, black sweat of the gigantic Scorpion as it raises its tail to sting me, the earth catches fire, the meadows burn to white ashes, Mount Etna spits fire back at me, the ice melts on mountaintops, rivers boil over their banks, I pull the vulnerable world with me in my fate, the incandescent chariot searing my body, the Babylonian Euphrates is alight, the Nile flees in mortal terror and hides its source, all existence laments, and then Jupiter hurls his lethal bolt of lightning which bores right through me, burning me and dashing me out of the chariot of life, the horses break free and I am flung like a blazing star to earth, my body implodes in a hissing stream, my corpse like a charred rock in the water.

Suddenly I notice how quiet it is in the classroom. They stare at me as if they have never seen me before, and to regain my composure I turn my back on all those eyes, green ones too, and write on the blackboard, as if it were not also written in the books in front of them:

HIC • SITUS • EST • PHAETHON • CURRUS
AURIGA • PATERNI
QUEM • SI • NON • TENUIT • MAGNIS
TAMEN • EXCIDIT • AUSIS

Here lies Phaethon, driver of Phoebus' chariot. Though he failed, he had ventured. Metrically my rendering was a disaster. And I had omitted that my (his!) body had been buried by water nymphs – why, goodness knows.

When the bell rang the pupils left immediately, more quickly than usual. Maria Zeinstra came over to my desk and asked: 'Do you always get so worked up?'

'Sorry,' I said.

'No, I thought it was great. And it's a fantastic story, I didn't know it. Was that the end or does it go on?'

And I told her about Phaethon's sisters, the Heliads, who changed into trees out of grief over their brother's death. 'The way your rat changed into larvae, and then beetles.'

'A roundabout way. But it isn't the same.'

I wanted to tell her how magnificently Ovid describes the transformation into trees, how the mother, seeking to embrace her daughters for the last time, breaks away the bark and twigs framing their receding features, and how drops of blood ooze from the branches. Women, trees, blood, amber. But it was complicated enough as it was.

'All those changes of mine are metaphors for yours.'

'Mine?'

'Well, in nature, I mean. Only without the gods. There's no one to do it for us, we do it ourselves.'

'Do what?'

'Change.'

'Once we're dead, yes, but then we get the help of sexton beetles.'

'It must be an enormous job to roll us up. That would make a pretty big carrion pellet. Pink.' I could picture the scene. My small hands folded inwards, my thinker's head poked into my belly.

She laughed. 'We have other personnel for that. Maggots,

worms. Very refined, too.' She paused. Suddenly she looked about fourteen. 'Do you believe in an afterlife?'

'No,' I replied, truthfully. I am not even sure we exist at all, I wanted to say, and then I went and said it.

'Oh, come off it.' It sounded very North Hollandish. But suddenly she grabbed me by the lapels.

'Let's go for a drink.' And in the same breath, stabbing her finger against my chest: 'And what about this then? Doesn't this exist either?'

'This is my body,' I said. It sounded pedantic.

'Yes, so Jesus Christ said, too. You do concede that it exists.'

'Oh yes.'

'So what do you call it? "Me", "I", something like that?'

'Is your "I" the same as ten years ago? Or the same as fifty years from now?'

'I hope I will be gone by then. But tell me exactly what *you* think we are, then.'

'A cluster of composite, endlessly altering circumstances and functions which we address as "I". What else can I say? We act as if it is fixed and unchangeable, but it changes all the time, until it is discarded. But we keep on referring to it as "I". It's a sort of profession of the body.'

'Wow.'

'No, I mean it. This more or less random body or this collection of functions is required to be me during its lifetime. That sounds rather like some kind of job. Or doesn't it? Don't you agree?'

'You're slightly mad if you ask me,' she said. 'But you tell a good story. And now I want a drink.'

All right, she thought I was a funny little geezer, but my charred Phaethon had impressed her, I was very obviously available, and she was out for revenge. What makes Greek tragedies great is that this brand of psychological nonsense doesn't enter into it at all. I had wanted to tell her that too, but unfortunately conversations consist for the most part of things one does not say. We are descendants, we do not have mythical lives, but psychological ones. And we know everything, we are always our own chorus.

'What I hate most about the whole affair,' she said, 'is that it's such a cliché.' She was referring to Herfst and d'India, of course, and I wasn't quite sure yet whether she was right. The worst of it was of course d'India's mysteriousness. All the rest – young, pretty, pupil and teacher – that was the cliché. The mystery lay in the power the pupil had acquired.

'Do you see what I mean?' Yes, I could see very well. What I could not see, but I didn't say so, was why, of all people, d'India had chosen this imperial prat. But Plato had already coined a magic formula for that: 'Love is in the one who loves, not in the one who is loved.' It would be part of her life for ever, it was a mistake, but she was entitled to that. It was all right for me, I had come close to something that resembled love for the first time in my life. Maria Zeinstra, being one of the free, took her freedom for granted; she cut straight through everything, it was as if this was the first time I had anything to do with the Dutch, or indeed with the *hoi polloi*. But one can't say such things.

She stood in a frozen dance posture between my four walls with my four thousand books and said: 'I'm not illiterate myself, but this is going too far. D'you live here alone?'

'With Bat,' I said. Bat was my cat. 'I don't expect you'll even see him, because he's very shy.' Five minutes later she was lying on the sofa with Bat sprawled on top of her, the last rays of sunlight setting her red hair alight, two languid bodies, purring and murmuring, and I stood there as if I were the extension of my bookcases, waiting to be admitted into their intimacy. Bookish, somewhat ethereal women, they had been my domain until now, from timid to bitter, and all of them had been very good at explaining what was wrong with me. 'Bloody know-all', or 'If you ask me you don't even notice if I'm here or not', were often-heard complaints, along with 'Must you read *all* the time?' and 'Do you ever think of anyone else?' Well, I did as it happens, but on such occasions it was not of them. Besides, I simply had to get back to my books straightaway, because the company of most people, once the predictable events have taken their course, does not inspire conversation on my part. Indeed I had grown skilled at getting rid of people, so that my circle was eventually limited to humans of the female sex who had the same idea as I. Tea, sympathy, urges, and subsequently the turning of pages of a book. Growling red-haired women who knew all about sexton beetles and egg chambers were different, especially if they were curled on the divan with my cat in an undulating sequence of bellies, breasts, outstretched arms, laughing green eyes, if they pulled me towards them, took off my glasses, removed their clothes (to judge by the changing colours in my blurred vision) and said all sorts of things that I could not quite make out. Perhaps I even said the things people say in such circumstances. All I know is that everything was changing all the time, and that this had to be something like happiness.

When it was over I felt as if I had swum the Channel. I retrieved my glasses and saw her leave with a wave. Bat looked at me as if he was about to gain the power of speech. I drank half a bottle of Calvados and played the *Ritorno d'Ulisse in patria* until the downstairs neighbours protested. Memory of lust is the most elusive of all, once lust becomes just an idea it becomes its own contradiction: absent, and hence unthinkable. I know that I suddenly saw myself that evening, a man alone in a cube, surrounded by invisible others in adjacent cubes, and with tens of thousands of pages around me filled with descriptions of the same, but ever distinct, emotions of real or invented personages. I was moved by myself.

I would never write such a page, but the emotion I had felt during those past hours was mine for ever. She had shown me a garden that had been closed to me. I was still shut out, but at least I had caught a glimpse of it. Glimpse is the wrong word. I had heard it. She had made a sound that did not belong to the world, that I had never heard before. It was the sound of a child, and at the same time of a pain no words can describe. Where that sound came from it must be impossible to live.

The Sons of Angus MacElster

Joyce Carol Oates

A true tale of Cape Breton Island, Nova Scotia, 1923

T his insult not to be borne. Not by the MacElster sons who were so proud. From New Glasgow to Port Hawkesbury to Glace Bay at the wind-buffeted easternmost tip of Cape Breton Island, where the accursed family lived, it was spoken of. All who knew of the scandal laughed, marvelled, shook their heads over it. The MacElsters! – that wild crew! Six strapping sons and but a single daughter no man dared approach for fear of old Angus and his sons, heavy drinkers, tavern brawlers, what can you expect? Yet what old Angus MacElster did, and to his own wife, you'd scarcely believe: he'd been gone for three months on a coal-bearing merchant ship out of Halifax, returning home to Glace Bay on a wet-dripping April midday, his handsome ruin of a face wind-burned and ruddy with drink, driving with two other merchant seamen who lived in the Bay area, old friends of his, and at the tall weatherworn woodframe house on Mull Street overlooking the harbour he dropped his soiled gear, freshened up and spent a brief half-hour in the company of Mrs MacElster, and the nervous daughter Katy now twenty years old and still living at home. Angus stood before the icebox devouring cold meatloaf with his fingers, breaking off morsels with his stubby gnarled fingers, and washing down his lunch in haste with ale he'd brought with him in several clinking bottles in the pockets of his sheepskin jacket, then it was off to the Mare's Neck as usual, and drinking with his old companions, how like old times it was, and never any improvement in the man's treatment of his wife. Returned to Glace Bay for three weeks before he'd ship out again and already there was a hint of trouble, it was Katy put the call to Rob, the eldest son, and Rob drove over at once from Sydney in a car borrowed from his employer at the pulp mill under the pretext of a family emergency, and Cal in his delivery van drove over from Briton Cove, and there was Alistair hurrying from New Skye, and John Rory and John Allan and I, the youngest, live here in Glace Bay where we'd been born, freely we admit we'd been drinking too, you must drink to prepare yourself for the hurtful old man we loved with a fierce hateful love, the heated love of boys for their father, even a father who has long betrayed them with his absence, and the wilful withholding of his love, yet we longed like craven dogs to receive his father's blessing, any careless touch of his gnarly hand, we longed to receive his rough wet despairing kisses on the lips of the kind he'd given us long ago when we were boys, before the age of ten, so the very memory of such kisses is uncertain to us, ever shifting and capricious as the fog in the harbour every morning of our waking lives. *Even at that late hour, our hearts might yet have been won.*

Except: unknown to us our mother had gone in reckless despair to the Mare's Neck to seek our father, and the two quarrelled in the street where idlers gathered to gawk, at the foot of New Harbor Street in a chill glistening wind, and we would be told that he'd raised a hand to her and she'd cried *Disgusting! How can you! – disgusting! God curse you!* tears shining on her cheeks, and her hair the colour of tarnished silver loosened in the wind, and she'd pushed at the old man which you must never do, you must never touch the old man for it is like bringing a lighted match to straw, you can witness the wild blue flame leaping up his body, leaping in his eyes, his eyes bulging like a horse's and red-veined with drink, the flame in his greying red hair the colour of fading sumac in autumn, and in a rage he seizes the collar of her old cardigan sweater she'd knitted years ago, seizes it and tears it, and as idlers from the several pubs of New Harbor Street stare in astonishment he tears her dress open, cursing her, *Cow! Sodden cow! Look at you, ugly sodden cow!* ripping her clothes from her, exposing our cringing mother in the halter-like white cotton brassière she must wear to contain her enormous breasts, milk-pale flaccid breasts hanging nearly to her waist which she tries to hide with her arms, our mother publicly shamed pleading with our father *Angus, no! Stop! I beg you, God help you – no!* Yet in his drunken rage Angus MacElster strips his wife of thirty-six years near-naked, as the poor woman shrieks and sobs at the foot of New Harbor Street, and a loose crowd of beyond twenty men has gathered to watch, some of them grinning and laughing but most of them plainly shocked, even the drunks are shocked by a man so publicly humiliating his wife, and his wife a stout middle-aged woman with greying hair, until at last Angus MacElster is persuaded to leave his wife alone, to back off and leave the poor hysterically weeping woman alone, one or two of the men wrap her in their jackets, hide her nakedness, even as old Angus turns aside with a wave of his hand in disgust and stumbles off to Mull Street three blocks away yet not to the tall weatherworn woodframe house, but instead to the old barn at the rear, muttering and cursing and laughing to himself. Angus sinks insensible into the straw, like a horse in its stall in a luxuriance of sleep where, when we were small boys, he'd spent many a night even in winter, returning late to the house and not caring to blunder into our mother's domain not out of fear of her wrath nor even of his own wrath turned against her but simply because he was drawn to sleeping in the barn, in his clothes, in his boots, luxuriant in such deep dreamless animal sleep as we, his sons, waited inside the house shuddering and shivering in anticipation of his return, his heavy footsteps on the stairs, yet yearning for his return as a dog yearns for the return of the very master who will kick him, praying he would not cuff us, or beat us, or kick us, or yank at our coarse red curls so like his own in that teasing tenderness of our father's that seemed to us far crueller than actual cruelty for at such times you were meant to smile and not cringe, you were meant to love him and not fear him, you were meant to obey him and not turn mutinous, you were meant to honour your father and not loathe him, still less were you meant to pray for his death, steeped in sin as you were, even at a young age, even in childhood touched by the curse of the MacElsters, emigrated from the wind-ravaged highlands north of Inverness to the new world with blood, it was rumoured, on their hands, and murder in their hearts. And there at the house when we arrived was our mother weeping deranged with shock and humiliation, her mouth bloodied, and Katy tending to her white-faced and shaking as if she too had been stripped naked in the street, and would be the scandalised talk of all who knew the MacElsters and countless others who did not, from Glace Bay to Port Hawkesbury to New Glasgow and beyond, talk to endure for years, for decades, for generations to this very day: and seeming to know this as a fact, Angus's six sons wasted no time, we strode into the barn known to us as a dream inhabited nightly, that place of boyhood chores, of boyhood play, badly weather-worn, with missing boards and rotted shingles loosened by wind, glaring-eyed Rob has taken up the double-edged axe where it was leaning against the doorframe, and Cal the resourceful one has brought from home a twelve-inch fish-gutting knife, Alistair has a wicked pair of shears, John Rory and John Allan have their matching hunting knives of eight-inch stainless steel, and I have a newly honed butcher's knife from my own house, from out of my own kitchen where my young wife will miss it, and the six of us enter the barn to see the old man snoring in the twilight, in a patch of damp straw, and panting we circle him, our eyes gleaming like those of feral creatures glimpsed by lamplight in the dusk, and Rob is the first to shout for him to *Wake! wake up, old man!* – for it seems wrong to murder a sixty-one-year-old man snoring on his back, fatty-muscled torso exposed, arms and legs sprawled in a bliss of drunken oblivion, and at once old Angus opens his eyes, his bulging red-veined horse's eyes, blinking up at us, knowing us, naming us one by one his six MacElster sons as damned as he, and yet *even at this late hour our hearts might yet be won.* Except, being the man he is, old Angus curses us, calls us young shits, spits at us, tries to stumble to his feet to fight us, even as the first of our blows strikes, Rob's double-edged axe like electricity leaping out of the very air, and there's the flash of Cal's fish-gutting knife, and Alistair's shears used for stabbing, and the fine-honed razor-sharp blades of John and John Allan and me, blades sharp enough and strong enough to pierce the hide of the very devil himself, and in a fever of shouts and laughter we strike, and tear, and lunge, and stab, and pierce, and gut, and make of the old man's wind-roughened skin a lacy-bloody shroud and of his bones brittle sticks as easily broken as dried twigs, and of his terrible eyes cheap baubles to be gouged out and ground into the dirt beneath our boots, and of his hard skull a mere clay pot to be smashed into bits, and of his blood gushing hot and shamed on to the straw and the dirt floor of the barn a glistening stream bearing bits of cobweb, dust and straw as if a sluice were opened, and we leap about shouting with laughter for this is a game, is it? – will the steaming poison-blood of Angus MacElster singe our boots? – sully our boots? – will some of us be tainted by this blood and others, the more agile, the more blessed, will not?

This old family tale come to me from my father's father Charles MacElster, the eldest son of Cal.

Sophia Walters Shaw

Patricia Duncker

y name is Sophia. But there are three of us. There have always been three of us, and the other two are here with me now. We go everywhere together. The taller of the other two has sandy hair and freckles. He looks pigeon-chested, unconvincing, but in fact he is surprisingly agile and very strong. His name is Walters. The third one of us is the most dangerous. He is the quiet one, the dark one, the one with the shaved head. A delicate spiky down covers his skull as it grows out. Whenever we construct one of our operations he shaves his head. It is a formal ritual, a preparation. It is as if he needs to alter his appearance irrevocably before he is able to act. He becomes a slightly different person. His name is Shaw. He has no other name. I think that we are all slightly different when we are working, but he takes the trouble to look different. Walters and I are never disguised. We appear to be who we always are. He is unassuming, but authoritative. I am the woman who is very well dressed. I began to dress up years ago. I never take risks.

I think of us, not as three single people, but as one. We are intimately connected. It is as if my identity is hyphenated, like the modern woman, who, when she marries, settles for a half-way house, keeping her own name, but adding those of her husbands: Sophia Walters Shaw. I cannot imagine being separated from the others. It is as if there have always been three of us. But that is not so.

We first met through the agency. I was something of a wild card then. I was twenty-one. I had dropped out of college, a thing that women never do, or at least not the women who intend to become wives, and I was heavily in debt. I sat about aggressively in waiting rooms, waiting to be interviewed by banks, social security officials and prospective employers, legs splayed apart, wearing a black mini-skirt and sheer black tights, peppered with ladders and holes. I wanted to be noticed. I was asking for it, up for it, out to get it any way I could.

Walters was the first man who offered me a job. He was the front man at the general office, supposedly managed by the agency. He looked innocent enough behind his barrage of telephones and his computer with a screensave of floating coloured fish, a gormless flotilla of shifting purples and greens. He sat very still, with his hands on the table before him. None of the pens in his little brown tray had ever been used. I noticed that. I remember thinking: there isn't a secretary. If this outfit had been for real there'd have been a secretary, banging away at the order forms, memos and files of clients' desires. But there was none of that in this front office. This office is a stage set. This man does no work here. He's never written on that pad, never even looked at that calendar. He does it all through the computer. This man acts as front of house.

So I sat there, chewing gum and deliberately trying to look insolent. We eye-balled each other for a minute or so. I didn't say anything. Neither did he. It's up to you to ask questions, mate. I could see that he already had me down as a cheeky bitch, the kind they bundle up and cart off every day. But I could also see that he didn't dislike me. He kept his hands folded on the table in front of him. Then he said,

'Stand up.'

I did.

'Pull up your skirt.'

There were only four inches of skirt to haul up above my cunt, but I pulled it right up to my waist anyway and he got a close-up eyeful of my shredded tights, my standard-issue black knickers, no lace, and the spiky pubic hair around my crotch. I don't shave like most other women do, or at least the women who want to be wives. Why bother? Why should I? Walters looked me over carefully.

'That'll do.'

I pulled my skirt down again.

'Turn around.'

I turned my back on him.

'Take off your T-shirt and bra,' he ordered, his voice utterly neutral and indifferent, as if he was asking me to find a file among the boxes outside.

I did as he asked.

'Now pick up the chair you were sitting on and raise it above your head.'

I was a little taken aback at this. The chair was made of iron tubes and plastic-covered foam with a rough green surface. It was heavy and awkward. But I swim twice a week and I work out at the municipal gym. I keep fit. Really, it wasn't that difficult. I swung the chair into the air, setting my legs apart so that I kept my balance. The mini-skirt creased up into folds around my arse.

'Hold it there.'

I thought he was going to walk around the desk and inspect the shape and fall of my breasts. After all, he would be paying me. I would be one of his girls. The agency has the right to have first look at the goods. But he didn't. I glanced over my shoulder and he caught my eye. But he hadn't moved. His hands were still folded on the desk before him. My muscles were beginning to shiver with tension.

'Two minutes,' he said calmly.

But it was longer than that. I must have held that heavy pipe-frame chair above my head for a full four minutes before I'd had enough. I swung round and slammed it down on the desk, dislocating one of the telephones and sending the computer mouse flying over the edge. The gulping fish vanished from the screen and my own face, sulky and shut, with all my basic details appeared before me:

SOPHIA
d. of b.
daughter of . . .
present occupation: unemployed
ex-student in Harrington Wives college
no siblings, one parent still living
clean driving licence

'That's enough,' I snapped.

He didn't look at my breasts, but at my face.

'Exactly so,' was all he said as he swung the computer round, out of my sight. I got dressed again without bothering to turn away from him. I was pissed off. He wasn't going to humiliate me quite so easily. I didn't give a shit about his fucking agency. I'd get another job somewhere else. Better paid. Maybe even in one of the international airports or with the sex police. Where you just took your clothes off, or opened your legs, and where you didn't have to perform fucking circus tricks. I picked up my jacket off the floor and was about to stalk out when he said,

'Don't lose your temper. Sit down.'

I glared at him.

'You'll have to take the chair off the desk first.'

He hadn't moved. Don't play silly buggers with me, mate. But I decided to give it a go. I took the chair off the table and banged it down on the plastic floor. I took my time sitting down again. He waited. Not a muscle on his face was out of place.

'All right,' he smiled slightly, 'let's do business.'

We sat staring at one another.

'I would like you to consider a position with us as a reception hostess. We will probably keep you in this country to begin with, but, if all goes well, I would hope to send you abroad for a year or two. Either Germany or the Far East, to complete your training. I may be proved wrong, but it seems to me that you have the potential to be very successful in our line of work.'

I said nothing whatever. I didn't think much of his flannel. I was still pissed off.

'My name is Walters,' he said. 'You will be answerable directly to me.'

The first club in which I worked was called The Underworld. My code name was Cyane. Walters explained that I was named after a fountain in Sicily. I thought that it sounded very exotic. We all had code names. Some of them were very odd: Arizona City, Westworld, Violet Gorilla, Dodge Kitty, Boudicca, Red Rita, Boy Clio, Benton, Guido, Rampant Strap. The names were already attached to our identity disks. We were given no choice. I wondered if Walters had made them all up. Most of our clients were Japanese business men. You had to be a member, but it was possible to join at the door if you had a valid computer identity card and all the details, including the codes, corresponded in the citizens' identity data base. That was one of my jobs as reception hostess: to run back-up identity checks on their disks to see if they were counterfeit, or if they were police, just visiting. If I found out that they were police I never turned them away, just pressed the Visitors button so that Walters knew the house was spiked that night and could make sure that we kept the show nice and clean for the evening. That's not a problem. We just warn the boys and girls and they do routines that are within the limits. And for all the bloody bits we just run simulations.

We only ever had one raid that I knew about and that was the raid which closed us down: the infamous Jungle Show. We were even interrogated by the Race Police. And that had never happened before. The Jungle Show was an old-fashioned scenario, very popular and passionately anticipated by our older clients, women and men. I never could detect a gender bias in their tastes. Our principal performer was a big black man with a handsome set of genitals. Huge, black and uncannily hairy. He did the whole thing in a cage with exotic flowering plants and a soundtrack of African drums and jungle cries. His partner was a young German girl, small, blonde, with large breasts. Her pubic hair was very dark. Walters didn't want her to shave, but he made her dye it blonde, which she told me took ages and stained her shower with yellow streaks, so that it looked as if she was given to urinating down the drain. But then, when he looked her over before the rehearsals, Walters suddenly changed his mind and told me to shave it all off. Her skin was very fragile and soft. I used a safety razor, but I was still terrified that I would cut her. She didn't speak much English. But I think 'Vorsicht! Vorsicht!' must mean Be Careful. And she kept saying that she was pretty pissed off with Walters. She maintained that he never knew what he wanted. In any case, old videos of the original act showed that the woman kept all her pubic hair.

I didn't bother with the rehearsals, although they appeared to involve an excessive amount of screaming. Well, if you work in the industry you lose interest in the soft acts pretty quickly. They're all much the same and whether they're any good or not is up to the individual performers. But the Jungle Show, while classed as a soft act, aroused a lot of interest because it had the cachet of being illegal and first performed right back in the 1960s before any of us were born. Walters came down to the dress rehearsal and decided that the cage should be suspended in the middle of the floor, just above the audience, so that the angles from which the show could be viewed were very exciting. He could charge more if the clients could see the action right up close. Walters is a showman to his fingertips. He knows what will make money and pack them in. Not that we could advertise any of it beforehand, given that the whole thing was illegal. But I knew the form. We'd done this before. Make sure that the whisper goes round well in advance. That was my job really. I developed a sequence of euphemisms: a very special show, nothing like it seen anywhere in town for over seventy years, old videos so very hard to get, a chance to see a real rave from the grave, and a hot night out. The clients get to know the codes. Everything I said meant that it was retro, illegal and violent.

One of the girls asked me why it was prohibited and I wasn't sure. So I asked Walters. By then we did have quite a good working relationship, even if he was a bit monosyllabic.

'It promotes hatred of black people,' said Walters, as if he had very little interest in the question.

I was mystified. At least half of our clients are black. We were downloading the new computer information disks into our system at the time and a quick glance down the list tells you everything: Ngato, Zwelo, Afrekete, Kabilye – they're all black names.

'Why should the Jungle Show do that?' I looked into the flickering green screen, mystified.

'Watch the dress rehearsal,' snapped Walters, indifferent.

I did, and then I understood what he meant. The show was bestial in the grand tradition. Our black star was presented like a gorilla in leopard skins with brutal, violent appetites and no imagination whatsoever. The act emphasised violence and fear rather than sadistic complicity, which is now so much the fashion. I prefer a lucid, calculated sadism. It seems cleaner, and more just. The German girl flung herself into her role. She played the victim all the way, right down to her shaved pubic mound. She cowered in the corners, tried to cover herself with foliage, and was absolutely convincing as a helpless abject prisoner, down to her last, heaving, sweating gasp. But the performance was all about slavering brute lust, well out of control. Our black star presented a creature that was barely human. He was mere animal heat and priapic cruelty. I think that we were all rather shocked.

It struck me as odd that acts like this had ever been popular. I've never studied the sexual theatre of the mid-twentieth century and once I'd seen the Jungle Show, I didn't want to do so. But on the night we were sold out. All the clients were at least thirty years older than we were. It wasn't a market I had ever dreamed about. Yet they were all still there, shouting, gyrating and urging the players on as if they were massed round a bear pit. The public was every bit as raw and crude as the performers. I peered round the barriers from reception as often as I dared during the evening, to watch both the audience and the act. To me the Jungle Show seemed brutal, self-indulgent and lacking in nuance.

I'm a leather girl myself. So I enjoy the modern SM leather shows, orgies in the multi-user dungeon, with powerful roles for the women. I've never taken part in the show of course. Walters always kept me either as front of house or circulating on the floor. I was his eyes and ears among the public. On the leather nights, however, he allowed me to dress the part. None of those soft, femme, low-cut black dresses. No, I looked like the real thing, tight black leather suit, chains and studs. My only concession to femininity was a black leather rose behind my left ear. I always had offers on leather evenings. Not bad money either. Quite substantial sums. But private work was strictly forbidden. You negotiated your own salary with the agency. And some of the artists, not just the men, were very highly paid. I wasn't complaining. I earned just as much that night as the black stud in the Jungle Show. Walters used to say that I was worth it, what with my SM style and my computer skills.

On the night of the Jungle Show, when we were all nervous and tense, waiting for the off, Walters came downstairs. He told me to send the take at the door and the entire identity records straight up to his offices as soon as we had shut down the entrance and the show had begun. I was wearing a leather dress and my black rose. He added up the entrance bookings, plucked the black rose from my hair and then kissed my throat very, very softly.

'Well done,' was all he said, 'you've collected a very fine haul in your sexual net. You are my favourite dominatrix, the one that all the family can enjoy.'

I hardly recognised anybody who came into the club that night. I just checked their IDs, expressionless. And charged them the extortionate entrance fee Walters had dreamed up for the Jungle Show. The punters looked like pickled mummies. Some had stretched face-lifts and paint inches thick. The men were hideous, with folded jowls and savage eyes. I only remembered one of them, the one who withheld his ID chip. I stretched out my hand to receive the card and he closed his own over mine. I felt the chill of his heavy, golden rings and looked up. He was huge, with a thick moustache and assassin's eyes. He must have been nearly sixty. His once dark hair was riddled with grey streaks. He was wearing an old-fashioned dinner jacket and a black bow tie.

'Just tell your boss that his guests have come.'

He nodded to my minders, dismissing us all. One huge hand clamped around the elbow of the woman who was with him. In the narrow entrance to The Underworld, I looked straight into her face. She was afraid, terribly afraid.

Here was the frail, blonde face of a woman who lived in gracious spaces, surrounded by delicate, expensive things. She wore no paint at all. She was pale, her huge eyes dilated with apprehension and alarm. She was not here in this dark, permissive space of her own volition. She was not a free agent, as I am. She cannot have been more than eighteen years old. She was being forced. She was too young, too weak, too confused to resist. I looked at the soft lawn hiding her breasts. The dress was covered in thousands of tiny green flowers, embedded in silk. In this world of pounding, violent dark, she was a precious thing, being dragged down, down, down.

I pressed the internal line on the comsystem.

'Walters? Your guests are here.'

'Thank you.'

He was utterly non-committal, quite unsurprised. I wanted to know who she was. I was wise enough not to ask.

The police turned up in force well after two when the show was nearly over. The German girl was bleeding from lashes and tooth marks on her arse and thighs. Her thrilling screams were perfectly genuine. She was begging the audience to help her escape from the cage. Our black player was quite crazed. I wondered if he was flying on coke. He was by now stark naked and his body was painted with red and black stripes which glimmered under the floods. The woman was tied up to a totem pole with her ankles in fetters, supposedly last worn by slaves. He was screaming about sexual revenge on the white tyrants. The audience was ecstatic. The woman was bent forward, bleating piteously. I wondered how much she was being paid and if Walters had made it clear that when we did retro, we went all the way. Verismo. Down to the last detail. We very seldom actually kill our performers, largely because the cost of the show, in security terms, puts it well beyond the reach of our usual clientele. There are specialist clubs for all that. But they're small, exclusive and have government security clearance.

When I next looked into the main house the black star was buggering the woman in a sequence of violent thrusts and the public were standing on their chairs, screaming. The cavern was filled with broken glass and smoke. I went back to the door and settled down with my usual thugs, checking the security zones from the computer. I saw them coming just a second or two before they crashed roaring through the door.

Police. All masked, heavily armed. One of them stuck a gun in my stomach and yelled,

'Get away from that screen, you fat bitch!' I engineered a fall backwards, which gave me the chance to press the Visitors button. The thing is actually green, rather than red, and marked OPEN LAVATORY DOORS, one of our private jokes. I also managed to unplug the computer. This caused the entire system to utter a groan as it closed down. One of my bouncers took a swing at the officer pointing a gun at my stomach. Usually, we don't attack the police, but he was taken by surprise. Nobody pulled the trigger, but three men fell upon him, pounding his chest and head with a mixture of fists and the steel shafts of their weapons. We could hear yells from the interior of the cavern, mixing with the twentieth-century disco music, as the show was stopped short, well before the climax. I teetered up from the floor in my short leather dress and black high heels, pulling at my skirt, apparently in an attempt to make myself decent. As I did so I slid the information disk from the computer inside the elastic of my knickers. The disks are tiny, about the size of the small coins which used to be legal tender in this country, but have long since been discontinued. I planned to squeeze the thing up into my vagina and get rid of it before I was strip-searched. Police procedure is pretty standard. They usually search you before they let you go, on the grounds that what you take out of the police security zones is likely to be a lot more dangerous and more valuable than anything you could ever take in. The information on our disks is confidential and in the usual run of things clubs are not required to give them up. But we were, almost certainly, about to lose our licence. I had the real disk safely lodged in my most intimate crevices. The only list that the police could now find was the mail-order confirmation list, the names of people who had never stepped inside The Underworld in their lives and had probably never done anything riskier than order a leather suit, scented condoms and a silver-plated dildo. In fact, that list is littered with High Court judges, Cabinet ministers and ecclesiastical dignitaries of every religious persuasion.

We were thrown into closed vans and removed in a cloud of howling noise. Walters was flung onto the same bench in the police zone waiting room. He thudded down beside me. He was remarkably calm. As soon as the officer in charge had taken all our details and drifted away, he leaned over and hissed in my ear,

'You have a handsome bruise swelling up on your left cheek, my dear. I assume that you also have other things hidden on your person.'

'Well hidden.'

He nodded, then looked away. He seemed pleased, even slightly amused. He might have been smiling.

'Stand up, you smug fat cunt,' snapped one of the officers, 'you're spending at least one night in the cells.'

I was dragged away and I didn't see Walters for the rest of that night, nor all the next day, nor the night after that. I was locked up alone in a tiny graffiti-ridden cell with nothing but a couple of planks covered in a scratchy grey blanket. I was given no food and no water. There was a shit bucket in the corner of the cell, but nothing with which to wipe yourself. The floor stank of urine. I suppose the last inmate hadn't even been given a bucket. I'd been in prison before. I knew what to expect.

The graffiti gave me something to read. Some of it was antique and dated back to the period of the Jungle Show. There were peculiar historic slogans, like ONE NUCLEAR BOMB CAN SPOIL YOUR WHOLE DAY, YOU CAN'T KILL THE SPIRIT and, most mysteriously, PORNOGRAPHY IS THE THEORY, RAPE IS THE PRACTICE. For us, pornography was like religion used to be, a condition of being, the way we thought, the way we earned our livings. And rape can't exist if all women, women everywhere, all of them, always say yes, yes, yes. I knew of no one who would think otherwise.

Walters himself came to bail me out. By the time he turned up, mid-morning on the second day, I felt humiliated, smelly and cross. You can only go on pissing in the same bucket that is never emptied with no lavatory at your disposal for just so many hours, without beginning to feel disgusting. And I was terrified of losing the disk.

The officer who let Walters into the cell was the same one who had called me a fat cunt. My well-aimed gob of spit got him on the cheek while he was fiddling with his keys. He would have hit me if Walters, now dressed in an elegant camel suit with a long grey leather coat slung over his shoulders, had not caught his arm.

'I apologise on her behalf, officer. She is clearly desperate for a shower and a change of clothes.'

'Take your fucking clothes off,' screamed the man and banged the cell door behind him. We were left alone for a moment in the tiny cell.

'They will strip-search you before they let you go,' he whispered. 'Take your clothes off and give them to me. Give everything to me.' He met my eye, pointedly.

'Didn't they get everyone in there anyway?' I started ripping off my clothes.

'The disk records everyone who passes through the doors.'

Walters held out his hand, irritated, urgent. Suddenly I knew that there were only two visitors who had not been hauled into the police zone: the green girl in her silken dress, covered in tiny flowers, and the man with the heavy rings of chilled gold.

Total strangers have seen me naked so many times that I have no difficulty undressing in front of Walters. He's one of the family. He had the grace to sniff the tiny disk appreciatively before slipping it into his pocket. Then he gathered up all my clothes, but held them at arm's length, suspended from his fingertips, while I trotted off to the shower, hugging my breasts.

A woman officer looked up my cunt and down my arse through one of those pencil torches with a magnifying eye at one end.

'Whadda you looking for?' I demanded smugly, as she peered between my legs.

'Drugs,' she hissed.

The Underworld had been closed down. All the windows and doors had been boarded up with fibre-glass panels covered with yellow KEEP OUT stickers. I went round in the morning and experienced an odd sense of loss, standing in front of the anonymous brick block where I had worked, for almost three years, five nights on, three nights off, six weeks' holiday on full pay, when you didn't know what to do with yourself. The club was home now. I knew all the dancers, all the sex workers, all the live show players, all their regular animals, all the bouncers and security men, all the illegal transsexuals we used to employ off the books, and Walters, the boss. Our boss. He was standing behind me in the public street, gazing at the anonymous shuttered door with THE UNDERWORLD in discreet blue neon, just above the arch and the descending staircase. The E was already disconnected.

I smelled betrayal and deceit. I turned on Walters.

'Why wasn't I questioned? Why wasn't I charged? Why are you and I free when everyone else is still in prison? You knew they were coming, didn't you?'

The sunlight catches the sheen on his hair. It is dyed. No man has hair that melting colour of red-gold. It is not natural. He is not natural. He is not even decent.

'My dear Sophia,' he takes my hand. I snatch it back. He shrugs. 'We are now considerably richer than we were three days ago and the police have hauled in an excellent catch. Who could only have been hauled into the public glare by something as primitive as our Jungle Show. Of course the entire event was a put-up job. Credit me with some taste. Did you think that I would have come up with a retro show like that as a commercial idea of my own? Heavens.'

'And the rest of us?' I yelled. 'You may be considerably richer. The rest of us have lost our jobs.'

Walters gazed into the middle distance, somewhat displeased.

'Those of you who were up to scratch will be re-deployed. But I will take this opportunity to shed a little excess weight. You, on the other hand, unless you have suddenly developed a social conscience, are more than welcome to accompany me to my new offices.'

I stood there, in the washed sunlight of a late spring, considering Walters's offer. He knew and I knew that I didn't have a lot of choice. In the old days women used to go to college and get themselves educated, just like the men do. There were many professions which accepted women and not so many social sanctions on what you did. There were wives and whores just like there are now. But those weren't the only choices. My mother's mother ran a taxi service: women drivers, women only. It's hard to imagine that now. She was married and earned her own money. Well, that's something that's no longer possible. You have to choose. You can either marry and never work or work your arse off and live at risk. I saw how my father treated my mother, and how poor she was when he dropped down dead, and I reckoned I'd rather take the risk. I chose my life when I went to work in The Underworld. That's when my mother threw me out. No daughter of hers would ever work as a whore. And if you choose to train as a whore, my girl, out you go. But I'd done my sums. It's the only industry where you can make a packet while you're young – if you can keep your head on, and your nose out of the coke. I told my mother what I thought. But she still believed that respectable women shouldn't harbour whores in their houses. That's the line they plug on the Internet screens. She meant it. So did I.

There were plenty of runaway girls in The Underworld. Some of them crept back to their families when they lost heart. Others put themselves down on the Marriage Lists and were eventually chosen by men who didn't ask too many questions.

I sometimes wonder what it would have been like to be married. And when I think how much more comfortable and easy it would have been I do get a queasy feeling of regret. It didn't seem hard to choose to be a whore when I was twenty. It gets harder. Maybe being a wife gets harder too. The Work Palaces are full of redundant or runaway wives. Whores always have something to sell. Even when we're old. We starve less. That's a fact. It's a hell of a life, but if you make enough money you can buy yourself out and that's that. A place in the sun well out of the way. In one of the desert countries, like Spain. You can't go on living in the north. Not once your ID has expired.

Old whores never die. But they do tend to disappear. Never been to Spain. They say it's wonderful. Your own villa with a terrace and a pool, irrigated acres of oranges and lots of well-known criminals for company.

Walters is still standing there, waiting for an answer.

'How much?'

'Twice what you earned in The Underworld.'

'Done.'

I hadn't any choice, but this was too generous. Immediately, I smelled a rat.

'What do I have to do?'

'Same kind of work. Some of it more confidential. See no evil. Hear no evil. Ask no evil.'

'So I've got to notice even less than I used to do?'

'Not necessarily. Just keep your mouth even more firmly shut.'

'And if I don't, I'll disappear.'

'Exactly so.'

Whores have no conscience. But, then, neither do their employers.

'Well, that's clear.'

'I always am.'

He looked me over.

'But we shall have to shed all this leather get-up and buy you some new clothes.'

And so I became front woman, computer woman, telephone woman, wonderfully well-dressed woman, the woman with the manicured nails. I was no ordinary woman. I was the first woman anybody heard in the air, or saw on the screen. I was therefore the first to meet Shaw.

I didn't even realise he was there. He walked in without knocking. I alerted security as a matter of course. No drama needed, not even a Visitors button. Just a gentle tap on the keyboard as if you're bringing up the screensave. In fact, you do bring up the screensave at the same time, and it's fixed with the codes, so that your work on the catalogue remains confidential, while you are dealing with the emergency.

'Do you have an appointment?'

He shook his head and sat down. The camera eye swivelled round to record all his movements. Not that there were any. He sat down facing me, with his hands on his knees, and ceased to move. It's very frightening to be in the presence of someone who is utterly still. His features were unintelligible. If I had to describe what he looks like, I'd be hard pressed to get it right. He is like a stoat: very concentrated, very calm, then one swift gesture. Which is all he needs. That first time, I just looked at him and he just stared at me, as cool as you please. Then he said,

'There was no need to summon security. I am your new colleague. My name is Shaw.'

As the years have passed my respect for Shaw has steadily grown. He is different from Walters. They are both quiet men, but Walters is always active, busy, engaged. Shaw has all the time in the world. He is like a professional undertaker. I do all the talking. Some clients call me the Cunt with Lip, but they aren't usually complaining.

There were two aspects to our work, the front job, which was an ordinary sex agency, like many others, catering for specialist tastes, for up-market clients, people in government or administrative branches of the state, and the dark side, the Special Jobs. These were not regular assignments and we always had very little time to prepare them. Sometimes they presented themselves like ordinary jobs. And I was only told at the last moment that this was a special. Like the first time. I think that you always remember your first time.

We had done a traditional dominatrix scenario in full

costume. I still wore leather for work. And liked doing so. I had whipped him till he bled, shouting my usual graphic torrent of filth which brought him instantly to orgasm. I quite enjoyed these jobs, as the client never touches you. That would spoil the effect. We were alone for hours. There was nothing unusual to report. Then I heard Walters, calling quietly from the door. I ordered the client to wait and be a good boy, or there'd be trouble, and stepped outside, puzzled. Walters never interferes. He lets me run my sessions any way I like. He knows that I'm a professional. But on this occasion Walters was very odd. He seemed very tense, on edge, but he said nothing. He walked me out into the garden. I stood there, masked and naked in my long black boots. I became very uneasy.

Then suddenly I saw Shaw, pulling the curtains in the living room where I had been working. I rushed back into the house.

The client was dead, his throat slit from ear to ear, his sperm drying in a small grim pool on the floor. But the slit throat wasn't the only mutilation. The corpse was disgusting. His entrails protruded from the sliced fat stomach and his penis, still unaccountably erect, poked at his flopping intestines. His blood oozed into the carpet. I felt sick and very angry. This was my first time, but I was already prepared to take pride in my work and to do a good job, thorough, untraceable. This bloated, repulsive heap was offensive on all counts. The work looked like that of an amateur, and very unconvincing.

Shaw stood by the windows, calmly cleaning his knives, without removing his black leather gloves. All the fluids and cloths he used were neatly folded and restored to his working case, which he then snapped shut. I stood before him, speechless with shock and rage. I pulled at my leather mask. It seemed to be nailed to my face.

'Oh, for God's sake, clear it up,' I yelled at Shaw.

Walters was already addressing himself to our pocket

computer, checking our emergency clearance. It came through in a series of muted beeps.

'You have half an hour,' said Walters mildly to me as if we were going out to dinner, 'go upstairs and wash.'

He had never even touched me, but it was as if the client's blood was on my hands and thighs. The room smelled musky with the stench of fresh sex and violent death.

'Couldn't we do better than this?' I raised my voice. Walters looked at me carefully, then lit a cigarette.

'We were asked to make the death look like a ritual killing for the sake of the press, Sophia. Your rule should be to see no evil, hear no evil, and ask no evil. I arrange the special assignments. I negotiate with the client. I assume responsibility and I do the research. This job, which you seem to find so untidily executed, has in fact been carried out in perfect accordance with our orders. I offer you and Shaw my warmest congratulations. Now do as I say and ask no further questions. I will excuse your outburst on this occasion simply because this was your first time.'

He would not excuse me again. I understood that at once. I stalked up the stairs and found myself padding across the thick pile in the master bedroom. There was a photograph of a pretty wife and three children on the glass dressing table. Where were they now? The client had been a family man. Most of them were family men. I shuddered at my masked face in the bathroom, then vomited into the sink. I had never done that before. When I peeled off the mask I found that I was shaking, not with distress for the bereaved family or horror that I had now become an accessory to violent murder. The client was a politician. He must have sent many others to their deaths as a matter of course. No, what shook me was the fact that we were not what we appeared to be. I had imagined that we were an independent exotic sex agency, in fact we were assassins. The client was not the real client. Walters had described this as my first time. There would therefore be other times. And it had been so easy. He had called us up himself. I remembered sending him the catalogue, exchanging e-mails on the Internet, spicing up his appetite, upping the price. We had already been paid for his murder, twice over.

Now every client would be one of my potential victims. And I would not know the true nature of the transaction until Shaw suddenly moved. What I did for a living had radically changed. I would have no difficulty in doing it again.

On that night, as the black slick of our limousine cruised away across the hills towards our city, passing the checkpoints, unchallenged, I felt the release of tension between the three of us. Walters let Shaw do the driving, which was unusual for him. Usually he drives and Shaw and I sit together, utterly silent in the back. Walters said nothing, but he took my hand and held it, all the way back, down the steep ravines and across the gorges, which separated the Heights from the city. I had no choice. He knew that I had no choice. My future lay with them, or nowhere. But even so, I willingly accepted the things I couldn't change.

And there were obscure advantages. We were not ordinary people, we were the angel-makers, marketing sex and death as a gourmet speciality. I felt closer to Walters and Shaw than I had ever done. There were no longer three of us. We were becoming one person.

Intimacy is a peculiar thing. Between lovers it can show itself in a glance, in the caress of a cheek, in a whispered breath. But the intimacy between killers is a more subtle bond. We are each other's muscles, hands and eyes. In Shaw's silence or in the tension I can sense in Walters's shoulders, in the small of his back and the tendons of his neck, the crouched theatricality of our collective strength, everything I read from the pace of our breath, I feel my own force, my own arm raised. Lovers come together, separate. But we no longer follow that rhythm. My part of our bargain is never degrading to me, for when I tempt the client towards me, opening my arms, my legs, I feel the other two bunched in my stomach, my thighs, waiting. I am the first to go forward onto the dangerous ground, our killing fields. But I am never alone. And now I will never be alone. They are my guardians and my keepers, my cold eyes, and my right hand.

The client wanted an ordinary, straightforward rape scenario: No. 2 in the catalogue, woman dressed not as whore, but as wife, lots of resistance, a bit of brutality, and then she loves it once she's forced. Then she's all over him, never known anything like it before, etc., etc. I've played it many, many times. Only the real sexual tossers ever order that one. Makes you wonder, sometimes. Walters gave me the brief without comment, but I noticed something, a rapid flicker in his gestures, the unnatural haste with which he fastened his briefcase, a glitter in his embrace. I scanned our orders. There was no mugshot of the client. He remained faceless.

'Who is he?'

'Ask no evil,' snapped Walters. Then he bent forward and kissed my nose. I had never seen Walters so throughly aroused. He was electric with anticipation. 'Dye your hair. Blonde. The client likes blondes.'

Walters knows him. So who is he?

But it was clear what manner of man he was when I saw where we were going, where he lived. We cruised up, up, up into the hills, luxurious in the leather and chrome of our limousine. Walters drove with ease and certainty. He knew the road. All the wealthy and the powerful live far outside the city. This man lived beyond the Heights. He lived on the slopes of the volcano. The view back down into the plains was surreal, glimmering. The road curved above us into a landscape of darkness. We saw high gates, with ornamental grotesques grinning from the ironwork in the car's lights as we hummed past. The villas were all hidden in the trees. Sometimes the guards bathed us in searchlights, checking our registration. No one attempted to stop us. As we passed the checkpoints Shaw's hands, relaxed and open, never moved from his knees. He was completely concentrated. I began to feel sick. Someone was waiting. Our path had been cleared. I had never been driven into these hills. We were rising into the residential area occupied by the highest reaches of the government. I understood why I had not been allowed to know who he was.

I stared at Shaw's profile in the flickering dark. His stillness was absolute, unreadable.

When we reached the massive gates and the checkpoint with armed guards, Walters sighed slightly, and I saw that his hands left damp marks on the wheel. I looked up and saw two huge stone hydras stretching out their necks towards one another across the arch. All our papers and our security IDs were checked again and again. We did not speak as the huge iron gates finally opened into the darkened gardens. As the car hummed to a halt we heard water idling in the fountains. The great doors stood open against the warm night. The illuminated flags drooped against their masts in the windless air. Shaw vanished into the gardens, but Walters remained beside me. He carried his black briefcase. I stood hesitant on the steps, glimpsing the wealth of great spaces, parquet and carpets, cabinets filled with African masks and totems, an encyclopaedia of cultures, collected under glass, polished, gleaming. The client was clearly erudite, cultivated. He owned hundreds of books. We passed from the great hall into the library. I saw a circular edifice of steps constructed to reach the topmost volumes. The room smelled of tobacco, long since obsolete among the general population. I recognised the smell. Only our most powerful clients still had the right to smoke. I could also catch the rich smell of spices: cloves, garlic, cinnamon. Who was he?

The palace appeared to be deserted. No servants bustled into the doorway, no animals scurried away. We stood patient, dark-coated, professional, waiting silent under the soft lamps. We were sombre as priests, visiting the bereaved. No one spoke. Walters placed a chair in the shadows for me, then leaned against one of the columns. He did not appear to be surprised that we were forced to wait. Nearly an hour passed.

Then one of the glass doors leading to the inner courtyard opened and a shadow appeared in the doorway. I could see into the courtyard. It had a glass dome covering the roof which was lit from beneath. The rectangle was overflowing with tropical and semi-tropical plants, hibiscus, bougainvillaea, lilies, cacti, palm trees – the inner garden was a micro-climate humming with the raw sounds of a tropical night and running water. A small gust of damp heat scudded across the hall from the open door.

'Come in.'

We advanced into a wall of humidity, an indoor greenhouse. I couldn't see the client's face, but he was wearing evening dress and smoking a cigar. He shook Walters's hand and there was a moment's displeasure, which I sensed, like a douche of cold water, as he looked me over.

'She's dressed like a whore. Send her upstairs. First floor, first left. Make her put on my wife's clothes. Then bring her back here.'

His voice was very calm, but had an eerie echo, as if he was speaking not from a place close to us, but from a long way away. I tried again to look into his face, but his features were always shadowed. Then I noticed his hands. He wore many cold, golden rings.

Shaw stood beside me. He touched my elbow gently and led me away up into the higher darkness of the house. Everywhere, I heard the trickle of running water. The interiors were very warm, fires were lit in all the grates, despite the mildness of the night. We entered a room of green mirrors. This was a woman's room, lavish as an Aladdin's cave. She had necklaces made with pure gold, pure raw lumps of gold, the gold you can only buy in the Indies, mined in the jungles. She had strings of black pearls and large brooches of onyx, set in gold. He dressed her in black and gold. But she preferred green. All her casual clothes, T-shirts, jeans, her house-coat, her swimming costume – I pulled out drawer after drawer – green, all green. She had two entirely different wardrobes, one lavish and heavy, underwear, night-gowns, evening dresses, full length, all in black, edged with threads of pure, real gold. Her other clothes – I skimmed the racks – were light fresh cottons and raw silks, all in yellow green, bottle green, sea green, forest green, aquamarine green. And then I found the dress I had seen her wearing, a soft lawn hiding her breasts and thousands of tiny green flowers embedded in silk. I snatched it out of the cupboard and turned to Shaw, who was standing, unmoving, by the window, gazing out into the illuminated dark.

'Will this fit me? What do you think?'

He looked carefully at the dress.

'It may be a little tight. She is slighter than you, but the same height.'

'You know her. Who is she? Who is she?'

Shaw closed his eyes slightly.

'Put it on.'

I ripped off my leather suit and folded the green silk over my body. Her shape had been suggested by the dress. My own showed through, bolder, less delicate, unashamed. I sat down in front of the mirror and put on her jewels, all her green stones, jade, pearl and moonstones flecked with green. I looked into the green-lipped shade of the mirror and saw again, superimposed on my own face, with all its lines of corruption and ambiguity, that pale fragile beauty that I had known at once to be a precious, alien thing. She was not one of us, she came from somewhere else, somewhere across the mountains. The scent of her impregnated the dress. Her face flickered before me. She was here, somewhere in this room, watching my gradual possession of who she once had been. I looked round quickly, the long drops of jade caressing my neck with cold. No one was there but Shaw. He had not moved from the window, but he was now wearing his black leather gloves, his supple, working gloves, a second skin on his cold hands. He had shaved his head.

I felt the prickle of horror all along my inner thighs.

'Shaw,' I whispered, and he moved closer, his hands hidden. 'Don't let him touch me. I beg you, don't let him touch me. I couldn't. Not with this client. Do you understand?'

A tremor passed through his face, like a ripple in calm water. I had never, ever asked this before. Shaw, intent and still as a crouching cougar, simply lowered his eyes.

'Come downstairs now,' was all he said.

I stood up.

The dress was long and loose at the hips, flowing outwards, rustling with her presence and the aroma of roses. I sensed the swaying raw silk billowing behind me. I felt taller, more graceful, as I descended the staircase. My steps echoed in the hallway. Her green slippers were one size too small for me, but I ignored the discomfort. It's not for long, it's not for long.

The rooms below seemed darker now, there were fewer lights. Walters had vanished, and Shaw, who had begun to descend the staircase behind me, was suddenly no longer there. I paused in the hallway, then stepped into the exotic garden. There were gravel walkways and everywhere, always invisible, the sound of running water. I examined the orchids, parasites cowering in the armpits of these heavy, lavish trees. Everything seemed huge, monstrous. The wet air clung to my face.

I heard his step on the pathway before me and then smelled his presence, tobacco and cinnamon. Now I could see his face.

I was expecting the grey-streaked hair, the killer's eyes and the heavy moustache. I remembered his cold, golden rings, crushing my hand, and the certainty of his authority. But he was not quite the same. Now the eyes were sunken back into the ancient face, the hair was thick, but quite white, the heavy face, white, cold, clean-shaven. He looked like a statue wearing a death mask. Layers of still fixity and cold thickened his gaze. He was as monstrous as his artificial tropics.

I had never been afraid of any of our clients. I usually see them at their most vulnerable, undignified, pitiful, pathetic. But this man was barely human. I was afraid of him.

I staggered backwards and cried out.

His eyes glazed over into smoky white balls.

I had reacted precisely as he had wished.

Then he was on top of me. I felt a black rush of wings and heard horses' hooves, rapidly approaching. His dead white face was all that I could see. His hands were around my throat. I heard my own voice, far away, inside the echo of his snarl, screaming and screaming.

Suddenly the head snapped back. The world steadied. A red slit appeared in the monster's throat. The weight against me surged away, and I found myself sobbing hysterically in Walters's arms. He carried me into the hallway and set me down upon the last step of the staircase. I clutched the marble banisters. Walters reappeared with a glass of pure water.

'Here, drink this.'

As I gulped it down Shaw stepped out of the tropical garden. He was unruffled, but his face was strangely drawn about the mouth. He carried no weapons. He was still wearing his black gloves.

'You take insane risks,' said Walters quietly, 'you moved too soon. Why didn't you wait? He could have killed all three of us.'

Shaw met his eye. He stood quite still, accepting the reprimand. Then he said,

'She was expendable so far as he was concerned. He intended to kill her.'

Walters paused, then nodded. He let his hand rest for a moment on my shoulder. I understood the gesture. There are three of us.

Walters closed the courtyard door without making a sound. He addressed himself entirely to Shaw.

'Where is his wife?'

'In the car.'

I looked up. We were taking her with us. Walters looked at the computer inside his watch.

'We wait another four minutes. Then we move. Can you walk?'

I could barely stand.

'My clothes?'

'Everything is already in the car,' said Walters.

I took off the green slippers and left them at the foot of the staircase. Walters leaned down and wiped my wet face with his own handkerchief. He put his arm around my waist, as if I were an invalid, and led me out on to the steps and into the cooling night. Shaw closed all the doors behind us.

The woman, dressed in Lincoln green, lay doubled up in the back seat. Her blonde hair gleamed in the dark.

'Put your jacket over her. Cover her hair,' ordered Walters.

I did as I was told. She was clearly drugged.

The car surged away down the long drive, past the

checkpoints. The soldiers showed no interest in our passing. We turned north, unchallenged, and headed towards the wild country. We had taken the opposite way to the one we had come. I sat wearing another woman's life along with her green silk and her jade earrings, while she lay, insensible in black leather beside me.

I could see the night world of open fields, little pockets of woodland, silent farms and cattle brooding in darkness, their white parts illuminated like a jigsaw with missing pieces. Shaw was driving fast. I overrode the computer locks and wound down the window, becoming calmer in the warm rushing air. I pulled my coat back from the woman's face. She was luminous, delicate, utterly beautiful. I gazed down at her still features, fascinated. Walters turned in his seat, and watched me for a moment. Then he proceeded quietly with his instructions.

'In ten minutes or so we will reach the airport. Our plane will be waiting. Shaw and I will get out. Only a woman can complete the last part of the operation. No man is allowed to enter the sacred spaces. It is therefore your responsibility. You will find the directions on the car's computer. Follow them to the letter. You will take her to the appointed place and deliver her up to her mother. The place will be a little surprising to you, because there will be nothing to see but open land, vineyards and a grove of cypress trees. If she is conscious by then, simply turn her loose in the open. She will come to no harm. Her mother will find her. If she is still asleep simply leave her on the bare earth in the grove and come away. You are strong enough to carry her unaided. Your return journey will appear on the computer before you. You have just over two hours. So drive fast. We are not going back to the city. Our time there is now over. We are under new orders. We serve another master. On no account, whatever she asks, must you give her any

explanations. You must say nothing. Nothing. Is that understood?'

I sat still, listening. Then I said,

'Can I keep her dress?'

Walters shrugged.

'That's up to you.'

He paused.

'Sophia, follow my orders to the letter. Give her no
information. No information whatsoever. Whatever she asks,
and whatever you feel. Say nothing.'

I nodded.

He turned back to the road.

I feel her hand, clutching my neck as she drags herself upright.
She is warm, golden.

'Oh . . . Why am I here? Who are you? Who are you?'

Her eyes meet mine in the mirror. I am following the red
computer lights, flickering on the dashboard before me. I do not
reply.

'But I know you!' She is sitting up now. 'You are the
reception hostess in The Underworld. The woman with eyes of
pure blue water. You are one of my husband's creatures. One of
his employees. Where is my husband?'

I do not reply. I do not react. I am under orders. I say
nothing. She clutches my arm. I shake her off.

'Who are you? Who are you? Why have you done this? Why
are you wearing my dress? Where did you find it? Why have I
been imprisoned?'

I say nothing whatever. She is clutching the car door and
crying. The automatic locks are in place. The car trembles and
jolts over the gravel and ruts on the white road before us.

At last, I speak to her.

'Is this your mother's house?'

Before us are acres of soft green, fresh with the dew of early day. The light shifts, from black to dark blue. I see the olive trees becoming silver in the dawn. To the left there is a grove of cypress trees, their dark, pointed shadows bolder against the light. Across the long slopes are acres of green vines. The goats' bells tinkle in the changing green shadows.

'Is this where you can find your mother?' The car's computer tells me that we have reached the place where I am to leave her. And indeed I see nothing, but vines, olives, and the whitening sky.

She looks out at the landscape, and then she howls, a long unearthly cry of grief and longing.

'Pull yourself together. Is this the right place?'

The car computer tells me that this is the right place. There is the little grove of cypress trees. I can hear running water and the rhythmic splash of a waterfall crumbling into a pool.

I shall hit her if she gets any more hysterical. My nerves are on edge. I smell her husband's blood on my breath, my face.

'You know it is,' she whispers, 'but this isn't real. I cannot be free. I have dreamed so often that I am transported here. By some miracle. But I don't know you. I don't know how to thank you. Will I ever see you again?'

I do not answer. I have been ordered to tell her nothing. I have no answers to her questions. She strokes my arm with an appalling timidity.

Her loveliness breaks over me. I look up into the tentative beauty of a woman whose life I cannot imagine, whose body sways with the fragility of spring. I belong to the unnatural world of concrete and darkness. We can never acknowledge each other.

'Who are you?' she begs. Who is it that she has to thank for giving her life back to her again? I cannot imagine. I open the car doors with an irritated click.

'Here. Take this.'

On to her lap I slam down the catalogue. She will finger it with horror. She will know us again. For we are imaged there, the creatures conjured from darkness to obey him. And there, folded into the glossy pages of daily perversion, directly over the orders of a man who relives his wife's rape for pleasure, again and again, is one name, our real name, scrawled in her husband's handwriting.

SOPHIA WALTERS SHAW

Narcissus and Echo

Nicole Ward Jouve

I t even had a lake.

The park was as magical as the castle. The lake held its own castle, slate green and blue. It shimmered when the long dark body of a carp swam close to the surface. Ducks diving propagated ripples all over it. It was all magic: not what mere academics like herself were used to. What a brilliant, brilliant idea to have a conference in such a place. A place worthy of Miranda.

There were going to be poets, musicians, actors, painters as well as academics. The creators were going to be present as strongly as the critics, those like herself who could only analyse, celebrate. More strongly. They mattered more. Wasn't Miranda herself a creator, who could turn her hand to, it seemed, everything? The most prolific, many-faceted writer of her age, some people said the greatest.

For a long time now the train, with its dust-smelling antique velvet seats, had rocked and stuttered and whistled its way through lakes and forests and gorges and castles perched on rocks, the slated roofs of keeps and gables glistening above expanses of dark firs. Then it had stopped. Dramatically, in the almost silence, and Heloise had known it was *the* stop. She had alighted. The station was empty, the station house like a chalet with its sculpted wooden eaves, its wooden balcony. Scores of people whom on the train she had mistaken for travellers bound for elsewhere, had alighted too. She would never have guessed the train held so many. Interesting-looking people, she had decided on the spot. Fascinating, really. Men with greying lion manes and strong facial bones, men with deep-set blue eyes under bristling eyebrows. Intense-looking older women with Joan of Arc haircuts and ponchos and the look of the famous about them, attractive-looking young women, some exquisitely pretty with high-heeled boots and flowing hair, others with pierced nostrils and black leather trousers, one with purple hair. Handsome young men, too handsome and what a pity, Heloise thought: in pairs. One tall old man with dazzling white hair, a monocle and a cape. Everyone elegant, or at least dress-conscious. Miranda attracted but the best; her own flamboyant elegance spilled over her admirers.

Miranda herself was not there. Of course: she would make her appearance at the appropriate time. And yet, Heloise reflected, she needn't do: wherever she went, she was bound to be the focus of all eyes. The most beautiful woman of them all. The greatest.

The castle *was* an enchantment. It did have the turrets and gables with conical slate roofs of the other castles that had tantalisingly loomed above the vast forests they had crossed on their way, but it also had a most attractive Renaissance granite façade, with baroque copings above the windows. From its gently sloping hill it stood above the lake that reflected it. What was so wonderful, Heloise thought as she wandered along the banks, dipped in and out of leafy avenues, of light and shade, crossed wild meadows and paths where the delicate pink of wild geraniums vied with the red-pink of the campions, was that here were no firs, but centuries-old deciduous trees. Beauties, some with trunks it would have taken two to embrace: elms, limes, oaks, graceful beeches. They were so stately, so sumptuously green in the princedom of early summer that Heloise could not help herself thinking that here were the models of the species – Ur-trees, the spirits of beeches and limes. The elms were untouched by any hint of a disease. The foliage, vast, shot through with light, filled with bird-song, had something pristine and powerful about it. Water murmured everywhere: brooks, rivulets. In many places the ground was spongy. Mosses and reeds. Marsh flowers bloomed. 'This place is replete with bulbs,' said a small dark man who wore sunglasses even in the shade. He had caught up with Heloise and was being both complimentary and ironic. 'In spring it is a feast of colours. Grape hyacinths, daffodils, primroses, scillas, wood anemones . . . And round the lake, especially on that bank over there, the ground is white with narcissi.'

Everything *was* magic. The huge library with its ancient leather-bound volumes, its golden-red shelves and wainscoting, where the talks, the lectures, would take place. The adorable eighteenth-century theatre with its folds of purple velvet, its baroque gilt scrolls, its sinuous balconies lined with purple velvet, edged with gold: there would be performances there! The equally baroque chapel, gold-laden, heavily painted, with profane, sumptuously attired Madonnas and saints. The altar piece, an ecstatic Virgin buoyed up on pinky-white clouds by Eros-like naked angels, all plump downy wings and curves and cuddly flesh. There would be singing there, an oratorio to Miranda's words. There were children's play-rooms in the attics, with dappled grey rocking-horses with red harnesses and worn flowery chintz armchairs. In one, a huge French doll's house sat on a Boulle cabinet. On the first storey, a languid doll lolled on a miniature Louis XVI yellow silk sofa, her yellow silk hair all elaborately piled above her exquisite china face. Handsome *marquis* and *marquises* leaned over the backs of chairs or against the mantelpiece and gazed with miniature china eyes in her direction, as if frozen in longing. But she had eyes only for the silver mirror whose handle, not bigger than a toothpick, she held in her miniature china hand.

She had, Miranda, made the most dramatic entrance: poised as if for an exit. They were all having cocktails on the paved terrace that overlooked the calm waters of the lake. In lake and sky, the golden-pink of the setting sun, barely streaked with cloud. Heloise was making friends with a Spanish woman analyst, a vivacious redhead, and her pal, a Finnish author of children's books. She was talking, she had her back to the castle, and then suddenly she'd noticed that all talk had died down. She'd turned around: bathed in the gold of the setting sun, framed in the doorway of the castle, exiting towards them but poised: Miranda. Poised on the threshold, like a model bursting in from backstage, suspended for a few seconds in the full flood of the projectors while ripples of stunned admiration run through the guests before she moves, walks down the catwalk. Tall Miranda, her hair gleaming gold and as she shook it ever so slightly, shook the golden mass, seeming to throw fire. She wore a trouser suit of shot silk, white and gleaming. There she stood for a few seconds, above them, framed in that doorway, as if transfixed, as if surprised by the large gathering. (She knew, she must have known, Heloise thought: Miranda had orchestrated it all, chosen whom she wanted, whom she didn't. Her secretaries would have seen to it.) But there she waved suddenly, as if barely able to overcome her startled delight: were they a hundred, two hundred who had ridden relays of trains, flown through the skies, driven thousands of miles, gathered from the four corners of the world to celebrate her, her work? There they were, admirers, exegetes, worshippers: would-be lovers, all. The setting sun was now suffusing them all in a warm gold, as if they were receiving the reflected glory of Miranda's own white and gold. And then she stepped forward, began to descend the stairs towards them, her high golden heels alighting gracefully on every stone step, poised every time as if she were floating on air, waving slightly like a tall-stemmed flower.

What followed had been worthy of that first appearance. The black-cloaked white-maned poet, who turned out to be the prestigious J***, had held them all enthralled by an eight-hour-long talk. Heloise would not have thought such talking, such listening was possible: but it was. Words appeared, Miranda's words, some sublime. Disappeared, fell to bits, fled, only to re-materialise in magical combinations, leaving a trail of fire as they went, catching fire from the original like a trail of sulphur from a lit match. They were entranced. Time had become space, an eerie fiery world, a world of fire-flies and dancing phosphorus. Arctic lights sang. They were startled by the lunch bell, they barely stopped to eat. And on it went. They forgot about tea-breaks, about cocktails. If the dinner-bell had not insistently gone on ringing, they would have sat there till midnight. Never, Heloise thought, have I been given such insight into Miranda's work.

It was overwhelming. In every way, she decided, as she made her way to her delightful tower bedroom. It was all curves. Elegant flower print on the bedstead, the curtains; roses in a vase on her elmwood writing-table with its reddish-blond sheen. The windows looked out two ways, towards the stables and towards the west corner of the lake, where it was at its most wooded, its most mysterious. There was an en-suite cabinet with an antique basin and a tiny window overlooking the stable yard: but neither toilet nor shower. Heloise went on a search, found toilets along the bends of corridors, in nooks and crannies. There was a shower two doors down from her own room; a door opposite intriguingly climbed a few rickety steps to an attic full of books and boxes, which itself led on to another winding staircase and more rooms. 'At least I can find the shower,' she muttered aloud and was making her way back to the staircase to her own corridor, when she almost bumped into a large bearded semi-naked man, handsome hairy torso above loins draped in a white bath sheet. He was stooping, and questioningly mumbled something that ended with: 'shower?' 'That way, down the steps,' Heloise smiled. 'No, I don't need it just now,' she added just in case. 'You go ahead.' 'Head' was all Heloise understood of his muttered answer, and she wondered whether he'd simply said he'd go ahead, then, or was cracking a joke about his needing to keep his head lowered so as not to hit it against the beams. It could have been an exciting, a promising encounter: Heloise wondered why it was not.

His name was Andy, she discovered that evening as she sat across from him at dinner. Short for Andreas K★★★, she further found, as he ceremoniously distributed his visiting card round the whole group who sat at their table. He was Miranda's translator into Ruritanian. It was thanks to his translations, to his passionate advocacy, that Miranda had such a following here. He it was who had persuaded Count and Countess D★★★, the owners of the castle, to host this international gathering. He had hangdog brown eyes that clung too long to your face, a sensuous mouth. Quite an eccentric: he walked in and out of the sessions without apparent regard for the speakers, entering and exiting through any of the multiple doors. He would sit conspicuously for a while, looking in Miranda's direction, then stand up and leave: each time he came back he wore a different hat. He had quite a collection: trilbies, American caps, Panama hats . . . Wherever he sat, or stood, his eyes remained riveted to Miranda's back. Her tall, straight back, almost boyish in its uprightness, her golden hair, her head attentively leaning towards whoever was speaking, or bent reflexively towards her knees. Even from the back, her shoulders draped in some exotic shawl or sharply outlined by the elegant cut of a close-fitting jacket, you could see she was beautiful. She drew eyes to her like a magnet. None so unswervingly as Andy's.

That *was* the mark of her beauty, of her work: that she could draw all kinds. Every form of seductiveness, every form of seduction too, gathered there. There was something, yes – virile? boyish – about her, both knight and page, strong and pliant, with something of the sinewy delicacy of a curled-haired Verrocchio youth. You wanted her to champion you: and if you *were* distressed, stressed, gravely ill, oppressed, one of the poor of the earth, Miranda would champion you. Mother you too. That was the weirdness of it. She was *both* Knight and Mother, both Percival and Demeter. Her youthful admirers, the young women who flocked to her, wrote papers, theses, books about her work, she protected like a mother hen: 'her daughters' she called them. She had a few sons too, gentle, often timid youths who served her silently, whom she in turns rebuffed and took under her wing. What was demanded in return was absolute, unswerving loyalty. No: dedication. Around, far away from, close to, Miranda, you could only admire. Reflect. Give her back something of her beauty, her creativity. Nothing else was allowed, at least for the likes of me, Heloise caught herself thinking almost bitterly, remembering how she'd hoped to get close, become Miranda's bosom friend – her lover, perhaps? Had she been tempted? For she was like a living flame, Miranda, that one time she'd hugged her tenderly, seduced her (Heloise did feel bitter, she now knew, hated herself for it). Miranda had hugged her, not because she really was fond of her, but because on the spur of the moment perhaps she'd felt like being charming, like being loving, and she'd overflowed in an impulse of benevolence and wrapped her in her arms, rubbed herself against her like a cat that then goes away indifferent, untouched, but having made itself yours for ever. For you could not forget how like a flame she'd been, flickering and rising and liquid in your arms, and you wanted this to happen again, you wanted it for real: but you knew you only counted in so far as you admired her, as you served her glory, as you were part of the reflecting crowd. So now Heloise held herself aloft in stiff watchfulness. That way she held Miranda at bay: she could not otherwise bear the death of hope, the feeling of rejection that came over her every time she came near Miranda, and Miranda called her as she would others too, 'my darling', as if you were special, as if you meant so much to her, and you were so moved – and you knew you were just being seduced all over again.

You could be one of the mirrors. It was as if they all, here, this audience rippling with anticipation and delight, listening in rapt silence as Miranda read her latest poems (and weren't they breathtaking, Heloise had to admit), it was as if they all were holding their little mirrors up to her and they merged into one huge watery mirror. They rippled and rolled and subsided as each gave his or her paper, and each was a tribute, a wave that rose and for a while gave back the brilliance of the sun shining upon it, then ebbed and died as the speaker sat to strong applause: for the mirroring had to go on, the moment of shining had to be reflected too. And the applause was like waves rolling back cartloads of pebbles as they ebbed.

In her turn then Miranda reflected. That was magic and terrible. When you had spoken your piece, suitably celebrated her work, she complimented you. She expressed her approval. Her delight, sometimes. Gave extraordinary praise, sometimes. Was overwhelmed, she said: once or twice. In the face of the poetic papers, the fairy-tale paper that evoked Beauty and the Beast. The speakers, all of them, were the Reader-Beast that held Miranda-Beauty for a while in the enchanted castle, as happened every time they held one of her books in their hands. They had lost their heart-rose to her, but that very loss had drawn her to them and they now held her for a while in fear and trembling, with hushed delicacy. They were so afraid, a wrong word (a suit too passionately pressed, Heloise wondered?) might make her fly back to her native kingdom. 'Beauty, will you marry me?' they all asked of Miranda's work as they read, as they listened. They knew she never would. But they were giving her a mirror, so that after she'd gone, she'd look perhaps and fondly remember perhaps, even if fleetingly, that they existed, that they were pining for her, dying, once the last page had been turned and the book closed, in their now deserted castle. And would the next book come, please?

Miranda's books were all about her, Heloise thought. Each poem one of her voices, each character in her plays a facet of her inexhaustible personality. In their illusion of capture they held her, held her books – Beast held Beauty. But they were the captivated ones. Was it because they each recognised themselves in what she wrote? Saw in her what they would ideally like to be? The object of their heart's desire? Untouchable, self-contained Miranda: the white-maned poet, on the first day, had celebrated her narcissism. She and himself, he'd said, were the most narcissistic people he'd ever known. Do not laugh, he'd added: you had to be narcissistic in order to be able to love. 'As long as it is not secondary narcissism,' the Spanish analyst had remarked to Heloise who was asking puzzled questions: 'What is secondary narcissism?' 'Ah well,' Pilar had laughed. 'Difficult to explain.'

Another paper also drew high praise from Miranda. Listening to it, Heloise had felt herself squirming, and so had Pilar and her Finnish friend Svenga (but was that because they were jealous?). It had been, really, a declaration of love. From a prestigious woman, a minister. There was Miranda, eyes lowered, blonde head bowed, pensive, touched, thrilled, embarrassed, who could tell? She had such self-control. Or was she so absorbed in her own self-image, in the reflections that came to her through them, that she did not care? Was she so used to everyone falling in love with her that it was now easy to take, take for granted, accept as simply her due, a form of homage that the world repeatedly paid to her beauty? There stood the woman, this high-profile, powerful woman, trembling, her heart in her mouth, she said, taking a terrible risk, she said, and the risk was to make her paper a thinly disguised declaration of love to Miranda in front of a crowd of over a hundred people. Listening to her, the poets she read, quoted, Wyatt, Donne, Byron, you would have thought that all the love poems in the world had been written for Miranda.

It grew, for Heloise, more and more difficult to take. Her own trouble troubled her, as she wandered round the lake, through the tall grass, under the centenarian beeches. As she clasped tree trunks in her arms, feeling foolish as she did, looking around first to make sure no one was about. She pressed her cheek, her breasts, her belly, against the trunk. It was rough and yet as she stroked it, its lichens and rusty mosses, strangely soft. She thought of Renaissance poems about nymphs hiding under the bark. She felt mothered, protected. Pillared. As if strength from the high-flowing sap got into her and she could for a while at least forget about all that trouble that Miranda, what was happening around Miranda, gave her.

She was in a storm of feelings. If only she had not been in love with Miranda, as everyone else was. Apart from that old woman with jet-black dyed hair who so audibly and visibly hated her. Smellingly too: she boldly farted when you sat next to her, releasing each fart as she slowly swung from buttock to buttock. She had been a great beauty herself once. She could not bear all that homage going to another. Why did she stay, thus eaten by envy, like a wicked fairy trapped at the princess's wedding feast? Captivated like the rest of them, surely. Safer in her hatred, no doubt, than the others were, than Heloise was, caught between her desire to be loved of Miranda and the knowledge Miranda would never love her – perhaps would never love anybody.

She could be so tender. She had a beautiful voice. She called you terms of endearment, 'my little foal', 'my fish'. You felt about to gallop, to leap: being called sweet names by Miranda was so blissful. She held out to each the promise of her love, she gave off the signs of love. She embraced you as if you were her child. She also looked at you with her huge golden, green eyes, literally shadowed by lashes thick as reeds round a pond. You avidly looked into them. You wanted to fall into them. Mother and irresistible lover both. For a moment she seemed as if she'd singled you out. She asked you about yourself. Perhaps that was it. You talked. She seemed to listen for a while, yet somehow you knew she was not there. She had withdrawn to somewhere else, she was looking at something else; your words ricocheted back to you. But you were held. You were captivated by the illusion of intimacy. You could not give it up. Some were keening more visibly, less guardedly than others. Andy for one, hovering with his faithful dog's eyes, making a show of himself with his hats and airs, agonising about his paper that was to be given on the last day but one and that he spent the nights re-writing. Twice, going to the toilet, Heloise met him wandering up and down cradling his typewriter like a baby in the attic room, looking for a spot where inspiration might strike.

She had to give it up, Heloise had decided long ago. Give up the hope of anything from Miranda. She had to keep her distance. Survival for her was at that price. It cost her dear. Her paper was more detached, more analytic than the others. As if she'd known what was coming, Miranda had sat on the side, not facing her in the front row as she had done with the other speakers. No praise had followed. She hadn't joined in the discussion. There had been no mirroring.

Heloise's old demons had rounded on her. She'd felt rejected. Competitive, envious. Just a bit more and I'll start farting, she'd thought, attempting to defuse what was rising in her. If she could have been chosen by Miranda, favoured in some way, she could have borne it: that she couldn't get what Miranda had. But how to compete? Beauty, power of mind and scope of achievement, magic of personality, in every area Miranda was unreachable. Even her past history, her family, were so romantic. Her magical father, the celebrated explorer, the one she called 'her strong brown river god', who had died in an archaeological expedition to the sources of the Nile and whom she made into an endless source of inspiration. Her anxious, solicitous, adorable mother, whose life was consecrated to her adored daughter – who, with ordinary, dutiful, fearful parents like Heloise's could possibly compete? Everything about Miranda was mythical. Heloise grubbed in the earth. She hated herself for her envy, it tore at her and she tore at herself for feeling it.

Wouldn't it be great if Miranda fell in love as they all had fallen in love with her? If she could get a taste of the torment she inflicted? For torment she did inflict. The people she rejected – those whose papers were criticised – or even that did not get the praise that was lavished on most, fell into a visible decline. You could see them go white as if they'd been bled, become invisible, vanish into the woodwork. Heloise tried to comfort them: was she tending to her own sorrow? One Italian film-maker, Francesca, a dark, intense woman with Anna Magnani's charcoal eyes, had stuttered over her paper. It had been cut short. She was having a breakdown. Heloise was drawn to her as if by a magnet. Her family, some Italian aristocrats, had known the count's. Friendship between the families went back a long time. She had spent summers in the castle with her sisters when they had been children. 'This place is fated,' she confided to Heloise. 'That lake is the horrors. Don't you know . . .? Of course you don't.' Veronica, the daughter of the house, Francesca's childhood friend, had committed suicide there. 'Thrown herself in where it is at its deepest, from that bank where the narcissi grow.' She'd stuffed herself full of sleeping pills, she must have sunk very quickly. Would have had trouble swimming anyway, so full of tangled weeds at the bottom. 'The top clarity of the waters is so deceptive. It's because it is so still, reflects so much. Deep down it is all muddy and murky. I know, we used to swim from the sand bank on the other side. Haven't you wondered why there are carp?' Francesca was gushing forth, she was pouring it all out now, how they as children had got up at dawn to swim and fish in the lake and how there had been this pink radiance that sometimes went red and seemed to set fire to the waters, how they'd played in those woods. And in the attic rooms, all the nooks and crannies and toys and treasure chests of the place. 'I used to so look forward to coming here. Playing with the other children, I could forget my mother. She could not cope with us children, she always pushed us away, rejected us. I grew up without a mother. This place was *it*, our children's games, it's the only mother I know. But even then, there was a sinister undercurrent. The count's brother was manic-depressive, he prowled around us, it was rumoured that . . . Never mind that. And the Mademoiselle, she was another one . . . Veronica was always strange. So highly strung . . . It took a while before it occurred to the family that she could be in the water. They'd searched high and low, even thought she might have eloped. While they were draining the lake, dredging up so much mud, so much blackness, the narcissi were coming into full bloom. All that white on the bank. All that darkness deep down. We were all there, remembering, remembering so much from the past and I kept thinking, "When she threw herself in, the narcissi must have been in sharp, pointed buds. How could she not have waited to see their blooming? She used to love them so, lie among them in her white muslin dress, her gold hair spread out . . ." Jilted by her first love, they thought. She was only sixteen.'

And now (Francesca kept pouring it out; they were in a wainscotted corridor and Heloise, who'd asked, who'd sympathised, felt herself cornered, under the siege of all that past, children running through those attics, and it seemed to her that the rocking-horse was creaking to and fro, and to and fro just there above their heads) – now, when Miranda cold-shouldered Francesca, ignored or interrupted her, it was like being rejected by her own cold unloving mother all over again. And all there was to fall back upon was this place, haunted by those memories. A place of drowning. 'She knows she is doing this to me. She knows. I am going mad and I can't help it. And I don't want her now to take me in her arms and make me better. I don't want to be babied. I'm not a baby,' Francesca had repeated several times, teeth clenched.

She was not a baby. She would not let Miranda treat her as such.

But she did. Next day before dinner, Miranda did go to Francesca, did make a fuss of her, did take her in her arms. Made her sit next to her at table. Francesca calmed down a bit after that. Heloise did not know whether she was moved or humiliated or angry. Or envious? Heavy: as if a spell could not be broken.

Interesting. There were some who did all right, because they were being praised, favoured. And some relatively detached older men and women who could somehow take not being

singled out – who watched, or who, though keening somewhere, were stoical enough to survive their keening. And a few
who were quite unaffected, most blissfully one self-contented
man, Johan, who evidently thought himself so wonderful, so
irresistible, whether with women or because he was so
convinced that whatever he did or said was the most brilliant
thing on earth, and he had to be in there asking questions that
turned into speeches and lavishing his charm on this or that
attractive woman. After one of his lengthier interventions, as he
showered the audience with what he evidently thought were
pearls of wisdom, Pilar had leaned towards Heloise and
whispered, 'That's secondary narcissism.'

But there were those who were sorely lacking in that.

One evening Heloise went on a long walk. She felt such a
need to wander away from it all. She'd walked out of the
grounds of the park, she'd climbed the steep road and on a bend
had caught sight of a tiny chapel in a clearing. It had a cupola
and small, narrow rounded windows, and inside – for the
creaking door had yielded after a shove – had not been locked –
was all round and peaceful embrace. There were no icons. The
stone was bare, with bits of plaster still hanging here and there,
with faded paint and bits of gold. There was a single bench.
Heloise had sat in the slowly fading light, the warm glow of
twilight. Into the night.

As she was crossing the hall on her return, glad to have missed
dinner, ready to go to bed, she was called by Johan. He was in
an armchair, deep in conversation with a brisk, pretty American
brunette. Laura. Heloise had exchanged a few words with her,
noted how acerbic she could be. 'Where have you been?' asked
Johan. 'You've missed quite a drama. Sit down.'

Laura was looking chastened. She told the story, relayed by
Johan. In his stuttering, insensitive way Andy had intruded in
the midst of a conversation she and other young women were

having. He'd been getting on her nerves anyway. She was always meeting him when she crossed this or that attic on her way down from her gabled bedroom high up in a tower. Half-naked sometimes. And he had that irritating habit of repeating bits of what you said, as if he wanted to cling to you, to draw your attention but didn't know how to. She couldn't bear impeded speech anyway. It rubbed her up the wrong way. So she'd said something ironic, something cutting like 'the man one can't get away from'. At that point he'd lashed out. A volley of abuse about women, something about young women who gave themselves airs and spent their lives trying to destroy men. 'Well, ruder than that,' Laura grinned, and Johan nodded ingratiatingly. He'd looked quite threatening, he was such a large, powerful man, like a bull suddenly let loose, and the young women there had been afraid. Then Johan and others had intervened, pulled him away. 'Eventually I managed to calm him down. I feel sorry for him,' Johan said. 'The poor man is in the middle of a breakdown. His wife is divorcing him, his life is caving in upon him. He's forgotten his pills. He's terribly worried about his paper, he so wants to impress Miranda, he's up half the night with it.' 'I'm so sorry,' Laura said, 'if I had known what a bad state he was in I wouldn't have . . .' She was a therapist. Another. There were quite a number there. Heloise felt herself looking at her quizzically. Johan was explaining that somebody had sedatives and had given him some, that Andy's pills were being sent express delivery. 'Do you know what a maternal man is?' he asked Heloise solemnly. 'Well, that's me. I have taken him to his bedroom and shown him where mine was and told him he could come and knock at any time if he feels troubled in the night. That way,' he beamed at Laura, 'the young women will feel protected.'

The next morning Heloise felt something gnawing at her. She was anxious on Andy's behalf, she told herself. His paper: he was due to give it later today. That was certain to be a disaster. As each day went by, it was as if the pressure on the papers was increasing. But if it was all on Andy's behalf, why, after such hesitation, had she locked her bedroom door last night? She'd told herself *she* was not frightened of men's violence. She had lived with it, she had been close to men having breakdowns. She'd even felt a little contemptuous of women who were afraid of so little, who fed excitedly on a bit of drama. But perhaps she'd been wrong? Perhaps precisely because there had been so much of that stuff in her life, a new crisis, however far removed, wakened old ones?

She was crossing the hall on her way to breakfast when she noticed Miranda, leaning against a deep window sill, her gold hair a halo in the morning light. Alone, which was unusual: whoever had been with her must have been sent for something. She raised her head and looked intensely in Heloise's direction, stretched out her hand appealingly. Heloise went over. Miranda looked fraught. 'Did you hear about the appalling explosion last night?' Heloise nodded. 'Johan and Laura told me.' 'How could that happen?' Miranda said between clenched teeth. She was seething with carefully suppressed anger, a delicate line between her brows, her nostrils quivering. 'I had given instructions. I had said that the madmen and madwomen were to be kept away. We had a list. I had no idea – no idea that he was like that.' 'Johan said his wife is divorcing him,' Heloise interposed. 'He is very worried about the children. He has forgotten his pills. He's been given some, they're bringing some more from B★★★. He'll calm down.' 'This is catastrophic,' Miranda continued as if she hadn't heard. 'I cannot have this.' 'But, Miranda' – Heloise feared she was being bold – 'he's here. He's part of us. He's part of our reality.' Miranda's eyes grew wide, grew dark. 'What?' she hissed. 'How can you say such a thing? This big foaming prick. He has nothing to do with me.' A little Japanese woman flew into the room, a white cashmere shawl in her arms. 'Here you are at last, my darling Jumiko,' Miranda said, turning her back to Heloise and wrapping herself in the shawl. 'Let's go in to breakfast.'

Andy stood up. A calm Canadian academic briefly but kindly introduced him. Everybody, it was clear, was conspiring to contain the thing as much as it could be contained. Were they all wincing internally as Heloise was? Andy started. Stopped and started again. A quotation. Then another. Quotations not even strung together. He was a translator, Heloise reminded herself. Perhaps if you were a translator you were especially dependent on other people's words? When called upon to say his own thing, all Andy could do was echo other people's words. They had a strange meaning in his mouth. He was looking at Miranda, heroically seated in her customary place in the front row, exhibiting again, Heloise thought, her admirable self-control. She did not once look up. What storms were going on inside that gracefully bowed head, under that exquisite head of curls? Heloise still saw in her mind's eyes the fine, chiselled white nostrils, quivering. She felt winded, as if she'd been punched in the stomach. There was devastation inside. Blackness. 'That big foaming prick.' Such hatred: of Andy, of men, of the uncontainable storms that broke the exquisite surface, disrupted the show, that was to be pure beauty. Andy was imitating the minister who had quoted poetry to declare her love. He was quoting. The quotations did not cohere. They were broken fragments. 'Why did I so love my friend La Boëtie?' Montaigne had written. 'Because he was he, because I was I.' He looked intently at Miranda, and Miranda, head bowed, eyes lowered, heard or did not.

It grew worse. Scattered fragments. Not shored against ruin. Echoes of what others had said, wandering, unwittingly echoing darker places, times. Heloise found herself thinking of Mr Dorrit's disastrous speech in Venice, when all his snobbish efforts to court the fine world collapse under the impact of his own breakdown, and the prison world returns to him, and he asks his daughter Amy in the face of the assembled grandees whether 'Bob was on the lock?' But at least, Heloise told herself, Andy is not shouting. He will stop. At some point he will stop. She thought of the little chapel where she'd sat the evening before. She put the little chapel around them. She invoked all the forces of mercy that were in the little chapel, asking that Andy, that they all, be helped through this. And, miraculously, she felt, there was no disaster. The echoes went on, then died down. The audience sat patiently through it. Andy stopped. The gentle Canadian thanked him chastely. Laura stood up. She said something kind, complimentary, clever. Such a surprise. Such a beautiful thing to happen.

Heloise felt relief. Exaltation even. Andy was leaving. The Canadian would drive him to the station. Help would be at hand, Johan assured her. On the way up the stairs, she came across Miranda, Jumiko trotting busily next to her, with the air of a solicitous nurse. 'I'm so relieved,' Heloise said. 'What do you mean, relieved?' Miranda spat, and she had her tragic face on. 'It was a catastrophe. I don't know what I'm going to do.' 'Miranda, it could have been a lot worse. Everybody rounded up, was so understanding and supportive. That's what matters,' and as she said it, and as Miranda stared at her, shaking her curls as if she thought she was mad too, Heloise thought, 'That's also a sign of what Miranda does to people, that we all rounded up to make it all right, to protect her – and ourselves – from worse.'

She was startled. She shook inwardly, and the shaking went through and through. At what she had seen: the blackness, but also the vulnerability. In one so strong. She had thought, admiringly, enviously, of Miranda's beauty and seductiveness, of her power to make herself the object of a cult. And, resentfully, of Miranda rejecting, casting people out. It had never occurred to her that Miranda needed to protect herself, that there was a need that possessed her, that drove her on. For the first time, that evening, Heloise felt compassion.

There had been a performance, with a soprano and tenor, of Miranda's latest libretto. A tragic love duo between Europa, rapt by Zeus in the shape of a bull, and her brother Cadmus sent by a cruel father to look for her – and never find her. So intense, so full of pleas to the unreachable, it was oratorio rather than duo. Brother and sister longed for each other, but each in thrall to an overwhelming power could only sing two solitary songs: intertwined, never meeting. It was beautiful, yes. But Heloise felt too shaken to respond as she felt she should. They stood on the terrace afterwards, under the full moon (and yet, Heloise thought, this is the décor for it, this is appropriate). A deep breathing rose from the trees, rippled the calm surface of the lake. People walked up to Miranda and to the composer who stood, elegant in his white jacket, self-effacing, one step behind, intimating he'd only been the servant of the text. People congratulated, raved. Heloise was holding back. But unexpectedly, on her way to refill her glass, she came up face to face with Miranda. And even more unexpectedly, here she was raving too. All that she had refused to see, to feel, whilst she was in the purple and gold theatre, rose in her: the pathos of that separation, the coming together that can never be. The beauty of the song, the only thing you can put in the way of the ever-unfulfilled longing. And then she noticed Miranda's face. Her eyes. They looked drowned. Intense and still, as if seen through a sheet of water. It was a watery face, the face of a drowning woman. Miranda was not seeing her, perhaps even not taking in what she was saying. She was seeing her own beauty in

Heloise's eyes, hearing her own song back through Heloise's words. All she wanted from Heloise, from anybody else, was the loving picture of her own splendour. That – herself – she longed for. That was her need. And it was absolute. Her eyes were lost – unseeing, so fascinated was she by what she was trying to grasp of herself, caught in the trap of her own beauty. And yet she needed Heloise. She needed them all, every one of them. She needed them to see herself, reflected, as she wanted to be. She was as much their captive as they were hers. And it was suddenly obvious why she could not stand the Beast, any Beast. The Beast had to turn into a Prince, but a Prince that would be the means for herself to know she was Beauty, a Prince that was nothing more than the mirror he had given her. That was the only use he could be.

Looking into the absolute need of Miranda's eyes, unseen by Miranda's eyes, Heloise was flooded by compassion.

'Miranda, I do love you,' she said.

Miranda smiled a vague, a weary smile. It did not matter that she could not hear what Heloise was saying.

Arachne

A.S. Byatt

S ome gods take on more reality as you grow older. You are caught up in, brush against, their original power in odd times and places. Ibsen remarked that the Greek gods went on living, whilst the Egyptian gods were dead as dry stones. Ezra Pound saw Aphrodite. Roberto Calasso says, as though it is a matter of common experience, that we can see that they are alive. Where? he was asked. In art galleries, he said. In the language.

When I was a small child, I was given books of Greek myths to read, sitting at the back of the class, after I had finished my set work, too fast. In those days, there was no question of belief. There were stories, and I used their accounts of gods and goddesses to diminish the importance of the Bible stories, which I was expected to believe, and recognised as the same sort of stories as the Greek, and the Norse, myths, only less attractive, less powerful, less real. They were all stories. Larger and more exciting than life (even though we were in the throes of a world war and my father was in the air in the Mediterranean) but stories.

So I arranged the gods in order of 'my favourites' as we did with colours, or film-stars. My favourite Greek goddess was Athene. The other important ones were all capricious and cruel. Hera, Aphrodite, Artemis, dangerous and beautiful. Athene was wise, just, independent, a half-seen helpful guiding presence to heroes like Perseus and the wandering Odysseus. She wore the dead snake-headed female monster as a buckler. Paris should have chosen her, but it was clear that he never would. She shouldn't have been undressed. Her armour, her helmet, were part of her dignity. Her virginity (a concept I didn't understand at all) was self-sufficiency. Better than the intertwined mother-and-daughter pair, Demeter and Persephone.

When we walked to school in the early morning the hedges were full of woven circles of light, sparkling and glistening with water-drops. They were, in their regularity of radius, their geometric intricacy, like the presence of some quite other reality, briefly manifest.

Michael Chinery, the entomologist, records that as a schoolboy he collected the webs draped on the hedges in slender loops made from privet twigs. He made, from layers of the webs, with the dew caught in them, 'a primitive sort of mirror'. A really good loop could be used, he writes, to bounce a ping-pong ball, an occupation which taught him about the elasticity of spider-silk.

Ovid's story of Athene and Arachne follows a long, convoluted tale-telling on Mount Helicon, in which the goddess is the audience for the Muses' narration of the revolt of Typhon, the rape of Proserpina, the metamorphosis of Cyane into falling water, and Arethusa into a subterranean river. The Muses, who address Athene as a greater artist than themselves, finally recount the challenge of the arrogant Pierides to their own harmonious supremacy in song, and the metamorphosis of the sisters into chattering magpies. This challenge puts Athene in mind of the Lydian girl, Arachne, who has claimed to be her equal in the art of spinning and weaving wool. The girl, Ovid tells us first of all, was motherless and low-born and ordinary.

Her father, Idmon, was a dyer, who dyed her wool with the purple dye of the murex. Her husband was of no importance, and she lived in a village. Ovid emphasises her ordinariness. She came from nowhere, but her skill was astounding. The nymphs of the vineyards left their sunny slopes to watch her, and the water nymphs rose dripping to see her at work.

One of the glories of Ovid's story-telling is his precision. His skill is to make his readers feel in their fingers, at the roots of their hair, the bodies and creatures his imagination inhabits. First, we have Arachne's commonness; next her skill. He describes her winding the rough yarn into a ball, teasing the wool in her fingers, drawing out the fleecy threads, fine as clouds, longer, longer, twirling the spindle with a practised thumb, embroidering with her needle. It is clear, the narrator says, that she must have been taught by Pallas. But Arachne denies this. Her skill is hers, grown in her, her own. Let the goddess show what she can do. If she were to lose, said Arachne (whose skill was all she had) then they could take anything, everything, it wouldn't matter.

Athene is associated with both the human artists in the *Metamorphoses* who are punished for hubris, for arrogance, for overweening delight in their skill. It was Athene who invented the flute, which Marsyas the satyr found where she had discarded it. She took a dislike to it, some authors say, because playing it distorted the gravity, the balance, of the player's face. Marsyas challenged the Lord of the Muses, the sun god Apollo and his lyre. Like Arachne, he risked everything. It was agreed that the victor would do whatever he pleased to the loser. The Muses were the judges. Apollo won, inevitably. He hung the faun from a tree, and flayed him alive. Raphael and Titian painted his agony, the beads of blood, the bursting flesh under the pelt. Michelangelo's St Bartholomew dangles his flayed skin from his fingertips; the folded, hanging face is Michelangelo's own. Flaying was seen as a way of releasing the spirit from the flesh, pure art from the earth. Dante in Paradise prayed to Apollo to break into his breast, to breathe in him as he did when he tore the faun, Marsyas, '*della vagina delle membre sue*', from the sheath of his skin.

Arachne's fate was less terrible, more earthy.

It is believed that Velázquez painted Las Hilanderas (The Spinners) *in about 1656, at the time when he painted* Las Meniñas. *In the foreground, five women are working, one at a spinning wheel, one carding, one winding a great ball of thread from a skein slung on a frame, one lifting or putting down a basket, one holding aside a scarlet curtain to cast light on the spinning. They are peaceful, intent working women, barefoot, with their sleeves rolled up to show strong, handsome, slender arms. The spinner, an older woman, has a finely-painted fine veil thrown round her head and shoulders. The girl with the ball of thread, seen from the back, has a blouse that reveals the nape of her neck and a shoulder-blade, a pretty ear and a delicate cheek. The floor is scattered with fragments of fleece; a fleece hangs bunched on a dark wall; a cat sleeps between the spinners' feet. Their clothes are dyed in dark reds and blues. They are working women, not allegorised Fates.*

Behind them, two high steps mount to a brightly-lit inner room. Within the door three fashionable ladies, in flowing silks, gold, blue and rose, silvery, are looking at a tapestry hung on a wall. The tapestry has a rich complicated floral border, with glinting gold threads. In it, winged putti can be seen descending through a blue sky shot with a tracery of clouds. At the bottom right-hand corner, half-obscured by the rich skirts of the blue-silk lady with her back to the onlooker, is a white bull on whose back is a bravura flurry of flesh and flying flame-coloured cloth, mounting in a tourbillon of motionless airy speed.

In front of the tapestry are two figures, who at first appear to be part of it. On the left, below and behind the gold-silk fine lady (who for some reason is next to a leaning cello), seen from behind, is a somewhat doll-like female figure, wearing a large helmet and a buckler (her lower half is behind the cello), raising a sketched naked arm, in menace or remonstrance. In the centre of the painting, in some sense, in the centre of the inner room, between the helmeted puppet and the bull, wearing an awkwardly constructed toga, olive, flame over a white blouse, is another female figure holding out one arm, low, demonstrating the tapestry perhaps, showing it to the onlookers. She is so far away her face is featureless, almost. The light, coming into both parts of the space from an invisible left window, is a visible shaft of brightness, which passes across the flat tapestry, the soft puppet-women, the shimmer of silk, to illuminate the strong arm and shoulders, the white blouse, the delicate skin, of the foreground woman with the ball of thread. The light catches in the threads, making their fineness visible, their transparence present.

For a long time, this painting was described as a genre painting. Velázquez was engaged in the planning and decorating of the royal apartments; he would have had occasion to visit the tapestry works of Santa Isabel in Madrid. One critic describes it as a painting of 'the quite meaningless events of daily life in a workshop . . . he painted what was there, without giving it any meaning'.

Later, the painting was identified as the fable of Arachne.

Pallas Athene chose to confront Arachne disguised as a decrepit old woman, with a false grey wig and trembling limbs. She appealed to the young woman's sense of respect for age and experience, and, playing the wise crone, suggested that it would be prudent to defer to the goddess. This dissimulation provoked in the young woman a fit of genuine, human petulance and nastiness. She told the old woman to save her suggestions for her daughter-in-law – or for her daughter – who, she sneered, were obliged to listen.

She insulted her. The problem, she said, was that the old creature was senile, and weak in the head. Anyway, she added, the goddess should come herself, if she was disturbed. The goddess was avoiding the contest.

Upon which, Athene revealed herself.

Ovid describes, not the divine glory, but the human flush in the girl's cheeks, which came, and faded, like the crimson in the dawn sky. With stolid courage and driven ambition, she persisted. She would be measured against the goddess. She would, she was certain, triumph. She knew what she could do.

After a moment of passion, Ovid likes to involve his readers in the detail of things, structures, bodies. He describes the setting up of the looms, the stretching of the warp, the threading of the woof, the darting shuttles, the notched teeth of the hammering slay. The notched teeth, in Latin, are *insecti dentes* – *insecti*, meaning 'cut into', jagged. He describes goddess and girl delighting in their work, their garments caught up so that they can move easily. He describes the beauty of the dyed threads, which, like the girl's flush of blood, he compares to the sky. Rich Tyrian purples, and all the shades, gradually, indistinguishably changing, like the huge stain of the rainbow after a storm, when a thousand colours shimmer on the wide curve in the air, and the eye cannot demarcate the transition from one tint to the next, though the rich edges shine clearly crimson, or violet. The artists weave into the rainbow bright shoots of cloth of gold.

The tapestries are narratives, old tales, shaped in threads of light and shade, bright and dark, glittering and subtle.

Needlework of all kinds is a woman's art. For that reason, perhaps, I hated it as a child. I remember trying to hem a dreadful bright purple apron in needlework lessons. I couldn't make the thread go forward. It went over and over producing lumps, bumps and knots, with no progression, stained with my blood, red and brown on grey-white (there was no purple thread – there was a war on). My grandmother, who was a dressmaker, and my aunt, who was an infant teacher, tried to interest me in embroidery in long winter evenings under flickering paraffin lamps. Chain stitch, satin stitch, feather stitch. My aunt used to teach the little boys in her class to sew, as well as the little girls; sometimes their mothers objected. I never lifted my nose far enough from the bloody point and the snarled threads, to see the pattern I was making, or following, for we embroidered on 'transfers', someone else's shadowed form of flowers and leaves in ghostly blue lines, ironed on to the linen we worked. The embroidery silks came in little skeins, intensely coloured – lemon yellow, buttercup, old gold, mustard, shading into orange and bronze. My grandmother also had huge balls of variegated silks, dyed in every shade of purple, from silvery-shadowed to deepest Tyrian, from violet to mauve to flaunting iris. She could, as I could not, make huge raised furls of solid satin-stitching, whorls of petals whose colours were dappled and shot with light and shadow, not like real flowers, but with an original shifting brilliance.

When I was at the end of my schooling, I was beginning to see that the gods were more real and dangerous than I had supposed as a small girl, reading my story-books. When I read *Aeneid VI*, where the golden bough shines on the shores of the underworld, and the Sibyl writhes in her cave, I felt a shiver down my spine which was recognition of power. When I read Racine's *Phèdre*, where Venus drives her claws and fangs into the human woman's flesh, when the woman dies in a fury of sun and blood and heat and terror with the gods in her veins and in the pitiless clear skies, I felt I had come into a more real, invisible world, where things were bright, not tedious, terrible, not humdrum. I had a glimpse of the strip of clarity between the prison gates.

On the eve of the exams, when all this was singing in my own blood, my headmistress, a sweet-spoken silver-haired woman, rose up to admonish the clever and encourage the gentle. She had, she said, written books and made tablecloths, and each was good in its kind, but tablecloths were more honest, and better, and gave more pleasure. She was proud, she said, of her tablecloths. They were useful. The implication was, that Racine was not.

Much later still, out of my own excessive distress over this pronouncement, I made a story, *Racine and the Tablecloth*. It was written partly to defend Racine and the gods in the blood against the schoolteachers who were encouraging my ambitious daughter to 'be a gardener, if she wanted to'. She didn't. She wanted to learn enough French to read Racine and go to university, but they wanted to persuade her that ambition was bad, competition was bad, French was for railway stations, human beings were for mild usefulness.

The story, however, unlike my eighteen-year-old self, was not against tablecloths. One of the minor delights of feminist re-thinkings, at that time, was an interest in female arts, the work of the needle, the quilt, the garment. Chaucer's and Spenser's fairy palaces are hung with tapestries that become alive, stitched trees that open into magic forests, hidden creatures who vanish over soft horizons, castles whose doors can be opened. Deeper than that, the movement, the intricate knotting and joining and change in tension and direction of a thread, became the image I had in my own mind of the things I wrote; you might have an expanse of rosy and flaming lights, you might have a tree of crimson and golden apples, but always you had the thread that persisted, connected, continued.

Into my story of my wrath and despair over Racine's blood and sunlight, I wove an image of my great-aunt Thirza, who was photographed when she was over eighty, in her house in Stoke-on-Trent, amongst her exquisitely bright tablecloths and cushions, embroidered on ivory satin, of the kind sold for wedding dresses. She was a mythical figure, my great-aunt Thirza. 'She had blonde hair so long she could sit on it,' my aunt would always say. I believe that as well as following the linear shadowed 'transfers' (like neo-Platonic 'forms') she sometimes invented her own fruit and flowers, boughs and garlands. I have several of the cushions still. The silks are still bright. In my story my great-aunt Thirza stood for my ordinary origins, and her own bright work, for women making things in snatched time. But she was not allied with my levelling, lady-like headmistress, who haunts my dreams still, the nay-sayer, the antagonist, the fairy godmother who turned gold threads back into dull straw.

Ovid describes the woven scenes in detail. Pallas Athene weaves the forms of civic and divine order, the hills of ancient Athens, and the quarrel over the naming of the city. On that occasion, she was opposed to Poseidon and both gods gave gifts to the city. Ovid follows the tradition in which Poseidon strikes the rough cliff with his trident, and causes a great salt spring to gush out. Other writers (including Pérez de Moya whose *Philosophia Secreta* was in Velázquez's library) say that after the blow a white horse sprang from the rock. Ovid's Athene does not weave the horse. She weaves the twelve gods, on their twelve high thrones full of exalted gravity and grace. She knows their faces, and depicts them, including Jupiter in majesty. She depicts herself, too, upright, armed, with shield, spear and helmet. She shows her own gift to the city – the olive tree,

also springing from the rock, silvery-green and thickset
with the delectable fruit. The lords of life are amazed at the
lovely plant. Athene weaves in the figure of Victory,
crowning her for her gift, naming the city Athens. She is the
bringer of rooted peace and plenty.

In the four corners of her web, symmetrically, she weaves
four scenes of human presumption and punishment. These,
like Ovid's poem, in which they are images within images,
show metamorphoses. They are addressed to Arachne; they
portend pain and terror. There are Rhodope and Haemus,
once mortal challengers, now high, bleak mountains. There
is the Pygmaean queen, changed by Juno into a crane, and
Antigone, another victim of Juno's anger, white-feathered,
clapping a rattling bill, an ungainly stork. And there is
Cinyras, lying on the white marble steps of a temple,
weeping, it appears, for his daughters, whose cold limbs
have been transmuted into the steps on which he lies.

Round this work, which is about power, and judgement,
Athene weaves a border of olive branches, her own peaceful
tree.

*Velázquez is the great court painter. No one has bettered his icons of
power and divine right, Hapsburgs on high delicate, mythical horses,
princesses rigid in the stiff huge silk frames of their panniered dresses and
fantastic crimped and ribboned hair. His princes and princesses are
human beings and representatives of majesty and piety: the living man
is the symbol of himself. Critics using books of emblems and iconology
have read* Las Hilanderas *as a painting in honour of nobility, since this
is the meaning of the cello in Ripa's* Iconologia. *Others have read the
silken static ladies as other arts – Music, Architecture, if Arachne is
Painting. What strikes the onlooker most about them is the fluent skill,
the lightness and brightness, with which Velázquez has rendered the
shimmer and transparency of the stuff of which their dresses are made,*

the stuff whose elements are being spun together by the working women in the foreground.

I find it hard to see how this painting, cello or no cello, can be about nobility. The court ladies are mild and disinterested; the drama, the meaning of the painting is in the foreground, and on the back wall, in the sea and sky of the tapestry.

And Arachne's tapestry? She too wove tales of shape-shifting and metamorphosis. Hers were not tales of impertinent women, but of erotomanic gods, full of randy energy, infiltrating the world of the creatures, even of metals, to trick, to impregnate defenceless girls. Here is Europa, rushed away into the ocean by the silky white bull; Asterie, struggling in talons; Leda, pinned down by a battering pinion. Here is grave Jove slipping from form to form – eagle, swan, bull, satyr, human shepherd, spotted snake, shower of gold, rearing cone of pure flame. Here is Neptune – bull, ram, horse, great bird, bounding dolphin. Apollo as shepherd, as hawk, as golden lion; Bacchus using grapes as a tease; Saturn in horse-form, engendering the centaur. All is deception. Ovid's writing here is full of glee and movement, wickedness and writhing. There is more in Arachne's tapestry than there would be space for in any work of shuttle and wool, more forms, more human bodies, more rape, more birth, a plenitude of flux. Round her border, Ovid tells us, Arachne wove flowers and twining ivy.

Arachne's tapestry is Ovid's poem, a rush of beings, a rush of animal, vegetable and mineral constantly coming into shape and constantly undone and re-forming.

In Athene's tapestry, the work is divided into clear spaces, each with its content. It can be visualised, like a church window, thrones, faces, hills, sky, trident and water, spear and olive; the human punishments are at the corners, and smaller.

Neither Pallas Athene, nor Envy himself, Ovid writes, could find a flaw in Arachne's work.

The golden-haired goddess was enraged by the woman's success. She tore up the beautiful web. She pulled apart the briefly visible image of divine deceits, rapes and violation. Still furious, she turned on the mortal woman, still holding her wooden shuttle, and beat her on the head with it, three or four blows.

The tapestry in Las Hilanderas *represents the Rape of Europa. It represents, to be precise, Titian's painting of the Rape of Europa, which was in the Spanish royal collection when Velázquez was in charge of the decoration of the Escorial. The king also owned a copy of Titian's painting by Rubens. Velázquez has increased the space of sky and cloud, compared to Titian's luminous stormy sea-coast and sunset colours. His expanse of painted pale blue, representing silk, representing air, gives a trompe-l'oeil vista of open space at the back of his painted space. His flying cupids are more ethereal, less fleshly than Titian's. Velázquez was the painter whose company Rubens sought when he was working in Spain; it is thought Velázquez may have watched him make his copies of Titian, including* The Rape of Europa. *Velázquez's tribute to both painters is thus an act both of homage and competition. He has painted the Titian, the Rubens, but converted the surface to woven silk, with ripples of creasing, a heavy border, with folds, and rays of light from a real, not an illusory window traversing from the high left hand to the flurry of coral skirts on the bull-back. (Though all the light is an illusion, of which Velázquez is the maker.)*

In his library, besides Ovid, he had Pérez de Moya's Philosophia Secreta, *a compendium of myths and legends, moralised. Pérez de Moya's account of the duel between Arachne and Minerva argues that 'This metamorphosis is given to us to show that no matter how skilled*

*anyone may be in any art, there may come, later, another who will
outdo him, adding new things, as happens in all branches of knowledge,
for as Aristotle says, Time is a great co-worker, and through time, the
arts are changed and enhanced.'*

*This appears, at least, to suggest that Arachne won the contest.
'Vengeance,' he says, changed her into a spider.*

*Velázquez was in a line, a thread, of emulation, of reworking, from
Ovid to Titian to Rubens. He added the painting of light on textiles.
He added the spinners.*

It is a shock to realise that perhaps Arachne won. That was not
the way we learned it as children. I have never heard it
suggested that Marsyas played better than Apollo. Only that his
skill was nature, and Apollo's was art. Ovid gave Arachne all the
lively images. He gave her his own style, as Velázquez gave her
Titian's skill and his own, whilst his doll-like goddess puts up a
puppet-arm.

Italo Calvino, in his brilliant essay on Ovid and Universal
Contiguity, argues that we not only cannot, but must not try to
come down on either side in the contest. Is Ovid, he asks, on
the side of Athene or Arachne? He answers,

'Neither the one nor the other. In the vast catalogue of myths
that the entire poem in fact is, the myth of Athene and Arachne
may in its turn contain two smaller catalogues, aimed in
opposing ideological directions: one to induce holy terror, the
other to incite people to irreverence and moral relativity.
Anyone who inferred from this that the poem should be read in
the first way (since Arachne's challenge is cruelly punished) or in
the second (since the poetic rendering favours the guilty victim)
would be making a mistake.' The *Metamorphoses*, says Calvino,
contain all the tales, the images, the renderings. The nature of
myth is not to be resolved into one meaning or another. It is a
fluid, endlessly interconnected web.

Most people think Athene simply pointed at Arachne, and said, 'For your presumption, become a spider.' This is not so, according to Ovid. The act of transformation was partly merciful. Arachne, Ovid tells us, could not endure being beaten on the head by a goddess, and put a rope round her proud, pretty neck, to hang herself. When Athene saw her hanging there, she was filled with pity, lifted her and told her to live – but to go on hanging from a thread, she and her descendants, for ever. And she sprinkled the girl with Hecate's herb.

And once again, Ovid's precise imagination inhabits a painfully changing body. Arachne's poisoned hair fell off, he says and with her hair her nose, and her ears. Her head withered and shrank; her body diminished and diminished; only her fingers remained, fringing her belly as fine legs. And from that remaining belly she spins still, the long spider-threads, the silk. She practises her old art, making webs, weaving the intricate threads.

Velázquez probably knew Philostratos' *Eikones*. These are (probably) second-century Athenian descriptions of paintings, either seen or imagined, either exercises in ekphrastic description or inventions of visual forms in the brain. One of these is called the Webs. It opens with a description of Penelope, tending her weaving, endlessly unpicked and reworked. You can hear the shuttle, says Philostratos, you can see Penelope's tears, like melting snow. This is human pathos, but the true praise, the enthusiasm for the art-work, is given to the painter's skill with the spiders and their webs. The painter has shown the fine threads, and the spinners. The writer knows his spiders. He praises both orb-webs and funnel-webs, 'a quadruple thread, like an anchoring cable, fixed to the corners of the web, from which its fine tissues hang in concentric circles, held together by radii. The workers run along the threads to repair them where they are stretched or torn.'

He describes the painted beasts themselves, too, 'bristled and blotched, as in nature, presenting to the eye an aspect both menacing and savage'. He describes the flies caught in the shining traps and devoured by the spinners – 'one is held by a leg, one by the tip of the wing – one has its head already eaten away'. He praises the painter for accuracy of observation, and for delicacy and mastery of fine brush-work – consider, he says, the way in which the finest threads have been rendered.

Las Hilanderas, *as a painting, is not in good condition. Its colours are darkened and stained. It has been enlarged, around the central image. But it can be seen to be a painting about light, about the rendering of light as it catches and makes visible threads so fine that they are made of pure light, shimmering silk tissues with the light running in bright darts and shoots on the gloss. The spinning-wheel is a whirr of moving radii; the thread held in her ball and skein by the pretty worker is quite different in quality from the translucent veiling around the head of the spinning women, and different from the gauzy draperies over the fashionable ladies' satins. Light catches strands of hair differently again, and the soft thick pelt of the solid cat.*

Las Hilanderas *resembles* Velázquez's *Christ in the House of Martha and Mary. Both have a foreground full of solid human working women, and a scene of mythic, or spiritual 'meaning' sketched in an alcove, or an embrasure. Mary, who has chosen the better part, the contemplative life, sits at the Master's feet, as Athene and Arachne stand before the woven scene, ambiguously in and out of the work of art, the frame, a picture on a wall, or real characters in the same, or an exemplary tale, neither art nor life, but hovering, as myths and visions do, between two worlds.*

What is painted with love, in both pictures, is the working women. The angry, sulky, resentful cook with her pestle, an embodiment of Martha's indignation at being cumbered with much serving. The spinners, full of movement, deploying their skill, using their bodies unselfconsciously. In both cases, the painting is about the way light catches objects in the world. The source of light in Christ in the House of Martha and Mary *is not the Lord, in his armchair, but the fish and eggs, the garlic roots, glittering, gleaming, shining with cream and silver and white.* Las Hilanderas *is mapped by circles and radiant radii, light catching threads, a spinning-wheel, the struts of a ladder, the circle of white thread in the woman's glistening hair. The painting is about vision and skill. Velázquez is painting not only the Fable of Arachne, and the Rape of Europa, but light at its work, the eye discerning the forms of light, the skill of the human artist who with a fine brush and an exquisite touch makes maps and delineates the visible and invisible world at the point where they touch.*

I began my first novel with a description of air visible in heat, of light on a lawn. I described warm currents snaking in visible rivers across the grass, and the light flung between the shorn blades of grass 'like crossed threads of spun glass, silver, green and white'. The choice of image was instinctive; I now think that there is something in visible forms of light, threads, currents, or the dust–motes turning in a beam from a window, which very early arouses our aesthetic sense. There is such a beam, or column, descending diagonally across *The Rape of Europa* in *Las Hilanderas*. I do not know why it is so moving. I associate it with the Platonic forms of perfection, the transcend-ent order whose shapes we discern in the solid world, and draw, or paint, or build. I believed, until I checked to write this piece, that I had finished my lawn with a description of the network of bright wet threads left by the 'aerial dispersal of spiderlings'. I remember discovering the phrase and being delighted by its precision and beauty. Either it was elsewhere, or it was an editorial sacrifice. Spider's webs, like sea-shells, like leaf-skeletons, are sudden visual reminders of a geometric regularity inherent in the mess and excess of the world. The orb-webs are Fibonacci spirals, like some snail-shells, like sunflower seeds, like the growth of branches from trunk and twigs from branches. They move us; we call them beautiful. I invented a character who preserved his sanity by mapping the world with geometrical webs and connections, making mud safe, and bulking tree-trunks regular and lovely. I think I became interested in painting because I was interested in the mapping of the visibility of light.

Spider's webs are also, of course, traps, for flies, dusty festoons on the bristles of brooms, tatters of the uninhabited.

Some real spiders

Spiders are predatory, carnivorous arthropods. They belong to the group Chelicerata, which includes the king crabs (Merostoma) and the Arachnida, which includes, besides spiders, harvestmen, scorpions, pseudoscorpions, ticks and mites. There are over 40,000 known spider species, and more are constantly discovered. Spiders proper belong to the order Araneae; they have eight legs and venomous fangs (chelicerae). They have varying numbers (between three and six) of silk-spinning glands attached to spinnerets. Only the orb-web spiders produce the viscid silk, or glue, which attaches their threads. Other uses of spider-silk are drag-lines and life-lines, ballooning on air currents, wrapping prey, cocooning eggs. Cribellate spiders make cribellate silk which they brush and fluff, with microscopic teeth on their hind legs (the calamistrum), into microscopic loops, which they deploy in ribbons, or hackle-bands, to entangle hapless flying things. Spiders have been on the earth for at least 400 million years, and were spinning silk to our knowledge at least 300 million years ago. They range from bird-eaters to tiny money-spiders. They drink their prey, after breaking down its tissues with venom. They can be devoted mothers, tending eggs and spiderlings, leaving their own bodies as the final meal for their emerging offspring. Some eat their mates; some cohabit amiably. Some jump, some spit, some wait, fingering their threads, in the base of burrows. Jean-Henri Fabre enticed tarantulas with a jumping ear of barley and I have seen a Brazilian Indian do the same with a twig for a dark monster in the jungle. They moult repeatedly, taking hours, or days, emerging pale and soft, taking colour again slowly.

They can be very beautiful, complicated creatures. They can resemble leaves, seeds, pebbles, ghosts, stained with rose, with russet, with slate-grey, with moss-green; they can appear to be laughing masks (*Zilla diodia*), or hanging bats, jet beads, or crackled porcelain. *Cyclosa oculata* has an octopus-like fin and a pair of eyes like a gravely-staring goddess. *Argiope iomennichi* is an orb-web spider striped in creamy-yellow, wavering black and dark gold. The Araneidae spin webs with a lattice at the hub, no hole, and a signal-line connecting the orb of silk to the creature's hidden retreat. They can decorate their lovely traps with bands of silk across the diameter.

Literary spiders

Sir Thomas Browne observed the mathematical regularity of the spinners in *The Garden of Cyrus, or the Quincunx*. Discussing the

'Rhomboidall decussations' of perspective painters and lapidaries, he writes, 'But this is no law unto the woof of the neat *Retiarie* Spider, which seems to weave without transversion, and by the union of right lines to make out a continued surface, which is beyond the common art of Textury, and may still nettle *Minerva* the Goddesse of that mystery. And he that shall hatch the little seeds, either found in small webs, or white round Egges, carried under the bellies of some Spiders, and behold how at their first production in boxes, they will presently fill the same with their webbs, may observe the early and untaught finger of nature, and how they are natively provided with a stock, sufficient for such Texture.'

And Jonathan Edwards, the eighteenth-century American divine, at the age of eleven observed for himself, with delicate diagrams and precise mathematical measurements, the aerial dispersal, or ballooning, of spiders.

'In very calm and serene days in the forementioned time of year [the latter end of August and beginning of September], standing at some distance behind the end of an house or some other opake body, so as just to hide the disk of the sun and keep off his dazzling rays, and looking closely along by the side of it, I have seen a vast multitude of little shining webs, and glistening strings, brightly reflecting the sunbeams, and some of them of great length, and of such a height, that one would think they were tacked to the vault of the heavens, and would be burnt like tow in the sun, and make a very beautiful, pleasing, as well as surprising appearance. It is wonderful at what a distance, these webs may be plainly seen. Some that are at a great distance appear (it cannot be less than) several thousand times as big as they ought.

'But that which is most astonishing, is, that very often appears at the end of these webs, spiders sailing in the air with them;

which I have often beheld with wonderment and pleasure, and showed to others.'

Wonderment, pleasure, precision. Edwards observed the silk production and calculated the gravity of the tiny fliers. He observed that they always flew towards the sea, and supposed ('for it is unreasonable to suppose that they have sense enough to stop themselves when they come near the sea') that 'at the end of the year they are swept away into the sea, and buried in the ocean, and leave nothing behind them but their eggs, for a new stock next year'.

Jonathan Swift saw spiders darkly as self-involved, dirty and poisonous. His spider, in *The Battle of the Books*, represents the overweening Moderns, whilst his wholesome bee, ranging widely, represented the liberal Ancients. The allegorical spider praises himself as 'a domestic animal . . . This large castle, (to show my improvements in the mathematics) is all built with my own hands, and the materials extracted altogether out of my own person.' The bee retorts that it is a question 'whether is the nobler being of the two, that which, by a lazy contemplation of four inches round, by an overweening pride, feeding and engendering on itself, turns all into excrement and venom, producing nothing at all but flybane and a cobweb; or that which, by a universal range, with long search, much study, true judgement and distinction of things, brings home honey and wax'.

Swift's spiders are allegorised humans. Whereas his contemporary, Alexander Pope, was shiveringly sensitive to the possibilities of inhuman sensibilities in other creatures. Why has not Man a microscopic eye, he enquired, and answered himself, For this plain reason, Man is not a Fly. We are constructed neither to see mites, nor,

tremblingly alive all o'er
To smart and agonise at every pore.
Or, quick effluvia darting through the brain
Die of a rose, in aromatic pain.

His sensuous imagination briefly inhabited the 'green myriads in the peopled grass' and noted the spinners at work:

The spider's touch, how exquisitely fine!
Feels at each thread, and lives along the line.

Real spiders

Real spiders may have two, four, six or eight eyes. Some cave-living spiders have no eyes at all. Most have eight eyes, arranged in two or three rows, in patterns varying with their families. These are not compound eyes, like the flies, not faceted, but with a simple lens, and retina. Mostly they have poor sight, with the exception of the hunting spiders. Jumping spiders have large central eyes that can see sharp images as far as twelve inches away. Ogre-faced or gladiator spiders have huge eyes that can gather and concentrate light, so that they can work, and chase, at night. Most spiders, however, rely on scent and vibrations to construct the world they perceive.

Literary spiders

The most startling and most beautiful literary spiders I know were made by Emily Dickinson, student of Jonathan Edwards, poet of genius. Oddly, though she was a woman, and she praised her spiders as artists, they were all, improbably, male in her terms. Some of her spiders are not much more than whimsy:

> The spider as an Artist
> Has never been employed
> Though his surpassing Merit
> Is freely certified
>
> By every Broom and Bridget
> Throughout a Christian Land –
> Neglected Son of Genius
> I take thee by the Hand.

Or

> The Spider holds a Silver Ball
> In unperceived Hands –
> And dancing softly to Himself
> His Yarn of Pearl – unwinds –
>
> He plies from Nought to Nought –
> In unsubstantial Trade –
> Supplants our Tapestries with His –
> In half the period –
>
> An Hour to rear supreme
> His Continents of Light –
> Then dangle from the Housewife's Broom
> His Boundaries – forgot –

Circumference was one of Dickinson's favourite words, and she delighted in changes of scale and focus. She could describe a visitation of a spider (it has been suggested that she was describing a visit to the water-closet) as though it was a vision of eternity crossing time:

Alone and in a Circumstance
Reluctant to be told
A spider on my reticence
Assiduously crawled

And so much more at Home than I
Immediately grew
I felt myself a visitor
And hurriedly withdrew

Revisiting my late abode
With articles of claim
I found it quietly assumed
As a Gymnasium
Where Tax asleep and Title off
The inmates of the Air
Perpetual presumption took
As each were special Heir –
If any strike me on the street
I can return the Blow
If any take my property
According to the Law
The Statute is my Learned friend
But what redress can be
For an offense nor here nor there
So not in Equity –
That Larceny of time and mind
The marrow of the Day
By spider, or forbid it Lord
That I should specify.

Here the creature is the demonic, the visitant, who disrupts the
daily and the domestic. Spiders cohabit with us, trailing their
other reality through and across our rooms and thoughts. Emily

Dickinson's most gnomic spider makes an eternal circle. It is still male.

> A Spider sewed at Night
> Without a Light
> Upon an Arc of White
>
> If Ruff it was of Dame
> Or Shroud of Gnome
> Himself himself inform.
>
> Of Immortality
> His Strategy
> Was Physiognomy.

That is, the spider's geometry is the shape of the circle, the face of the infinite. Not the woman, but the spinner, is the Immortal.

In *Possession* I invented a woman poet who wrote about spiders, and her spider was both Swift's ugly beast and Dickinson's architect of order. Christabel's poem was called 'Ariachne's Broken Woof' after the beautiful textual crux in Shakespeare's *Troilus and Cressida*, where the betrayed hero cries out that an indivisible creature has split apart like sky and earth:

> And yet the spacious breadth of this division
> Admits no orifice for a point as subtle
> As Ariachne's broken woof to enter.

A spider-thread? The thread with which Ariadne led her lover from the maze which housed the monster? The two become one.

Christabel's spider.

From so blotched and cramped a creature
Painfully teased out
With ugly fingers, filaments of wonder
Bright snares about
Lost buzzing things, an order fine and bright
Geometry threading water, catching light.

Women are still weaving light and shifting shapes into tapestries. In 1998, I saw an exhibition of work by Danish women who had made images of earth and sky, creatures and presences, Northern Arachnes. The materials were old and new – silk and wool, but also glittering plastic strings and threads, feathers and slivers of wood. Kari Guddal dyed more than 300 tonnes of wool on flax to make a shimmer of blue silver light in a cleft of earth browns and deep darkness. Lisbeth Graem, in sisal, flax and wool, turned a red sky off Bergen into a woven red cloud inhabited by mysterious vanishing shapes, women or vases. Grete Balle, in 'The snow like a wall against the sky' woven in sumach, paper yarn, flax and silk, turned an expanse of snow on a mountainside of granite and schist into a shimmering flat contour, surrounded by blues, pine greens and a hint of sand and terracotta. These are the changing appearances of air and earth and light woven into a threaded surface, described by the lovely words 'haute lisse'. Then there is Hanne Skyum's 'Skumringsflut', Dusk Flight, repeated, scattered flying silhouettes of ducks, in shadowy sand-grey fawns and muted creams – abstract shapes of flight, stretched, tumbling, outspread, flickering, bunched, effort and floating of wings, on the most extraordinary groundcolour, blood-dark, brown-black, at once richly solid and deeply receding as weaving can be, simultaneously. All these images owe something to modern technology as well as to ancient visions – the duck forms are the result of repeated photographic records, the mountains are computer-constructed. Skyum's imagination inhabits the hunched flap, the soar of wings as Ovid's did.

Annette Graae's 'Daemoner' are four tall figures, shadowy but bright, with sharp mask-eyes. They are both very modern figures, moving elegant bodies in modern clothes, and ancient haunting spirits, glittering at the edge of consciousness. They are dancers, they are imps. One is red, one blue, one black and one white and silver. All are threatening, faintly dangerous, and attractively lively. Their variable shimmer is made of many materials. The white daemon is woven of parcel-string, fruit-tree netting, strips of material from old frocks, and traditional yarns like flax, silk and viscose, with silvery lycra. The black daemon has strips of velvet from an old dress woven into flax, silk and lycra. The red daemon is bright with Thai silk, strips of cloth, velvet, bast-yarn and flax, and the blue one is parcel-string, flax yarn and viscose yarn. Graae says she wanted the texture of the work to be brittle. The creatures are metamor-phoses of other forms, other shapes, other ways of holding matter together. Graae says her daemons are both bad and good, Latin demons and Greek daemons. They are part of the Ovidian earth, leaning against bars in modern cities, poised to change, or vanish.

Real spiders

And can we use the spider-silk, so tenuous, so strong? In the eighteenth century a Monsieur Bon made gloves and stockings from it. It was not commercially practical. Réaumur estimated that 663,552 spiders (he did not specify the species) would be needed to spin a single pound of silk. We do use the fine silk of the black widow spider to divide the field of view in some optical gadgets. Some tropical fishermen use the webs of the golden orb-web spider (*Nephila*) as nets. These spiders, says Michael Chinery, to whom I am indebted for this and much other information, produce 700 metres of silk per creature, and their silk has indeed been used to make tapestries. And in the *New Scientist*, in the week when I wrote this piece, it was reported that in Quebec researchers plan to make biosteel from spider-silk spun by goats. This beautiful, strong fibre would be biodegradable, and strong enough to stop bullets. Spider-silk is a rock-solid protein, spun into a whisper-thin thread, hardened as the threads tauten into a crystalline cable. Natural silk, the scientists have found, is stronger and more elastic than high-tensile steel, or the Kevlar used in body-armour. Using bacteria to produce the protein made only snarls and insoluble knots. But mammals secrete milk as spiders secrete silk – in skin-like, epethelial cells, held in a space, or lumen, where shear stresses on the protein are minimised.

There was the goddess, with the snake-haired woman on her shield, who turned men to stone, and sea-weed to coral, and the magic aegis on her breast. She could appear in a beam of sunlight, or move from invisibility to visibility in a sigh in the leaves, a shiver in the air. And here, at the other end of the scale, is spider-silk, a protein, nurtured, like Jove, by goat's milk, held in a space, or lumen, to make the durable crystals of an invulnerable chain-mail. What we see is a clue only to the force, and the beauty, and the order and the complexity, of what we don't see. Gods, or spider-silk.

Leda

Paul Griffiths

i t will have been by water   so by water   your
body spreading itself   do you remember the
island in the lake   so by water   and the softness
oozes between   your foot falls more slowly
through this   through the cool vegetable debris
the lax waste we were swimming   we   together
to the island as I looked   you looked like   nor my body and the
flutter   a flicker of a wing at my thighs   my white limbs
disappearing with each stroke toward   your head behind a little
way   a beat   reaching out your white hand   your orange-
toured face uncertain in the water   among the trees on the
island my hand   your hand feathering   and the other softness
the wing   as this July morning breaks you ply quite lazily over
the folded waves till you come to extol   so by water   your
body spreads itself   do you remember the lake islet where soft
vegetable debris oozed up   through the lax waste we swam
we   a beat   my white limbs with each stroke toward   your head
a little way   reach out your white palm amid the trees   your
red-toured face above the water   as this July day breaks you ply
lazily over the folded waves till you come to extol   you looked
like   a flicker of a feather at my thighs   together to some islet as
I saw   do you remember   my pale limbs beat toward   your face
a little way   amid trees your pale palm   islet   soft vegetable
debris oozed up   as a July day bursts you ply lazily over folded
waves till you come to extol   it will occur by water   so by

158

water   your body spreads itself   you seemed to be   do you
remember   us as a pair swam   islet   a flare at *m*y legs   you wear
a fire arrow at your wrist   you offer yourself   as a still day bursts
you ply lazily over folde*d* waves till you arrive to extol   as it still
bursts you ply la*z*ily over *w*aves till you arrive to extol   occur
by   so by   you offer your   you appear to be   you recall   us as a
pair play   islet   a flare   a flavour of fire   you offer yourself   as
it still bursts you ply coolly over a pool till you arrive to extol
us as a pa*i*r   a beat   a flare at   so by   lax stuff   a valley you
vault   you of*f*er your   as October bursts you pl*y* o*v*er a pool to
extol   as late boats steal across   a bell   a breast to please   us as
best   recollect a pool   as October *b*ursts explorers pleat a pool to
*e*xtol or to parrot a taut plutocrat   tux à la Proust   a last axolotl
laps   lust lost   at a cool coast   as actors at a crux across a pool

Leto's Flight

Marina Warner

L eto licked the girl's head, working with her tongue at the flakes of skin on the scalp and loosening the fine dark hairs that, sparse as they were on the newborn infant's head, albumen had wadded together. The savour was whey-like, saline, and came at her taste buds in starbursts, as strong as sherbet, and as surprising, so much more powerful than the tiny forms of her twin babies could ever have prompted her to imagine. She swallowed, but her throat was dry and it was difficult to make the saliva flow. Here and there, her tongue discovered a speck of shell, and she crunched it, lightly, hoping the calcium might replenish her sapped forces a little. The babies had been entwined as one and hidden inside her; now there they were, two of them, miraculous entities, separate, different from one another, a boy and a girl, lying beside her, needy. And she was not prepared, but a raw recruit to motherhood; and apart from the babies, she was alone. Shell and bone, albumen, lymph and milk: could they survive by exchanges of their substance, their fluids, their flesh?

The pelican might peck her own breast till the blood flowed into the open beaks of her young, or so Doris had told her, voluptuously, when Leto was a little girl and Doris was dreaming of dynasties. Leto had laughed, but inwardly she thought the pelican silly – a dead or weakened mother was no good to anyone, least of all her children. Surely there were sounder strategies for survival – the little sea mouse lifts the thick eyelashes of the whale so that it can see where it is going and so is allowed to ride on the whale's back and share its feeding grounds; the tiny toothpicker fishes that swim into the jaws of huge ocean predators and clean their triple rows of teeth feed from the parasites swarming in the host's gums and so stave off rottenness and toothache, and the shark or stingray or whatever realises where its best interests lie and does not snap, but lets the small fry prosper.

This was the turn Leto's thoughts were taking.

The baby girl had three crowns on her scalp, the usual central whorl, a second behind her left ear, another at the peak of her forehead; her thin dark hair spiralled, as if her head had been idly drawn on by the designer of shells – when Leto was flying from her lover and he, bird, fish, beast, man, was pursuing her, they had skimmed and swooped over the surface of the water together, and Leto knew her children were born of saltwater, of marshland and reedbeds and the tang of the mist hanging in the fringed river where it ran into the sea.

When she had managed to make a small improvement to the girl, she turned to the boy, to loosen the rime on his, narrower, head and longer, even lighter limbs. She worked her teeth and tongue to make saliva, and succeeded in bringing some spittle to her swollen lips. The babies' salty natal flesh might give her meagre nourishment but could not quench her, only exacerbate her thirst. Yet the sight, the feel, the smell of the twins made something inside her leap brokenly, the slow legato of her normal breathing had been jolted into a wild rhythm and she was whirling to it.

A daughter, a son, twins, babies: she could not quite say 'my' daughter, 'my' son – after the clandestine closeness of the last months their new apartness from her made her feel her unbelonging, her own strangeness and separation. That daughter, that son, those babies.

Setting the boy down in his cotton wrap on the ground, she lifted the scrap of tunic the little girl was wearing to look at her body; it was smeary and wrinkled, the limbs very thin and purplish-red, with a dark down streaked here and there. The abdomen was smooth, no bud of flesh peeping stickily from the child's taut tummy; there had been no umbilical cord for her hatchlings.

She bent her head to the infant body again and gently plied her tongue over the parts that still seemed caked in the dried fluids of the albumen sac. Leto felt her daughter squirm with pleasure in response, and all of a sudden, the baby flexed her limbs, her legs and arms working together in a quick, surprisingly gymnastic movement. As she did so, she opened her eyes: slate black with a blueish bloom, like damsons. They did not focus on Leto at her ministry; the child could not yet see the mother.

Flies droned near; she brushed them off the babies, but let them settle and buzz in her sweat and lesions, too tired to struggle against their persistence. That surcease of all the turmoil and pain of these last days might enfold her, carry her down far far below wakefulness, deep into the felted dark of extinction, where even a candle flame would sputter and fail, so utterly saturated would be the soft deep texture of that oblivion. And yet, deeper even than this yearning for no pain, for numbness, for death even, the nestlings at her flank lit a taper inside her: her mind was forming pictures of the future, of schemes she must attempt, of means she must use. These plans were physic; they administered a fluttering, winged medicine to her ordeals. Her needs and her children's began to assert their claims on her: she wanted water. To drink, to wash. She dreamed of a clean basin and a brimming ewer and linen napkins and talc and rosewater and lotion and dry, scented towels. The memory of a sweet taste rose in her throat, a buttered pancake flavour, runny with syrup flavoured and sprinkled with almonds and pistachios as Doris served in the mornings when she came in to wake Leto in the Citadel. The bathrooms made the Citadel where Cunmar ruled one of the most luxurious military fortresses in the world, so travellers from elsewhere marvelled. She thought of him and she cleaved to him, in spite of everything, for he had trembled when he held her and made her own child's body feel as tall as a thunderhead in its power over him; she thought of him, of his big, battered frame with the map on it of his adventures, in scars and holes and pits under the mesh of his pelt, how he lounged in the cistern with only his big toes and his cock poking up above the froth as she and Doris splashed him and soaped him and sluiced him.

A choking pain rose in her throat; her chin started to quiver and hot needles stabbed her eyes. She fell back against the ground, anger and fear scorching her cheeks and neck as she clasped the girl in her arms, lying alongside her son.

Consciousness came and went; Leto drifted in and out of this place where she found herself, where no lights in the distance guided her to human habitation. The late night air was soft-fingered, though, unlike the desert below the crag of the Citadel; so she was farther away than she had thought, somewhere near the coast and the warm onshore winds of the dunes and freshwater ponds trapped behind them. Water. Her tongue swelled against her palate and rasped and she was dreaming, ablaze with wanting to drink, to drink deep, to plunge into cool dark water and merge into its flow. She rolled on to her side; put out a hand to the baby boy she had laid down on the ground. He lay very still. She could have used one of his father's slippers for a cradle, or hung it from her back and carried him in it. The boy had come out second, and was more purple-skinned and his few matted curls kelp-dark; from his position he was staring up at her and his sister, unblinkingly as if she were as far away as the sky.

One smooth blue egg, then another, a feeling of huge relief from a load, as after a bout of constipation. And then, a long time ago, a face near hers, gibbering: 'You're to be killed, and your bastards too.'

How clumsy they had been together, the messenger on his murderous errand shrieking at her, foam flecking his lips. He was clownish, grappling with her with one hand and trying to stab her with the other, she thrashing and kicking: two drunks flailing at each other and staggering. Had Cunmar thought she would come quietly? Did Porphyria his wife really think Leto would just roll over and die? That she would not struggle under attack?

When she went down to the stables to help Sebald groom the horses, she would watch the mares' patience at the trough and want to hit them. But hitting only made them meeker. Would they never rebel, toss the hay from the mangers in contempt, refuse to be pacified? In that cool arcaded precinct below the Citadel, they munched the hay Sebald baled for them, their tender velvet lips curling over the dry stalks, blowing through their quivering nostrils and inflating their bellies as they fed as if playing themselves like bagpipes. Leto would smell the sweetness in their feed, and her teeth would clench with impatience. That miserable supply was enough to keep them captive, standing and chomping on the same diet all winter long.

That is why I am not the same, Leto knew at eight years old, that is why a girl is not a mare. I will not be patient. I will not learn patience.

Her spirit was fired up by the births, not cowed; like a mother cat disturbed after littering, she spat and hissed at the hitman Cunmar had sent – or if not Cunmar, then Porphyria conspiring with that son of hers, no doubt, whom Cunmar had planned would save Leto from disgrace. Instead, she found herself facing her friend the groom, the bearer now of different orders and she was screaming at him and struggling until he was cursing and crying out himself in a muddle of pain and pleading. Sebald did not know how to handle a slip of a girl who had just given birth, with her babies clamped to her. He could not get a hold of her without feeling the shame of his orders to take her and kill them all three and so she was able to sink her teeth into his sword arm until the bone under the muscle stopped her bite. She clamped her jaws tight as she could and held on through his howling till the gouts of blood in her mouth sickened her. At fourteen, she still had sharp teeth; Leto's favourite foods were fruit and sweets and they do not blunt the ivory like meat.

Leto felt her shoulder where the dagger had cut her on its passage towards her throat and the long time since Sebald had wounded her stretched from where she lay under the sky to the farthest star.

She laughed, the sound was dry and clacked against her dry tongue. The death messenger, he who had been her ally, her childhood friend, the stable boy Cunmar appointed to watch her when she had been transferred back to the Citadel, he had accepted the errand. Cowards! All of them. Not to do it themselves. And to think she would not put up a fight.

It was when the dagger slipped and cut her shoulder that she had bitten him.

And to think that Sebald knew her, that he had known her since she was six and was first sent to the Citadel. In his heart of hearts he must have hoped that she would fight tooth and nail.

She was rank as a hyena; she must find water.

Doris had pulled her out of the Citadel and down the steps and into the street, pushed her up on to a cart with her babies – Leto had howled when they took them out of her arms, but someone gagged her, but then they were back with her and they were being hauled up on to the load. Someone threw a cloth, soaking wet and cold and minty, on to her face, then covered them all up under a scratchy blanket; it was a nightsoil cart, free to move through the Quarters without question at night. Lidded buckets, but they still stank. Even through the gauze soaked in peppermint held over her mouth and nose she caught whiffs of corrupt meats and hot fresh waste.

Crazed Sebald, weeping at the order for her death, he'd clutched her in a kind of embrace.

She probed her shoulder, where his tears and her blood had mingled. She was foul with her own emissions as well; her dress was stiff with stains, from the birth, from the struggle, from the flight. So foul she smelled like the lair of a whole pack of hyenas after a carrion feast.

Again, pools of fresh water formed and smiled at her, calling to her with a sound of flutes and pipes and bells – to slip down and dance in their depths, to be washed clean.

She drifted asleep, but fitfully. The small fists of the baby, kneading at her breast, woke her; the boy beside her was mewling, too small to wail more loudly than a kitten. She sat up, bundling her scraps of clothing under them to support their small bodies, and arranged them in her lap. They were only mites, but she was too weak to bear their weight in her arms while they fed. Her breasts were hard from the milk, and the infants' tiny hard gums closed on her flow, clamped tightly as sea-shells to rock as the tide rises.

She must find water, she must find food, she must find shelter.

She looked about her to get her bearings. Clothes, too. And people; people who might help the three of them.

They were in a stone building that had once served as a byre, perhaps, but had lost its roof and was no longer in use; the scanty straw under them was grey and brittle. A twisted tree was growing from one corner, its crooked branches silhouetted like script in black ink against the sky, where the stars were fading now and a bird, far above the ground where she was huddled, was singing to the first light of dawn visible from its vantage point. It was trilling to another, who answered, displaying more frills and rills. She could not see them, though they sounded strong enough to pick her up in their beaks and soar upwards with her and the twins together.

She tried to puzzle out where she might be: it was May, so the dawn was not so early. Though it felt to her as if she had been carted for a lifetime last night, the whole journey could not have taken longer than two hours; if she was right, and the mild warmth of the morning air indicated the presence of the sea, they must have taken the coast road – south? She only had her thin, silk slippers on her feet – the pair of indoor shoes embroidered in silver thread that she was wearing when Sebald appeared in her bedroom with his orders and his knife. Her thirst scraped in her throat, worse than her hunger; she was lumpen with the sore weight of it; next time she fed the babies, they would empty her, drain her to a flaccid camel's hump.

When she looked outside the byre, she realised where they had left her: in a necropolis, among the tombs. Though Sebald had not been able, at the last, to fulfil his orders, he had left her where she might have been buried anyway. She could hear him give Porphyria his report: 'Yes, ma'am, you can rest assured that you will hear no more of Leto or her babies – they are disposed of – in the burial ground of . . .' Maybe he had cut the heart from a calf to show her to prove it, a bloody lump – 'This is all that's left of her, ma'am.' And Porphyria's eyes would glitter.

Leto felt her own fill at the news of her own death. 'She was such a pretty little thing – had spirit. Shame she was taken so young,' Porphyria would murmur to the court, her lids lowered to hide her pleasure.

People would perhaps be coming in the morning to this place, to tend the graves of their loved ones; she must try and appeal to them. But all around the Citadel, the villages had been embroiled in the war for years, she knew; they could be on anyone's side. Or on nobody's.

Leto had no goods of any kind with her. Still, she gave every indication of her status, she knew, with her indoor feet and her pale face and hands. This might anger them, that she brought them nothing. She felt at her neck – the gold chain and the phylactery he had given her after the first time. She undid it with shaky hands and knotted it into a corner of the boy's wrap. She could trade it – for milk, for apricots. She craved a ripe apricot.

Someone might see her as a bargaining counter, they might hold her for a possible ransom. She should try and convey this, before they did her and the babies harm – three mouths to feed after such a time of shortages.

They could not stay where they had been left; they needed to move from the cemetery. The sun would bake them; that single crooked tree gave no shade. She began to prepare herself to leave, before the sun rose higher. The children were wrapped in their cotton cradle blankets, which were damp and acrid, a smell of raw silage, but she tied one to her back and one to her breast; they were quiet, drowsy with feeding and perhaps still stunned by their entry into the world; she was grateful for this, though it alarmed her, too, as if they might already be failing.

★

Leto and the twins left the byre. The ground of the cemetery was broken; dusty sharp plants, already sere from the springtime sun, had worked stones loose from their matrix of rock; this was lizard and tortoise and snake terrain. She tried to pick out greener patches, where water lay perhaps concealed under the earth. Around her, some tombs stood freely, here and there marked by pillar of honeyed stone with carved inscriptions; others were niches dug in the rock, empty, riddling the ground at random. She looked down into one: no water, only the pocked colander of the limestone where the rainfall drained away. She remembered the scrap silver after one of the metalworkers in the Topaz Quarter had punched out slugs to make charms for a bracelet, leaving behind a curious, indecipherable template that could be melted down and used again. Could this be happening to all the dead who lay here in the higgledy-piggledy scattering of tombs? Would their flesh be melted down to be recast in another, perfected form?

Some more tombs, banked one above the other in ledges on one side of the area, were marked with sigils in the Greek style. They were hollowed out from the rocky outcrop that lay ahead of her and formed a natural amphitheatre, as if the dead lying in their sarcophagi on the shelves were an audience awaiting the grand spectacle of doom to begin on the stage towards which Leto was making her slow progress, her thin cloth soles giving her no protection on the jagged stones and slithering on the larger, smoother slabs. Some of the rock tombs were sealed by blank slabs; yet more were empty, awaiting occupancy or looted, dark gaps in the spongy rock. They would give shelter – and shade, Leto noted. In a cleft that ran slantwise across the rockface to its foot she saw tufts of greener, bushier plants, marking a kind of trail; she made her way towards it, slowed by the difficulty of the ground.

She heard something shuffle and clatter, and stopped. A

tortoise appeared, clambering pigeon-toed over the uneven stones, manoeuvring to find the fulcrum of each obstacle beneath it, and toppling down into the crevice between, on to its back. It retracted its limbs, then began to wave them scrabbling for purchase on the air above, its gnarled dark head twisting in panic. Leto found that she could still laugh at its plight, so much more helpless than her own; she bent to the yellow and black cryptic shell, and righted it. The tortoise pulled in its limbs, but she could see its eye, like light at the bottom of a well glinting on the surface of the black water. Did tortoises get thirsty? Was it heading for water?

She picked it up; it would make a first plaything for her babies.

The cleft was moist and springing with plants; she tugged up green grasses and sucked their stems as she had done when a child; their dew gave back for a moment's respite the familiar scale and contours to her tongue. She took heart and followed the damp track of growth; there was no surface water, but there might be a stream farther on, springing inside the rocks.

The greenery took her down a narrow fissure between two escarpments of the tomb, and the temperature of the air cooled, turned musty; in the interior chamber, a dark green slab of water, fly-blown over most of its surface. She knelt to it, splashed the larvae aside and dipped into its silk, bent her face to the liquid sluicing through her cupped hands and drank.

It was acrid; pungent, too. An animals' watering hole, of course. Fouled by their piss and worse.

Then she recognised the animal by the gamy odour stirring from the recesses of the cave; she knew she was in a den used by wolves.

Then, from the shadows beyond the pool, she saw the she-wolf, ambling towards her, her powerful shoulders moving to her stride and her long narrow head cocked.

Leto left off drinking, put one hand over the head of her baby daughter against her breast, tied with the stole, and the other on the head of her baby son on her back, where it lay against her neck. Though she had felt so dry-mouthed and sere she'd thought there was no fluid left anywhere inside her, a hot dribble spurted from between her legs, the heat of it searing her soreness there from the birth of her twins.

But the wolf did not gather pace and did not collect its limbs to pounce on her, but came steadily on until Leto could see that the tilt of her head was not menacing, and then she spoke and said, 'Don't be scared. Saw you dumped here last night, so I's watching out for you before dawn this morning before you woke up. Not much takes a wolf by surprise, you know.'

Leto held tight on to the baby at her breast; began picking at the material that held the boy to her back because she wanted to take him into her arms, to shield him, too. If the wolf was beguiling her.

'I patrolled the area, in fact . . .' the she-wolf tossed her narrow grey head to indicate a higher point in the rocks above the cave, 'kept a look out after they left you. Didn't want some swarm of something nasty crawling over you – the blood and all that. Though there wasn't much of it and no afterbirth! Now that did take me aback, in spite of what I said earlier. I thought they might come back, the enemy, people you call them, might change their minds, do you and the babes an injury.' She stressed the word babes. Her long pink tongue showed itself between her thin jaws, in a smile that was less wolfish than nurse-like, a coaxing look, urging confidence on her patient. She was very close to Leto now, and her breath was hot and smelly, but Leto did not recoil, for there was convincing smiling kindness in her words, her glowing eye, her flossy pale ears, her lithe furry flanks. 'They exposed you on the hillside. They do that. Lucky they didn't pierce your feet.' The she-wolf's voice was throaty, her tone drily humorous.

'They wanted you to die. I suppose that way they feel less guilty – not dealing the *coup de grâce* but trusting to the elements – or to beasts like us,' and she chuckled, 'to do it for them. But they don't know the intricacy of our loyalties and our thinking. And besides, our kind can't be done away with so easily.'

Leto began to cry, against her will, with the hunger, the fright, the darkness, the reprieve; she was made helpless by the foul water and the animal's sympathy.

'We'll wait till nightfall, and I'll take you to the water hole I use. It's in the valley, on the other side of this outcrop, in the direction of the sea. Meanwhile, as you noticed, there's the pool here, though it's not the freshest. And if your milk is dry and thin, you and your babes can drink mine – my own cubs are so lively they excite more than enough from their mother! It'd be a relief to me.' She drew Leto deeper into the cave, and indicated, with a toss of her narrow head, a tangle of fur, sharp ears, the lambent lights of four round orbs. Leto was trembling. But she trusted the she-wolf, and began unwinding the sodden bundle of her twins that, by comparison to her host's surroundings, was almost fragrant.

To Leto the fetor in the cave was nothing; for the first time since Porphyria discovered her with Cunmar, she was safe.

The she-wolf sang to Leto and the twins during the days she stayed in her den. She intoned a rasping, sad, tuneless kind of a lullaby that began in her throat as a rumble and left her jaws as a thin howl, and it spread heaviness through Leto that neverthe-less soothed her. As she grasped the song, she added her high quivering voice to the song and then, to the steady intake and exhalation of breath, she and her babies slept quietly.

The cubs played with the tortoise, sniffing inside the shell, trying to coax it to poke out its limbs. It refused, of course, and in its fright, crapped green smears, which the cubs investigated curiously, beating their short, plumed tails on the cave floor in excitement.

The wolf also shared food with her: Leto picked out the marrow from a bone with a stiff grass blade and, after the twins had suckled the wolf's milk, she tried it, too, for she wanted to be able to satisfy her babies herself, and replenish her body so that her own juices would spill over too.

Her rescuer understood that Leto did not have the energy to do much more than listen. But she gave her plenty of advice.

'Don't let any of this put you off life – or put you off sex either, for that matter! There's many more where Cunmar came from. Sometimes you've just got to sit out the evil in your fate. It's got to be cleared from the air, like the weight of a storm before it breaks and lifts and brightens the summer again. You've started young, so there's lots of time. On the human scale, you'll still be a young woman when this lot' – she eyed Leto's babies tenderly, humorously – 'are giving you trouble with *their* mistakes.'

'Why did he let her?' Leto managed to wail. 'He could have stopped her. He said he loved me. He promised to take care of me – he said he would always love me.'

The she-wolf looked pityingly at the human girl.

But at the evident picture of her distress she relented, and offered her a consolatory question or two, to cheer her: 'But did he know? Are you sure?'

'*She*'s done it before.' Leto glanced upwards to the roof of the cave, to where the stars would be, had they been outside under the night sky. 'She won't let him go, even though he's miserable with her and they don't have any sex, that's what he said. The other girls were nothing, he said. He said he didn't care for anyone as much as he cared for me.'

The wolf clicked disapproval. 'Love! You don't have to love

someone to have sex with them! You people are always justifying yourselves with huge passions and big promises. What hypocrisy, what abuse, all in the name of love! You're a child, Leto, you're still simple as sky after rain. But you'll find the less candid shadows far more kindly and their colours, once you get your eyes used to the dark, so much more interesting.' She patted a cub out of the way, as it tried to attract its mother's attention. 'Later, can't you see I'm saying something important to our guest! *You* listen, too. Married men. Full of declarations, full of reproaches, full of remorse. Full of wind. Full of *shit*. Avoid them. Or if you can't, try not to believe a word they say. They're different, different from us creatures, different from you people, different from women, from mothers, from our kind.

'And part of their power lies in your belief in that power, remember. Don't give them that satisfaction.'

Tell me how do you know all this? Leto wanted to cry out. But her head was throbbing and her throat was lumpy and thick, in spite of the she-wolf's milk and the morsels of marrow she had eaten. Nothing the animal told her stopped the pain. In fact, as she had found this comparative safety, sustenance, shelter, the memories were growing fiercer; she would like to tear them out of her head with teeth as sharp as her new protector's.

The crickets were chafing loudly among the dust and stones when Leto was strong enough to leave the mountain cave and set out down the rocks on the other side from the necropolis towards the freshwater lagoon that lay behind a sand bar near the shore. They were walking south, their accompanying shadows moving beside them over the terrain in long thin ribbons, scribbling their presence.

The wolf was uneasy; her nose pointed and detected

movement, the salt sweat of working bodies. 'We should have started after dark,' she muttered.

Leto was headstrong; she insisted she must find water, people, somewhere to go. She could not stay in the wolf's den for ever, with no clothes for herself or the babies and no water that was not fouled.

She was stumbling in haste on the uneven, precipitous path; in her depleted state, with the babies tied to her front and back, she was clumsy.

'Here,' said the wolf, 'give me one of them.' She butted Leto's son with her narrow muzzle. 'I'll carry him.' Her own cubs were trotting behind her, as light on their feet as if they were tumbleweed on the breeze.

At first, Leto resisted, and kept on, stumbling, towards the shore; she still had her silk slippers on, for thin and frayed as they were, they gave her soft feet a little protection against the sharpness of the stony ground. But they also made her slither when the slabs were broad and smooth.

The sea's surface was shining in her eyes, a stretched skin, gilded and tooled, that threw back from its surface the horizontal shafts of the late sun like a struck gong.

The wolf stopped, now and then, and sniffed. 'There are people about. More people than usual. We have to turn back.'

'No!' Leto wailed. She so longed for water, she could have faced a crowd, naked.

'Give me the boy,' said the wolf. 'We'll move more nimbly.' Gently, her muzzle closed on the dirty rags that swaddled the infant. Her own cubs frisked, making three times the distance as they scampered ahead, tacked back, tumbled in a flurry of limbs together, picked themselves up and gambolled on.

They saw the water below them, a wide smile of silver with the smith's small hammer blows setting it to glitter. The sight of it lightened Leto's step and she almost began to run, turning her head now and then to make sure the wolf, with the baby in its jaws, was not taking a different path.

'Wait till dusk,' whispered the wolf. 'Don't go so fast. They'll have gone by then.'

But Leto ran, with her daughter on her back, as soon as they reached the marshy ground around the lagoon; she pushed through the reeds, feeling the suction of the wet earth tug at her slippers.

She undid the scrap of material that held her daughter to her back, and taking her tightly in her arms, walked into the water as she was, closing her eyes as the cool thick silk of the flow clasped her and soothed the hot soreness of her feet and legs and between her legs. She must not lose her footing, not with the baby on her hip, who was looking up at her slightly cross-eyed, with furrowed brow, as if perplexed by her mother's immersion.

The lagoon was mud-bottomed, and swallowed one of her shoes; she felt the silt move smoothly between her toes. With her free arm she splashed her face; the baby looked even more puzzled, poised to howl in protest. Leto turned back, to find a point of access, a kind of beach, where she could set the baby down while she bathed.

The wolf was calling to her, softly, through the darkness from a screen of reeds.

'Leto, we're here. This way. Wait. You're too exposed there.'

But she ignored the animal, and sank deep into the dark water, into its coolness, drinking it into every pore and cranny of her sore dry body, inside and outside, through her mouth and eyes and floated . . .

When she surfaced, she heard calls from the shore, and shook the water out of her ears.

'What, in hell's name, are you doing?' The words bounced

on the surface of the lagoon towards her, clear as the opening phrase of a tune.

'*Get out of there, now!*'

She saw men emerging from the reeds, with cut sheaves on their shoulders. Her baby was there; she began to struggle to reach the shore. But she was feeble from the privations of the last few days, and the water stuck round her legs and the mud shackled her ankles.

'You . . .'

'. . . and your fucking baby . . .'

'*Get out!*'

'Strangers.'

'You and your kind . . .'

'*Go back where you belong.*'

'You don't belong here.'

'Not here.'

'None of your sort . . .'

'Can ever stay here.'

'*This is our home.*'

'Not yours.'

Their cursing reached her in rags and tatters, flying lashes, a sting of pain on one side of her head. She put her hand up and felt a warm pulpiness above her ear, in her hair, where the stone had hit her. She looked across the dancing water to the shore; shapes were moving in the reeds; she caught shouts, gathering huddles, figures bending. She saw the streak of the wolf's form move higher, beyond the reeds. She fancied she heard the animal howl, but no, the papoose still hung from her narrow mouth. The animal was leaving her, with her son, running for cover in the caves riddling the cliff, she could not do otherwise, or could she?

More stones drove into the water near her; another caught her on the head again; she floundered, the refreshing element in which she was swimming suddenly heavy as sheet metal, preventing her from moving, from climbing out of its clasp. She grasped at the rushes to find her balance and push her way to the shore.

Her daughter. A group of shadows on the inlet criss-crossed where she had laid the baby down.

Her dress was stuck to her; she kept her arms crossed over her body as she clambered out through the silt towards them.

'Come on out, lady!' sang out a jeering voice.

Then another, 'Let's have ourselves a party!'

Her head was swelling, full of turbid cloud; she staggered towards them.

The wolf, where was her friend, her guide, her protector, her saviour? Where was the wolf?

She reached the bank. They had the baby; one of them was cradling her, making goo-goo noises.

'Oooh, ooh, what a pretty little creature! Who'd ever think your mother was a whore?' He threw the child in the air, made as if to let her crash, caught her and danced her up again. 'Dance a baby diddy, what shall daddy do with ye?'

He threw the infant across to another figure, passing her like a ball.

Leto was among them now, whirling to catch her daughter as they chucked her from one to another. The baby was roaring, a red and purple scrap, her tiny limbs spreadeagled like a flying bat as they played. One of the men grabbed Leto as she struggled to catch her child; he clutched at her breasts under her wet clothes, twisted her round by them and pushed his face into her mouth. She twisted and pushed, using her nails, her teeth, until at last, with a supreme effort she leaped to catch her daughter and, holding her close, fell to the ground, crouched over her.

A kick made her fall sideways but she kept curled tight

around the peach-soft flesh of the baby, who was slimy with tears and other oozings of her terror.

'This is our water,' shouted one man in her ear.

'Don't you ever come near it again with your dirty brat,' another was shouting over her, a giant looming against the sky.

Yet another kicked her, 'Next time, we'll kill you and your runt.'

'You'd be better off if we did – you dirty cunt,' said another, with a laugh.

'Trash like you.'

A blow caught her full in the small of the back; they were beating her with something whippy and wet and flat – the rushes they had been gathering in the lagoon. Their panting rose as they lashed her; she curled up more tightly over her baby.

'Taking our water . . .'

'Taking our food . . .'

'From the mouths of our children.'

'Robbing us blind.'

'Taking our houses.'

'Whore.'

'Teaching our women your dirty ways.'

'Filth.'

'Whore.'

'Stranger.'

'Don't you ever dare come here again.'

'Keep away from us.'

'For ever.'

One dabbled his fingers round her neck, tore out her gold earrings – she was glad she had remembered to take off her necklace.

They had cutlasses; they had been slashing at the reeds with them.

One man tussled now to pin her legs, another at her shoulders to turn her over. Their breath was coming in short, hoarse bursts.

Through her swollen lids she saw them, jagged flashes and flickers, like scraps of leaves tormented by a storm wind that tossed shadows against a moon.

She prayed, to no god whom she could name, but to all the powers and thrones and dominations she had ever known or half known or guessed or dreamed. She did not see her life pass before her, but through the broken roaring and grunts and curses and maulings and beatings she saw her lover again. She saw Cunmar's eyes above hers, the pupils widening into a corridor to the velvet where the far stars swim as he bent to kiss her. She saw his wife in her fury, and her pain. She saw her friend, her servant, Sebald, who'd been sent to kill her, and Doris, her nurse, who'd bundled her on to the nightsoil cart. And she felt for them all a piercing longing, for their love, for their mercy.

'I couldn't help loving him,' she cried. 'He wrapped his long limbs and dipped me in his hot sweet honey words till I flowed for him. Forgive me, help me, let me and my babies live. His babies, the children of our loving. For he did love me, I know he did. And I loved him.'

She prayed to the angels of love, whoever they were, who infuse men and women with the capacity for passion and for gentleness, with the potential of courage and sacrifice, with sympathy and with forgiveness. So she believed.

Nothing came, no answer, no stirring. Only the rage of the assault burned her body, her breasts, her thighs, her sex.

This was the inexplicable hatred that gripped the cities, strangled the nations, tortured and butchered the peoples.

Then she heard her: the she-wolf was howling from the ridge. Leto picked up the high keening noise through all the tumult as the men scrabbled over her, and then she felt them freeze. Her attackers were rising, in disarray; screaming at one another. They rushed, themselves now animal in their panic, a quarry raised and scattered by beaters in the chase. Some ran in terror, dropping everything; others, more thrifty, hesitated, casting about to salvage the harvest of reeds they had been cutting.

The she-wolf was loping down through the dunes towards them; they could track the sound of her battle cry as she came.

A flying missile of fur and spit, the animal hurled herself on to the shore of the inlet, scattering the remaining men; one of them turned and stood and slashed at the animal with his cutlass, but she was snarling, crouched back on her haunches, and he dared not close with the bared canines that glinted in the darkness, and he, too, turned to flee with the others.

But there were no others; not any longer. How had they disappeared so swiftly? So silently? First he had picked up their cries of panic, their footsteps stumbling through the reeds and on the dry ground, but now he could see nothing, hear nothing, except the shrill song of the crickets beyond the wolf's snarling.

Then he too began to leave the man he knew himself to be. He stood, transfixed by the slaver from the wolf's jaws. Semen smeared on his stomach, blood stains on his mouth, his arms, his legs, he could not run as he felt a bolt of something damp and wet snake over him and cover him and begin to shrink and condense him; his flesh, as it diminished, turned clammy. His fingers grew longer, skin grew between the digits of his bare toes, and knobs and gnarls swelled over his bones; when he tried to cry out, his voice came out in a feeble gulp; when he tried to run, he found he was jumping on his new thin, green legs; so he dived headlong into the water with a wild croak; there, he joined his fellows, half-sunk into the mud, their bulging eyes big with alarm, the pulse in their crops racing to the terror in their changed hearts.

Leto lifted herself with the last ounce of her strength so that the baby, pressed underneath her into the sand, might be eased and breathe.

The wolf was near her; she placed a paw on her shoulder to turn her over.

The baby nuzzled; there was blood in her mother's milk.

The wolf cleaned her wounds, gently. Her tongue was lithe and thorough. She murmured, 'I've stowed the baby boy with my cubs deep in the rocks up there – they'll not be found.'

But she could not bring Leto back from the darkness where she was plummeting.

There, Leto was crying silently as it furled her in its cloudy arms.

'The boy's safe, I've kept him safe. She, too, the girl, she'll survive,' said the wolf. 'And Leto, Leto, come back. So will you.'

Antiquity's Lust

M.J. Fitzgerald

A t that time Tereus took the hand of Procne in marriage, looking into her eyes with a smile that made her tremble and look into his eyes with a smile, aware of him standing tall and straight in the kingdom of Athens, straddling the world with ease, dazzling the king with his armour and plumed helmet, shining in the court of Pandion her father, and casting his light on white columns as he led his bride into the dance.

But shades skulked behind columns, moved with the dance to avoid the brightness. And where they laid fingers of fury the black veins hidden in the heart of marble were made visible. The murmuring curse went unheard in the joyous clamour of the wedding feast, the piercing thin laughter was ignored when Tereus bowed to Procne's sister, the child Philomela, who blushed to be dancing with the warrior her sister would be honouring and serving in marriage.

But oh so far away, she thought as she stepped on bare feet to the rhythm of lyre and reed, and tears coursed down her cheeks even as she danced. Tereus was moved; you will come, he said to the child, you will come to Thrace as soon as the king your father permits his youngest to go, I promise, we will give him no rest in our insistence, be at ease, Philomela, wipe the diamond drops from your cheeks, laugh and make merry, do not be sad to sadden our happiness. And Philomela smiled through her tears.

As the Furies turned to Aeolus to lend them favourable winds, Procne, still in her bridal gown, wept against the broad shoulders of the father whom she loved, threw her arms around the fragile neck of her sister, gawky with unrealised girlhood, and buried her face in her curls, bidding her be strong, while she herself wet Philomela's hair with her tears.

And the tears stained red streaks into Philomela's black hair; but Tereus shone in the kingdom of Athens, and shone in the heart of Procne his bride, who followed him, forfeiting the security of guards, the indulgence of dark nurses, the playing by streams, the company of soft-spoken girls, the games of princesses, the couch she has shared with her sister, the security of Athens.

Philomela forgot her games and her friends, looking out where the white sails were being swallowed by blue sea and sky; she saw ominous birds hovering in formation, unmoving in the cloudless horizon long after the ship had disappeared, until the setting sun appeared to scorch them from view. She yearned for Procne, who would again beat her in races along the sandy beaches, and whom she would finally overtake, slicing the saltwater with strong arms. There was no comfort in the bed without the nightly tales of wonders, Diana and Daphne, gentle Narcissus and Hyacinth, swift-footed Mercury and Eros bearing arms, Apollo and Mars, even taller, even stronger than Pandion their father, than Tereus.

Philomela brooded and grew in grace, never glancing at her reflection in glass or stream, careless of her slender beauty. She waited by the window to be the first to spot the messenger ship that brought word from her sister, ran down to the harbour pursued by the body of guards, the company of girls in attendance, danced impatiently to see, above the throng, the standard-bearer from the kingdom of Thrace, carrying tablets and scrolls, images in plaster of the child Itys, born in a far land from the sweet body of Procne her sister; not too much pain, no, no, and the grace of the child is such, Procne wrote, that – oh, but just look at the sketch that was made by the black slave skilled at such things, who is now decorating Itys' room with birds of paradise, and our rooms with paintings of Itys, asleep, laughing, crying, crawling, taking his first step. Eros himself may not have been as beautiful, if Venus can forgive such a boast in a mother.

The sister feared the Furies when she read these words, for already she had thought to have seen a menacing dwarf high up on the mast of the ship, cackling in imitation of seagulls. Don't, she wrote quickly, leaning against a rock by a stream in the forest where maybe the spirits that nourish discord could not see her, don't please, Procne, don't say such things, the Furies that are within the gods are so easily aroused, the Furies' sleep is so slight, even thought can awaken them, how much more can words etched in wax tablets. And she melted the writing in fear, hid the words beneath her own, tell me again, tell me some more, what is your country like, are there streams like the one I'm sitting by, where you can go and splash in soft water when the sea has encrusted your skin with salt? Are there mountains and hills, are there rocks and plains, and is the land tilled and hoed? Do vines and olive trees grow? And the court, and the companions; does Itys have a nurse like ours, black and comforting; and Tereus? Is he a king as our father is king, taking the counsel of his people? Is he a husband or merely a man?

When she had written these last words she looked around at the sudden onset of dusk, and shivered in the chill air as she rose to return. Where have you been, the nurse scolded her, escaping the watchfulness of guards, fleeing your protective companions. Philomela, my daughter, the king summoned her, you must not encourage our fearfulness for you by hiding thus,

you must stay within sight, to gladden our eyes with seeing you.
Only thus we will consider sending you far to bring your love
and ours to your sister and our daughter whom we sorely miss.

He is a man and fearful of the sweetness of husbands, Procne
wrote back, but my love can bear and forbear when I watch the
tenderness he withholds from me spill like a fountain of gold on
our child, who grows sturdy on legs that one day will be pillars
to carry our kingdom, who prattles and laughs, joyousness
incarnate. The land where I dwell is rugged, burned by a
relentless sun that withers the tender grasses. There is little
water, trickling streams that suffice to quench our thirst and
wash our bodies. Flowers are rare, and surrounded by thorns
that prohibit the gathering, but they spring up between cracks in
the dry earth, and fill the barrenness with colour suddenly,
between the wakening of dawn and the fall of night. It is beauty
of a kind, though not green as the kingdom of Athens.

You will come, Tereus my king and my husband has said. He
himself will bear letters to Pandion our father to urge your
coming when the next ship sets sail for Athens, after the great
heat of this land has spent itself, when the gift of rain is soothing
our bodies into movement after the immobility of summer. You
will come, little sister, and I will see your sweet face once again,
and hold you in the embrace I send you. What is mere greeting
now will become real, and my heart leaps with joy at the
thought. You will meet Itys my beloved son. No image, not
even the perfect portrait I send with these words, could ever
capture his grace, so fleeting yet endlessly renewed. Let Time be
as swift as Mercury, circling the earth on winged feet, and let
the days and nights be as brief as they are in the heavens where
the gods dwell, that I may see you and be with you through a
season that will slow down to an endless sunlit day. Itys has
taken the nib from my hand and sends his childish greeting with
the scrawl you can see. When is Philomela coming, he asks, is

Philomela coming? She is, I say laughing. And Tereus picks him up and throws him high in the air, to feel the terror of flight and the exhilarating security of his father's arms. You should hear his laughter, my sister. And you will.

The Thracian ship docked in the harbour of Athens before dawn could set to flight the dwellers of the night; the shades that had moved crab-like at the marriage feast, the birds that had hovered in the blue sky at the departure, the gull-cackling dwarf and the chill air gathered to greet Tereus. Silently they took their place in him, some behind his eyes, some in his mind, some in his heart, some in his loins. They stirred like worms in the king of Thrace, and Tereus was troubled by dreams and moaned in his sleep, rocked by the movement of the ship. The moan turned into the screech of an owl that woke Philomela from a deep sleep in a pool of blood. She cried her horror at the omen, running to the nurse, blood on the bed, among the white goose-down pillows and blankets, spattering the mosaic floor as she ran, leaving red footprints. It is no omen, the nurse laughed, taking the child's face in her hands, it is the beauty of womanhood being cast upon you.

But Philomela, fearful and shy, hid in her room, sending confused messages to her father, I cannot come to greet Tereus yet, she said, not yet. She sat by the window, looking at the docked ship lulled by the breeze, hearing mocking laughter in the music of the swaying high mast, while Tereus paced the white columned halls, went early on hunts with King Pandion. The Furies within him made him impatient, impatient with his courteous host, restless with irritations, so that arrows missed the target of deer, his belly tightened at the sight of foods on the banqueting tables, and the entertainment by graceful slaves awoke a rage he found difficult to control. He arose and paced the halls, left the court and strode the gardens and orchards to the fields beyond, returning late in the afternoon of the fifth day, the winds are favourable, if Philomela does not appear I will go at sunrise, he told Pandion. Be patient, my friend, the child is now a girl, and womanhood is not far behind. And women have their time and their season, and we would not have it otherwise, to have bestowed on us the gift of their beauty and the tenderness of their touch.

Here she is, Philomela my child. What beauty, my daughter, what beauty. Pandion stood still, in awe at the transformation, and Tereus turned to look at the girl. Neither Venus nor Diana could compare. Tereus' rage awoke, engorging the veins with blood that pulsed through his heart and spread a blush from his face to his rock-like chest, down his arms and legs. And the Furies within him whispered to take the child, now girl, now woman, take her and use her for the pleasure of his loins, take her now and take her again and again for nights and days, until the lust was satisfied. No admiration of her beauty, respect for the modesty of her manner, reverence for the innocence of her girlhood must come between him and the satisfaction of his furious pleasure. The urgency of his rage lent him restraint, and he hid the spirits that possessed him, urging the king to let the child leave at dawn, while the winds were favourable, and the journey could be brief that would bring his daughters together, that would bring his own dear love to his Procne.

And Philomela danced childishly around her father, joined in the plea, please dear father, my king and dear father, let me go. And as she danced, the dress was parted by malicious shades, showing Tereus her white thighs.

Are you so eager to go, to leave your old father alone? One daughter is lost to me, must you too be gone, Pandion spoke to his dancing elf. Oh no, dear father, I will not be gone for long, a season, a brief season, just a season to see Procne and know her life. When the winter winds and rains have ceased, when the new grass is sprouting and Narcissus is born again under the guise of white scented flowers, then I'll return and bring gifts, and speak words from Procne that only I can speak, and tell you of Itys in ways only I can tell.

I had hoped for a day or two, for pointless delay, Pandion smiled, as if my heart would be less sore. How we deceive ourselves, and how we toy to avoid pain. But my loss will be brief, he said, stroking Philomela's cool cheek, and an old man should live through winters alone to accustom him to the winter of death. I wish I could keep you by me and let you go, but only the gods have the gift of presence and absence, can give and receive with the same act. So go, my beloved daughter, and take a love that is no less strong to your beloved sister.

And Philomela danced with a heart made forgetful of omens, in pure joy at the anticipation of standing on the deck of the ship, of sleeping to the lullaby of mast and oar, to the gaiety of days surrounded by sea and sky; and then Procne. She could not contain her happiness.

But Tereus sliced through the black throat of the slave girl who accompanied the princess and tossed the body in the waves as soon as they were far enough from shore, hiding behind the shades of night. Under cover of darkness he entered Philomela's cabin, stifled the scream of the sleeping girl, split himself into her body with the violence of a warrior wielding a sword, with all the rage of all the Furies that inhabited him, bound her to the bed, gagged her to silence, and claimed to the soldiers that the princess was unwell. He himself would bring trays of choice foods to languishing Philomela, to entice her to health.

And throughout the nights the ship was at sea, not carrying any light that he may not see the large eyes of his victim watch the rage of his lust, he executed his violent pleasure on the bruised body. And when they reached the Thracian shore he carried the veiled girl to a covered cart and drove her alone to a remote steading deep in the infertile forest festering with alien creatures. He took the veil from her face, the gag from her mouth, eager for a cruder pleasure, for a further violence. She could shout all she wanted, not even Echo would come to her rescue. And Philomela finally knew her ravisher, altered beyond recognition by the Furies' possession of his soul. And she knew herself altered beyond recognition by the violations performed by Tereus. She spoke, letting the loss, the bewilderment, the terror seep out of her, and opening herself to righteous Furies that had stood by while their sisters engineered the perverse plot. She spoke with the quietness of hatred, her large eyes fixed upon the king of Thrace, diminished to a squirming dwarf:

'As long as I have tongue to speak I shall declare what you have done. I shall speak to the stones that surround me, to the wood that shapes this hut, and they will be altered by my words, and will speak by their alteration to worms and cockroaches, to spiders and flies. And from these creatures the word shall spread and reach the most remote corners of the world, until the gods that guard all things hear and shall give me the means to wreak my revenge and punish you for what you have done.'

But Tereus laughed his seagull cackle, as long as you have tongue you say. You will have no tongue, I'll take it and destroy it. He grasped Philomela's head, forcing her mouth to his pleasure. And while she still retched he pulled the pink tongue that had moved in speech and song, that had lain quiet when she slept and listened, that had been the instrument to tell her joy and pain. He sliced if off far in her throat and left the girl, pursued through the sterile wood by cries that did indeed displace stones and stir creatures. But only those without tongue dwelt at such depths, and Philomela lay among them, drinking the blood that did not course down her chest.

And the queen of Thrace was struck dumb when Tereus came

simulating mourning to tell her how her little sister had ceased dancing on nimble feet and was no more. Itys saw his mother's grief, the face that became suddenly lined, the hair streaked with white, how she wandered for days in hollow halls, in a desolation that took away all her strength, so that she could not carry her son, and never smiled; and he fell silent. And silence fell on the kingdom of Athens when word reached Pandion that Philomela had died, wasted by the mysterious illness to which she had succumbed after they sailed.

Tereus yielded to the Furies within him, returning to the steading again as the seasons changed, and again taking his pleasure of the maimed Philomela, regardless now of a beauty that was no more, delighting in perversion, indulging in cruelties that turned Philomela's heart to madness, and her mind to the ingenuities of escape. She made of her speechlessness an ally, and in the weeks when all the company she had was foreign guards and slave girls, she fashioned a make-shift loom from the wood of trees uprooted by storms, and wordlessly begged the silent help of Arachne to spin white and red thread of spider's webs and drops of her blood, laid sacrificial offerings to Pallas, that the message be made clear only to the queen who wandered the hollow hallways inconsolably, and fashioned a tapestry that told the monstrous actions of the king of Thrace in a code that only they knew from childhood games of spinning and weaving.

And the Furies, jealous of the successful havoc caused, at war with their sisters who dwelt within Tereus, determined to enter the soul of Procne: they smuggled the tapestry to the queen wrapped as a bodice around the bare skin of a slave girl skilled in the magic of healing, who had brought potions to soothe the bruised body of the prisoner, that Tereus may violate her again more quickly. Though the girl could not speak Procne's tongue, she came fearlessly, unravelled the tapestry and stood, unclothed and proud, giving her the gift that would unleash the chaos of conflagration between the burning Furies inhabiting Tereus and the icy sisters that entered Procne even as she read the coded message.

Nothing human would be held sacred in the war that followed, after Procne had swooped to the far steading, rescued her miserable sister and carried her to the palace, laid her on silk cushions, washed the body with her tears, poured ointments and wiped them with her hair. And as she saw and touched each welt, Procne's hatred grew colder, and when she saw the stump of tongue in poor Philomela's mouth, the perennial ice of glaciers reached her heart.

In silence she went to the hall where the king banqueted. Without speaking she looked at Tereus, raising the golden cup to his lips to drink the sweet wine from the kingdom of Athens, stretching his hand to the roast suckling, dipping it in savoury herbs and opening his mouth to receive the food. But when she caught sight of her son, her prattling child, her heart leaped with love. She took him into her arms, held him tight until he clambered down from her lap and ran to a guard, demanding to handle the long knife he carried. And as Procne observed him wielding the weapon like a sword, the natural instincts of motherhood were submerged by an avalanche: she saw merely the offspring not only of a man who had dared betray the trust of their marriage, a king who had betrayed the trust of his mission to Athens, but the tyrant who had tortured and monstrously gloated. She watched Itys turn to his father, and Tereus' face, so like his son's as he took the small hand to show him how best to grasp the sword to inflict death more suddenly and more completely. And the habit of love was buried. She smiled, she knew now what her revenge would be, the only revenge that would satisfy her Furies and give relief to Philomela's madness. When she rose and left the banqueting hall, the servants bowed and guards stood to attention, but her husband and child, too absorbed in their game, did not notice.

One more time, one last time the icy Furies were set momentarily to flight from Procne's soul, when the queen went to take Itys from his bed in the room decorated with birds of paradise, and saw the innocent curve of the child's cheek, the long lashes decorating the lids, the red lips disclosed in the shallow breath of the childish sleep, the limbs vulnerably sprawled, the sheet tossed to the floor in a dream. The mother's love rose like a ghost from its icy burial place and filled her eyes with tears even as she picked the child up in her arms to lead him to slaughter. Only when she met Philomela and saw the crazed face of her sister, heard the horrible regurgitations of her vain attempt to speak, did the ghost lie down in the icy tomb of hatred and revenge. Like tigresses with their prey the sisters carried the wakened child to a distant corner of the palace where his cries would not be heard.

And the innocent succumbed to the violence and the perception of the loss of his mother's love in the same instant, stretching tender-skinned arms to her and crying her name as she thrust the sword into his side and passed the weapon to Philomela, who sliced through the throat with the violence of her madness, and danced bearing the dripping sword aloft, leaving red footprints on the stone floor. The child was still moving when the sisters completed their task, cutting into the body, tearing Itys limb from limb, selecting the flesh to be boiled in herbs and the flesh to be roasted with spices, frenetic hatred ageing their faces and bodies into the shape of the Furies that dwelt within them: not dwarfs cackling in imitation of seagulls, but tall snake-haired Medusas.

And Procne decked herself in her most beautiful and seductive clothing, decorated her hair with jewelled combs and anointed her body with perfume from Venus. Not since Philomela's death have I felt this way, she sent message to Tereus, my love has rewakened and seeks to satisfy you in satisfying itself. I have prepared a banquet for us, just us, and no attendant and guard shall distract us from the anticipation of pleasure in the delight of eating and drinking. Come, my love, my husband, my king. Come to me. It is time we give Itys the gift of a sister. And in a daughter perhaps my sweet sister will be restored to me.

She decorated the table with flowers from the kingdom of Athens that had hung to dry in the ship on which Tereus had perpetrated his crime. She shaded the light from each lamp with leaves that cast shadows, and curtsied deep to Tereus when he came in a rattle of armour and sword. She looked into his eyes with a smile that made him tremble as he looked into her eyes with a smile.

And the tragedy constructed in a warring game by the Furies reached its conclusion: Tereus tasted with an appetite made keener by wine and the thought of seductions, and ate the choice boiled meat, the tender-pink roast. And when he called for Itys to share in the feast, mad Philomela appeared, her dark hair caked and her clothes stiff with dry blood. She laughed without speech and took a piece of the meat, cradled it in her arms like a baby and waved it in front of Tereus, frozen by her sudden presence, by her mad presence, by understanding. And she put the flesh of the king's son in her mouth, chewed and swallowed the sweetness of revenge.

They say the king pursued the two sisters who in their flight were changed to birds with red breasts and red-tipped wings. They say that Tereus too was changed into a bird, and that the sword he carried became the huge beak of a hoopoe.

Eurydice's Answer

Suniti Namjoshi

For Suki d. 27 July 1997
and Vana Akka d. 25 November 1997

A fterwards, especially when things don't work, when there is no victory, when all there is is the taste of failure, effort goes into understanding that taste, becoming familiar with it. It's the taste of greyness, the taste of a landscape in which all familiar features have become molten and mis-shapen. Eventually, the problem may be how to orient oneself, find a direction, even understand how to map such a landscape. And perhaps, someday, there might be other questions. How to make green this landscape? How flowers might be induced to grow upon it? Food too? Cauliflower and cabbages. Fruit. Pomegranates. But that brings back the splash of blood, brings back the immediate question at the point when the way forward doesn't matter, when the mother says to her daughter's lover: '*How could you? How could you look back? You had no right!*'

He doesn't say anything. He opens his mouth, then he closes it. There is something he might have said, but he doesn't say it. What might he have said? He might have said – suppose he says it: '*I didn't look back. She did!*'

Ceres, appalled, recognises the truth – that's how it had to be. She walks through the ashes, tasting something worse than failure. She tastes her own helplessness.

Then there comes a time when there are flowers, fruit – different fruits, different flowers – when they can try to ask questions, try to forgive. Themselves or her? They don't rightly know, but they can try. The mother speaks to her daughter. She tries to be understanding. The lover says nothing. He already understands, he knows. Her mother says, 'You must have looked back because you were frightened. You thought he was following. It's understandable. You looked back because he was following.'

Her daughter shakes her head, 'No, he wasn't following.'

Ceres puzzled, unable to understand. 'But he was there?'

'Yes.'

'He made you go back?'

'No.'

'*Then why did you go back?*'

All the passion in the world is in that question. The daughter knows this. She would like to be kind; but before she can answer Orpheus breaks in, '*She turned back because Hades smiled!*'

Eurydice shakes her head. 'He neither smiled nor frowned.'

'*Then why?*' Both of them loved her. Why did she betray them?

At last they must accept Eurydice's answer: 'I could not go any further. I was weary.'

Heart's Wings

Gabriel Josipovici

I t was her favourite passage. She was never as fond of Latin as she was of Greek literature and never, as far as I know, read any other poem of Ovid's. But few works of literature moved her as much as the story of Ceyx and Alcyone in Book XI of Ovid's *Metamorphoses*. I had brought home John Frederick Nims's 1965 reprint of Arthur Golding's 1567 translation, knowing her fondness for sixteenth-century poetry, her feeling that even the wonders of seventeenth-century English verse constituted a decline from the clarity, the precision, the innocence of the earlier period, an intrusion of the self which was to ruin European poetry in her eyes till it re-discovered its roots in the work of Yeats and Stevens and Montale, but I had not expected her to respond to it with quite the enthusiasm she did. After that Ovid for her was Golding (though I tried to interest her in some modern translations) and the best of Ovid was the story of Ceyx and Alcyone.

What was it about the story and its telling that moved her so? Fierce Daedalion and his gentle brother Ceyx were the sons of Lucifer, the morning star. Daedalion's beautiful daughter is wooed by both Hermes and Apollo and bears each a son. But her good fortune goes to her head. Rashly, she boasts that she is superior in every way to Diana and the incensed goddess shoots her dead for her presumption. Her father, mad with grief, flings himself from Parnassus, but Apollo takes pity on him and transforms him into a bird, a fierce hawk to reflect his war-like nature.

Ceyx, meanwhile, has married Alcyone, the daughter of Aeolus, the god of the winds. Now, disturbed by his brother's fate, he decides to consult an oracle, not the one at Delphi, which is close at hand but access to which is dangerous, since the road is infested with robbers, but the more distant oracle of Claros, best reached by sea. Alcyone pleads with him not to go, reminds him that the sea is even more dangerous than the land and that she, as the daughter of Aeolus, knows all about the unpredictability of the winds, how they can suddenly arise and destroy even the largest ship. If he is determined to set sail then let him at least take her with him; like that they will undergo danger together and if necessary die together. But Ceyx will not hear of it. If I go now, he says, I will be home in two months, don't force me to delay. Unwillingly she gives in. She accompanies him down to the beach, watches him board the vessel, and the two wave goodbye to each other, she from the shore, he from the stern, until they can see each other no longer. But she goes on gazing at the receding ship until it disappears over the horizon.

At first all goes well, as a pleasant breeze wafts them on their journey. But soon the breeze changes into a wind which grows more and more fierce. The sky darkens, the waves billow, and in no time at all the ship is being tossed on a stormy sea with the waves crashing against its sides. The sailors try to cope:

> Sum haalde asyde the Ores:
> Sum fensed in the Gallyes sydes, sum down the sayleclothes rend:
> Sum pump the water out, and sea to sea ageine doo send.
> Another hales the sayleyards downe. And while they did eche thing

Disorderly, the storm increast, and from each quarter fling
The wyndes with deadly foode,★ and bownce the raging
  waves togither.

At last the ship can take no more. The mast breaks, the waters
pour in, and it sinks to the bottom. Clinging to a piece of
wreckage, Ceyx calls out to his father Lucifer, to his father-in-
law Aeolus and to his beloved wife. All in vain. As he goes
under he is still uttering Alcyone's name, praying that his body
may be washed ashore so that 'by her most loving handes he
might be layd in grave'. That day, says the poet, 'Lightsum
Lucifer' was dim, hidden in mourning behind dark clouds.

Alcyone, knowing nothing of this, has been praying daily to
the gods to bring her husband home safely, but this soon starts to
embarrass Juno, who knows that the time for such prayers is
long past. She arranges for a dream to come to Alcyone to
inform her of the awful truth. In due course, as she lies sleeping,
Morpheus appears at her bed's head in the form of her husband,
'Pale, wan, stark naakt, and like a man that was but lately deade',
dripping wet from head to foot. He recounts what has happened
to him and begs her to rise up, put on her mourning garments
and perform the proper rituals: 'Let me not to Limbo go/
Unmoorned for', he says. She tries to embrace him but her arms
close round empty air. 'Tarry!' she cries out, 'whither flyste?
togither let us go.' Her own voice wakes her and now she
begins to lament in earnest, striking her cheeks with her fists,
pulling out her hair, tearing her robe from her breasts. I begged
you not to leave me, she says to him, but you would not listen.
How much better it would have been for us to die together, not
to have been divided as we are now. As it is, 'Already, absent in
the waves now tossed have I bee./Already have I perrished. And

★ Feud

yit the sea hath thee/Without mee.' I cannot go on living, she says, at least in death there is a sense in which we will be together once more, for 'Although in tumb the bones of us togither may not couch,/Yit in a graven Epitaph my name thy name shall touch.'

It is morning. She leaves the house and makes for the sea-shore, the place by the jetty where she had watched his boat depart. As she gazes out to sea, recalling every detail of that day, something catches her eye. She looks more closely and sees that it is the body of a man, rolling in the swell. Her heart goes out in pity for him and for the wife he has left behind, and then, suddenly, she recognises it: it is her husband, Ceyx: 'Then plainely shee did see/And know it, that it was her feere. She shreeked, It is he.' Clambering on to the jetty she rushes along it till she is just above the body, then hurls herself off the parapet into the sea.

But she never falls. Instead she skims the surface like a sea-bird on new-found wings. Uttering plaintive cries she settles on the body and tries to embrace it with her rough bill. Perhaps in response to this, or perhaps because of some movement of the waves, Ceyx lifts up his face to her, and in a moment he too has been transformed into a bird and is flying over the sea beside her. Together they loved, says the poet, and together they suffered, no parting followed them in their new-found form as birds. They mate, have young, and in the winter season, for seven days of calm, Alcyone broods over her nest on the surface of the waters while her father Aeolus reins in the winds and holds the waters smooth for the sake of his descendants.

What was it about the story and its telling that moved her so? She had lost her father when she was five and her mother when she was ten. Though she found it painful to talk about it, she had told me about it often enough, but while she was alive I somehow never made the imaginative effort to understand what this might have meant to her. After all, she was my mother, she was old and wise and there to comfort and protect me when I was troubled or in pain. The thought that she could herself be wounded and sorrowing, while I could understand it intellectually, I was never able to grasp emotionally. But now she is dead everything is different. I reread the story and try to enter her mind as she read. Of course there is no need to search for autobiographical explanations as to why certain works of art move us: there are thousands of reasons, we all know what loss and sorrow entail, we can all enter into the world of those who are bereaved. And yet I cannot help feeling that this passage out of all the myriad stories which make up the *Metamorphoses* moved her so because it spoke to her own experience.

As she grew older she grew more fearful. She, who had ensured our survival in France during the war; who had taken the decision, at forty-five, to leave the Egypt where she was born and where she had family and friends, for a foreign country where she did not even know if she would be allowed to settle, because that was necessary for my education; who had worked uncomplainingly through her forties and fifties at menial jobs to see me through school and university – she began, in her seventies and eighties, to dread being abandoned. Even a trip of a few days on my part filled her with anxiety – for me, for herself. She tried to hide it, knowing that I would take this as an attempt on her part to tie me down and so grow resentful, but she had never been good at hiding her emotions and in a way I loved her for that, though I did indeed resent that particular manifestation of it. It was then, I think, as she grew older and frailer, more and more reliant on me for the simplest practical things, but also shorn of the mental toughness which had seen her – and me – through so much – it was then that the demons she had fought so successfully to keep at bay all her life returned to lay siege to her body and mind. It was then that she began to feel again the terror of betrayal which first her father's illness and death and then her mother's illness and death had instilled into her and which she had managed to overcome for so long. Her husband's abandonment of her, pregnant and with a two-year-old child, in the middle of the war, can only have added to that, and the subsequent death, after only a few days, of her second child must have finally convinced her at some deep inarticulate level that nothing she loved could be held for long. Our subsequent life together gave her a new happiness and a new strength, of course, but then, as the years went by and she grew more and more reliant on me, she must have felt that if she lost me it would simply be more than she could bear.

Books are strange things. The mark of a classic is that it can speak afresh to each generation, and Ovid's *Metamorphoses* has been doing that since the book first saw the light of day. It spoke to Chaucer, who retold the story of Ceyx and Alcyone, dwelling on Iris' trip to the cave of the god of sleep, in the first part of his first major poem, which I had sent to Sacha from Oxford shortly after reading it, but which evoked little response from her then. It spoke to Arthur Golding in the sixteenth century and to Shakespeare and to Pound and Eliot. In the Golding translation it spoke to Sacha, in particular the story of Ceyx and Alcyone. Across all those centuries, across the barriers of language and culture, via a simple little tale of how the kingfisher came – as the ancients thought – to make her nest in the sea, she found her pain renewed and at the same time made bearable because spoken by another and spoken in memorable language: the language Ovid used and the language a sixteenth-century English translator used to turn the Latin into his own tongue. And now I too, as I try to come to terms with her death, read and take comfort from those words. Why? Partly because by reading what she herself read and loved I feel closer to her and she lives for me a little. And partly because of the story itself and the way it is told. For this is a tale as firmly rooted in the real as anything in Homer or the Bible. I am not talking about the Christian Bible but about the Hebrew Bible, what Christians call the Old Testament. Neither Sacha nor I ever believed in the Resurrection, and my discomfort with Christian funeral services has mainly stemmed from the feeling that the priest's pious words about the dead person now being with Christ in heaven, and how one day the bereaved will be reunited with their loved one, went against the bitter facts of loss and, being a kind of false comfort, would in the end bring no comfort at all. No doubt that is not how Christians feel, but it is how I have felt and I know that that is how she felt. On the other hand when King David says, about the son God has taken from him as punishment for his adultery with Bathsheba and his indirect murder of her husband Uriah: 'Can I bring him back again? I shall go to him, but he shall not return to me', the painful acknowledgement of a hard truth has something satisfying and even purgative about it. Yes, we think, that is how it is, I shall go to him, but he shall not return to me. That is the law of life and it is good to have it stated so simply and so well. And when Homer, speaking of Castor and Pollux, the two brothers whom their sister Helen thinks to be still alive and either in the Greek camp or at home in Greece, says: she was wrong, for 'her brothers lay/motionless in the arms of life-bestowing earth, long dead in Lakedaimon of their fathers', he is not only giving the listener information, not only highlighting what scholars call epic irony, but saying something profound about death itself: Helen's brothers are now buried in the earth and will never rise again, but the earth itself is life-giving, the source of all food, and they are after all buried where they would wish to be, in their dear native land. Death is part of a larger rhythm and we would do well to recognise and accept that, though this does not mean that we should not sorrow and lament the death of loved ones. Ovid's account is not so very different. He too recognises the finality of death. Ceyx and Alcyone will never be reunited in any of the senses in which we, in this life, can understand the term, for death changes everything, both the person who has died and the one who survives. It is the ultimate source of metamorphosis. What lends the story its special poignancy, what Sacha responded to when she first read it and what I now respond to as I reread it in the wake of her death, is the perception of the role of the grieving and longing heart: as Alcyone leaps from the jetty in despair she suddenly takes flight, and that flight is the literal expression of the heart's leap into oneness with the loved and lost person. It is her desire to be with him which transforms her: the wings of the heart and the wings of metamorphosis are one and the same. But the fact of metamorphosis underlines the hard truth that as their old selves they will never again be together:

And with her crocking neb then growen to slender bill and round,
Like one that wayld and moorned still shee made a moaning sound.

There is a further truth. The wings of the heart are also the wings of the imagination: as we read we enter into Alcyone's sorrow and loss and then into her miraculous gain, and we live it even as we recognise that it is possible only in the imagination.

Alcyone's story has been prepared for by the fate of Daedalion, but in his case, though Apollo takes pity on him 'and on the soodaine as hee hung/Did give him wings', he turns into the fierce and war-like creature he always was: a bird of prey. Ceyx and Alcyone, on the other hand, having once known the calm of a deep and trusting love, are transformed, after the anguish of separation, tempest, death, dream, lamentation, into birds of calm, bringing peace even to the sea in the midst of winter storms:

> And now Alcyon sitts
> In wintertime uppon her nest, which on the water flitts
> A sevennight. During all which tyme the sea is calme and still,
> And every man may to and from sayle saufly at his will.

Sacha went to her death in some physical pain after weeks of petty torment, but at the end she was at peace. She found the strength to call me to her and tell me she was tired of her body and felt the time had come to let it go. I have no fear of death, she said, I know it is the end. I want you to know that you made the latter part of my life as happy as it is possible to be. Reading Ovid's story I think again of that moment, but without pain, rather with a kind of pride and a sense of peace: heart's wings.

The Elysium Lifestyle Mansions

Margaret Atwood

S unset over the Pacific, a noble sight. I get a terrific view of it every evening, when it's not fogged in or raining that is. Amazing thing, sunset; I still enjoy it, even when seen through two layers of glass, and one of them curved. Time's winged chariot going down in flames, every single night, like a soccer ball on fire. Like the *Hindenburg*. Now there's one ticket I'm glad I cancelled. No Icarus yearnings for me! *Per ardua ad astra*, my fanny – who wants to go to the stars anyway? Now everyone knows they're only natural gas. Better to put your feet up and look out the window, right here on *terra*, though *firma* I must say is a joke. This whole coast will heave and crumble and sink from view sometime in the next million years or so, and California will have drifted up around Alaska, which will at least put a stop to the film industry, but I won't be around by then. Around here, that is.

Not that I warned anybody else about the *Hindenburg*. Older is not necessarily wiser, but it's definitely street-wiser, and I knew by then that no one would believe me. *Crazy old bat*, they'd have said; did say, in bygone times to memory dear. *Not playing with a full deck. Two bricks short of a load. Lights on, nobody home.* Best to keep your head down and yourself to yourself, and get the fuck out when Danger beckons with her coy but fleshless finger. Though sometimes I become distracted – I get too caught up in the slideshow of the distant future and fail to concentrate on my contingency plans, and that can be tricky. I almost got stuck in Moscow during the Revolution, though I did make it out with a thousand diamonds sewn into my corset. (The corset travelled separately, as it was by that time far too large for my diminished frame.) It cost me, but happily I could foresee which ones among the comrades were susceptible to bribery, and thank the Fates for the dependable cupidity of human nature. Without palm grease we'd all be subject to Justice, or someone's cranky idea of it, and then rat-a-tat-tat. Not that it isn't rat-a-tat anyway, much of the time, but still, it helps to be rich. 'Societal breakdown' is when the rats and the tats climb over the broken-glass walls and get into the *foie gras* and start raping the boss's wife. The rest is just *crime*.

Serves me right anyway. I was lollygagging, and I didn't snap out of it until the Bolshies were practically chewing down the door. What was I previewing? Peering in at the Moonwalk of the late sixties, as I recall – which was sheer indulgence on my part, especially since I know the whole thing was a fraud, filmed on the slag-heaps of Sudbury, Ontario, to give the Commies the nyah nyah heebie-jeebies. Did take the starch out of them, to an extent. But *space race*? Space farce is more like it. Amazing how everyone swallowed it whole, and still swallows it, despite the fact that the Yanks can barely get any of their other, later and supposedly technologically superior tin cans off the ground. So much for microchips. Nevertheless, I allowed myself to become too involved in the sheer spectacle of it, and also the sheer effrontery – I do admire a con job on a very large scale.

Or maybe it was the stock-market crash of '29 – figuring the angles. I sold short, and did quite well – I do quite well on the market generally, as you may imagine, which is how I can afford this dump. It was me who had the name changed: it used to be The Paradise Retirement Residences, but I got homesick. I had a couple of beds of daffodils planted out at the front to represent the Fields of Asphodel, though nobody gets the allusion. It's pearls before swine in the allusion department, around here.

I thought Tennyson was fairly plangent on the subject, in his day:

> It may be that the gulfs will wash us down:
> It may be we shall touch the Happy Isles,
> And see the great Achilles, whom we knew.

Not that Achilles was all that great – a sulk and bully, like so many of that lot – but still, the lines have a ring to them, and how was Tennyson to know? He wasn't there.

I dictated a fan letter to him, as I recall – I can do that if they take the cork out of the bottleneck and put their ears down close, and since they've invented those lapel microphones it's been a lot easier. (Some of my earlier stuff came out more than scrambled because the attendants were hard of hearing. I'm not apologising, mind you, just explaining.) I sent a note to Mr Disraeli as well, the year he named one of his novels after me. Not a very good novel, but in these latter days one must take what one can get, and a driblet or two of recognition is about all that can be expected.

Tennyson wasn't a patch on Virgil though. I especially like the part where he describes my hair standing on end with inspiration. I have it read over to me every half-century or so, though you can't find anyone with a decent accent any more.

How lovely it was to have hair.

Back to the present day. I do feel that The Elysium Lifestyle Mansions has a certain *je ne sais quoi*. It never hurts to be classy. Once I'd made my wishes known they had the gold lettering changed the next day, and why not, because I own this place; it, and much else besides – oil, gas, communications, high tech, entertainment, forced-labour shoes, the works – but all through front companies, naturally. It's an amusement for me, like a jigsaw puzzle: I used to do crewel work but this is more involving. So I sit at the centre of a tangled web. The rumours about my having been changed into a spider or a grasshopper or a heap of dust were not only false, they were just metaphor; still, much better to have folks believe you're a spider than to be aware that you're still more or less human, and fully functional, though somewhat diminished in size. Can you imagine what it would be worth to some in high places to have their very own infallible prophetess under lock and key, in a cupboard at Head Office? I'm priceless, I assure you.

But I like to run my own show. There must be ten phone lines at least going into this place, and twice as many computer screens. I am, you might say, the original Gnome of Zurich – the only one who looks the part, in any case – though I can't say I ever spent much time there. I'd have been too conspicuous – I'm pretty conspicuous anyway, carried around as I am in a three-foot-tall decanter – I can't eat out, it attracts stares, the sight of a large jar sitting in a chair. Someone might have got itchy fingers – thought they could make off with me tucked under the arm like a bundle of dry sticks and hold me up for ransom. I'd have seen them coming of course – I always do – but it's a drain on the energy. Like having five TV stations on at once. You have to focus.

But I was talking about Moscow. A similar thing happened in Vienna, end of the thirties, not to mention Pompeii, not to mention Carthage. Then there was Paris – I did tell Louis to get out of town, but being thick as a brick he didn't listen – and Armenia, not to mention Uganda, not to mention Cambodia. These package tourist jaunts aren't all they're cracked up to be. But such narrow escapes keep a girl on her toes, and anyway they do lighten the tedium. Century after century of greed and power-grabbing and empire-building, and then there's always the part where the empire starts getting artistic or a conscience and looking under the floorboards to see what's buried there, or I should say who's buried, and then there's a lot of breast-beating and *mea culpa* and the whole thing loses its nerve and goes to rat-shit. That's where the barbarians come in, and believe me they always do. Luckily I've known which ravening hordes to back. (Did I say I'm also into armament sales? Not nice, I grant you, but if I don't do it somebody else will. I don't shoot the guns, I only make them. Other folks pull the triggers. Don't blame me.)

We were much more candid in the old days. Winners got the loot and the women, losers got impaled on stakes or thrown off a cliff. No loose ends.

Too bad about Dido though. I liked her better than him. More zizz to her, you might say. The piety of Pious Aeneas is, was and always will be a definite pain in the bum.

Which brings me to my own story, the beginning of it I mean. The so-called romance. I find it refreshing to take my mind off the future for a while and dip into the past. At least it's over and done with; at least you aren't always waiting for the long-awaited other shoe to drop.

I was already a prophetess, though a young one then, and on reasonable terms with the boss. He dictated, I related; in those days you'd go into a trance, chewing the laurel leaves, breathing in the toxic fumes and so forth. I don't find that so necessary any longer, though I did drink absinthe for a while when you could still get it, and I had a pack-a-day habit for a while. Reverie-inducing, you might say, but I had to give it up because of my lungs.

Anyway. There he was, lurking around some stream or brook – they often did that, gods and men both, in the hope you'd be taking off your clothes for a quick wash – in the garb of a handsome shepherd or some such. You could always tell it was a god in disguise because they never got the details right. I mean, a shepherd with a golden bow? Give me strength.

Greetings, Phoebus Apollo, I said. He was disappointed that he'd been spotted – was counting maybe on a common-and-garden seduction, a quick roll in the shrubbery and no harm done, for which he wouldn't have had to pay. But now the cards were out on the table, and I was a hard negotiator even then. The deck was stacked, and not in my favour, but I was good-looking enough I suppose, and that's what counted. Where do I get these card metaphors? The Mississippi, in its heyday. Now that was fun.

Nowadays you'd call it a case of sexual harassment, but back then it was just the usual deal: a sex-for-perks trade. Being a god who set himself up against disorder – nothing in excess, bla bla – Apollo didn't like to indulge in plain rape, not like some of the others. He considered it beneath his dignity. Anyway he was one of the few who employed women, and he wouldn't have wanted to get a rep for abusing the staff. He didn't want to lose his nine-Muse cheering section.

You're a bright girl, he said. *You know what's what.* Nudge, wink. I flounced and pouted, he flattered and wheedled. Finally we got it down to a straight offer: nooky for him, immortality and the inside track for me.

I said I'd give it some thought.

You wonder why they can't stick to their own kind.

I was still living at home then, and commuting to work. I told my old mother. She could see further through a brick wall than most, which is partly where I got my talents.

Don't mix in with those gods, she said. *They're shifty. Anyway, what if there's a kid? You'd be related, and to that bunch! Killing their kids, burning up each other's mistresses, changing people into trees for no reason at all. I'd stay away from them if I was you.*

It's a bit late for that, and anyway it was the only job I could get, I said. *I don't see that I have much choice. After all he is a god.*

God or not, they only want the one thing, she said. *Whatever else, get your hands on the gift first. Otherwise he'll be away with the dawn and all you'll ever see is his heels.*

A done deal, I told Apollo, *but you ante up first*. So he did. He put his hand on my forehead. There was a kind of light, a kind of heat, though I can't say I felt any different right away. But I had to take his word for it.

So, tonight? he said. He didn't say *Your place or mine*. That's only in the movies. It would be the cave floor, in front of his own altar, as usual in such affairs.

I said I had my period. The next night it was a headache. And so on. I just kept stalling him.

Fact is, not much good had ever come to any girl who'd slept with a god. Anyway I didn't exactly lust after him; it was the hairdo, all those finicky little curls.

After a while Apollo got peeved. *Come across or else*, he said.

Or else what? I said. *If I really do have this immortality, there's nothing much you can threaten me with.*

You forgot something, he said.

What would that be? I said.

You forgot to ask for endless youth, he said. *You'll end up so old and shrivelled that people will think you're an insect. You'll long for death.*

All at once I saw it. There's always a catch with these gods. You can't win. *Wait a minute, let's talk*, I said. *Surely we can rearrange things.*

The gods themselves cannot recall their gifts, he said. Then he was off in a cloud of gold-dust. I heard a faint snickering.

At first I pushed all thoughts of the distant future aside. Just enjoy yourself while it lasts, was my motto. I still had to do a lot of prophesying though, there was a line-up every day, people wanting the usual scoops – birth, death, marriage, war, money, fame, and so on – and that keeps you busy, so the time passed quickly, and all of a sudden everyone I'd once known was dead, and after that it began to get tedious.

Tedious, and at the same time agonising. You see what's coming, you see what's coming again and yet again, it goes on and on, but you can't stop it. So much carnage, so much torture, so much howling. Yourself looking on, the last witness, dry-eyed.

They've spread it about that when I was hanging from the ceiling, in the cave at Cumae, in my first primitive bottle, people would come and ask – for their own amusement, I suppose, as at a zoo or freak show – *Sibyl, what do you want?* And I would say, *I want to die.*

This is another inaccuracy, another error in transcription. None of these journalists ever gets anything straight.

The god did not take away my youth. That would have disappeared anyway, in the natural course of things. He did something much worse. He made me like himself, like a god: he gave me knowledge, but knowledge without pity.

I never said *I want to die.*

I said *I want to cry.*

Disjecta Membra

Rosalind Belben

O HAMMOCK, swallow my laughter, lull a minor woe. I charmed the fellow tied to the door-post and slipped into the house at dusk and as recommended sought . . . for it's not all talk with me, uxorious though I am . . . to postpone the maid, eager to find my entry to the mistress smoothed, and luck would have it that this same maid, this slave, had eyes for me: the acquaintance, so nurtured, flourished and have I not always muttered to you that it's madness to dally first with the slave, in visiting the mistress I encountered the slave and so dallied, for she dropped into our brief conversation her birthplace, she's from Africa Proconsularis. HOW LONG it is since you swayed that other, nobler she in your strings, the one for whom no stirring lust, but love for the filial, who now calls home Africa, whither Cornelius Fidus must bear her off, far from her Pater and her native soil, whose Pater in his head brings cakes and blessings, it is her birthday, that dear daughter's, and will he treat her just as well, though he beg me to visit them and their Libyan shore. How could I fail to lap there if a little, the slave had come

he clapped the tablet shut and laid the stylus down

and tasted very sweet, so one thing led to another. Twice come, for removed a barbarian from farther in, from her bar-bar-

214

speaking tribe, so much she told me in her halting speech, not much more, mountain stronghold to two cities in high places to an island, so she spoke, an island, flatter than the sea. I must go back for more

he squinted at the sun

more of her stilted talk, it's quite quaint, she is afraid she'll lose her language, I wondered why, or what it meant to her, she cannot read or write so why mourn a distant tongue, or hope to return, no doubt '*caelum non animum mutant qui trans mare currunt*',[1] but unless she flattered me the pleasures are endowed with artistry in Rome. Once to Thugga was she hauled from farther south and there encountered a few of us among the Numidians, and north and south were stopped with kisses, she learned some tricks, and bathed, and bathed her mistress in a house that stood two streets above another sort, phallus erect outside the door, so giggled with more ornamental women, she met them when she went on the fetch of eggs

he gently swung

from this Thugga, that sounds a splendid city, all on a hill, sprawling high, above our miles of cereals, though much needing some Roman fist to put its architecture straight, with a circus highest as if to crown a mountain and seats wild for us to nestle up to ladies upon the rock that cradles it, from here uprooted to her flat lapping island she calls Circe's, and now we have the kernel of my desire for her, she slept and lay and fed and sipped

he wrote in an ever more constricted space

on enchanted soil, and was not, it seems, transformed in any

way, she intact from tribe to Sicca to Thugga whence in shape
the same to Circia,[2] named by the ancients Aeaea, to a fort close
by the westward sea. On that the sun sets crimson and makes
crimson blood of it, as I imagined, yet when I enquired as to the
herbs, the herb-clad hills, she said there were no hills. IT'S FLAT
where Circe abode, not wooded, no hills, not so many herbs. I
was somewhat deceived, my first she (the MUSE) has played with
my conceits . . . or did that other H. name hills . . . Wait, I shall
smear the wax plain black again. Not in my heart to be petulant
for in the discovering much joy was had, and it is art

TELLS ME of the garrison hilltop town of Sicca, from there, it
seems, she looked out deep into the mountains of Africa, one
gleans even from the ignorant that there is a source of sacred
water, a cult of Astarte had flourished above the citadel, the rock
formation is of a vulva and virgins were ferried there for rites. It
did gush, that is, we have great cisterns, and the lower source is
dedicated by our Roman soldiers to Venus . . . Two sources,
one goddess, I observed, or the same source at two founts. They
name such a remote fastness Sicca Veneria

he examined his nails

more an ardent ear into which flow the seed of stories, dallying
in the spirit of curiosity for hers. I ASKED, for the o so venerated
one tells of 'a land of thicket, oaks and wide watercourses', the
hills must have been mine, 'a low landscape' the Greek poet has
it, and she says the wind pulls the trees to pieces, there are date-
palms, at the watercourses she laughed with mouth open, many
a coarse tooth, the water is so scarce it trickles underground,
whence it must be won. The climate has changed, I instantly
averred. In ancient times more temperate. I went beyond her
understanding. The soil has blown into the sea, I offer. A god

did it, she asked. Does a skein of swans on occasion pass, I murmur, overhead.[3] Do you suppose, and I stroked her nape, if the goddess were to sigh . . . She corrected me: cranes. Often there were cranes. True that bathed in sun, she allowed, these islands, Circia and Circinitis, enjoy a magical climate all of their own, a surly day is rare. The flowers . . . Wind-flowers, I interjected . . . are small and lying. She clicked her tongue: grave doubt. Anemones like oak woods, no oak a stone-like land. Unless the top foot of the island was, as you say o master ha ha, sloughed off into the sea. Gardens of pomegranate and fig there are; poor barley, and vines and vegetables: toilers in them still spoke of a Greek 'princess' who'd come in distant times. The poet was fond of wooded islands. Could the oak be cork. She knows the cork-oak. Or cedar, cedar that blazed in Circe's hearth: was Virgil too mistaken.

SPEAKING OF wind, it does the wind die down. I was urged to relate how from the nectar-sprinkled blood of the dead Adonis, whom Venus loved, sprang a sanguinary anemone, though not on Circe's island, how he was to be alive each year in the hearts of men and how, at his adored pastime, the hunt of wild beasts . . . The slave was full of life and fire: Eshmun, she cried, Eshmun, fated to stand uneasily on the watch with his spear for the tusky boar that is coming to kill him. I see him, she breathed, his back to me, alert, ears strained, eyes on the least rustle in the qirmiz.[4] He will always die. And be reborn, I said . . . and you name him Eshmun. In Thugga they say he is the healing god, you Romans call him Aesculapius. You have confused Adonis with Aesculapius, I said, with some asperity. Not I myself, she said, fawning. I am a slave.

his thoughts wandered back to the island of Circia with its god-given weather

IS THERE to be found there, I enquired of her, a white flower with a black root?[5] I could watch the effort of memory: it took its course across her eyes as a chariot across the face of the sun. Square-fringed. I read the answer, and kissed the bafflement away. Cherished slave, there must be the hart Ulysses slew; but such beasts as the great high-horned deer can they be happy where no oak forests? Perhaps once pine. I am fated to be unhappy in Rome, she uttered; and was wounded when I smiled.

You will cross the Tyrrhene Sea, I said in a quiet tone, avoiding the dire straits, and so on almost to the Libyan shore.

O Circia, inimitable child of the sun, lying like a lily in the lap of the sea,[6] it is you, o island, as the years in history divide Aeneas and Dido, that yourself has been by poets amended.

as he swung the dappled shadows cast by the orange-trees brushed back and forth across his face

AND SO to the mistress.

Notes

1 They're still themselves, who cross the sea to different skies. Horace.
2 Cercia, anglicised.
3 Venus, making for Cyprus in her chariot, drawn by swans.
4 The kermès oak, *Quercus coccifera*.
5 Moly, given to Ulysses by Mercury to counter Circe's spells.
6 Circe's father was Helios, her mother the sea nymph Perse. Ovid was later to place Circe's home, as Virgil had done, on a wooded peninsula of the Italian coast.

Nightfall on the Romanian Coast

Paul West

I

Y ou know the statue at the Caffé San Giorgio, supposedly Saint George on horseback? Well, that's really your old scapegrace Ovid (call me Viddie) got up as a cavalier. Here in *Outre Tombe* I'm everywhere, skulking in the Morrone monastery, getting the monks to wash my penis, or in that huge, huge house of mine in town, that made dear old Rabelais gawp. All yours? He must have thought you could divide houses up like pies. Well, some folk do. No, I told him, *I* am *its*. Two homes actually, the other out there on the hill at Santa Lucia, among the ruins, where the spring called Love eggs us on. I wrote *Loves* there in between bouts with my fairy cockmother. There was buried treasure in that place, but I refused to let them dig for it, saying the place was protected by lions and tigers, wolves and bears and three callous anacondas. Once, some peasant wandered into one of the caves and found me there, writing, in a chamber full of barrels of silver and gold. I swung my big iron mace and scared him off, no doubt equipping him with fearsome dreams. Beware Viddie, I told him, Viddie the vicious. I used to careen through my ruins in a four-horse carriage to scare intruders away, making a terrible racket, just like an army on the march.

I'm a softie, really, accustomed to smiling without opening

my mouth. I'm observant too, always the one to notice that the intrusion in my left visual field is daffodils (they're over there, of course, each year renewing their hardy yellow, or the white floret in the yellow mouth like a whorelet in a whore's gash). Everyone said it: Viddie, one day they will send you away for – everything. You like to watch, and you like someone naked to watch you in the act of watching. Why are you so horny? Not because of oysters but because my organ twitches endlessly, playing lascivious music to itself like someone's nervous hand tapping a goblet with a little ivory stirring rod. You can't twitch all the time. We live in such a deviant, question-begging world. Talking shop with Rabelais the rouser, as often, I ask him if he has read the poet Semperius and he answers, 'I couldn't exactly say', which means No, he hasn't, but is unwilling to admit it. Or he would say, on other occasions, 'Forgive me, but I do not recall having a distinct opinion.' Shitnoodles to that. You might say anything to him and get the same evasion. 'Rab, Your Rabness, did you ever screw an ass?'

'In the ass? Whose ass is in question? Whose ass's ass?'

I read him a dirty poem instead about dropping a ring down Corinna's bosom, right between her tits, and it slithered down all the way, only to be trapped by those dangling lips. Why not a big ring through them, then, so I could lead and tug her around like a bullock? His Rabness does not like this idea, so I ask him why so little tupping, frigging, in his work, and he says his work reflects his life. So I sez, being the naughty man all over again, you don't assuage yourself except with a dead rabbit smothered in Ethiopian balsam?

And you know what he said next? 'I couldn't exactly say.' One conversation with him and you have plumbed the unclean mattress of his mind.

Twelve rooms I had, labelled mentally, and stuck to the job assigned to each – thus, I: Frontal, II: *A tergo*, III: Cunnilingus,

IV: Fellatio, V: Whipping, VI: Mutual self-defilement, as some call it, VII: Frotting – and so on, my only unfulfilled desire having been to be in all rooms at the same time with a different hussy. This is not love, Your Rabness, just jerking about lest I spend the whole day in thought. All that remains of our lovely country place is a long wall, part of the colonnade, where sometimes itinerant vendors sell Viddie beads, Viddie stones, Viddie's favourite flower (guess). The view now includes a jail, no doubt for groin offenders, profaners of things wholesome.

II

The function of insomnia is to make us try to write, or yell, what we otherwise wouldn't dare to, with various sad ghosts all looking on – Nerval, Cavafis, a few more. Unable to sleep, I blather away in mental prose like a manure heap observing its own decomposition, the aim of the exercise being to write one more poem, short or long, something worthy of my mysterious, shabby standing. But not a line comes, only a filtered memory of how she and I sneaked around town, only rarely dining out together, aware of a punitive dispensation mightier than we, but at the same time almost eager to be caught, not as blatant as Julia, picking up men in the Forum and screwing them by torchlight after-hours, abandoning herself to crazy parties on the Rostra. Nothing like that, but covert intensity. If you are partial to anything such, you know the feeling. Deserting the known planet for other ones in the conviction that something was lecherously there. It was a wonder we were still trotting or slinking around, on the loose, what with spies everywhere and the envious ever at their accustomed chore of celibate gusto. The speed at which things happened, when they did, leaves me still with an impression of compressed quicksilver, so much so that I have spent the time ever since then adjusting my poor body to celerity. Its coercive-propulsive power.

Julia *mère* was ganged while I took notes.

It was as crude as that. She invited it, calling out to me not to miss a certain feature of the orgy, almost as if she were not present, but high in a lighthouse, looking down. And no doubt it was an awful bore for her, she who made a profession of lustful loitering. She took no pleasure from it all, other than the constant one of flouting her father's rules. Did I take part? No, I always found, may the gods help me, that my own penis in the presence of half a dozen enraged specimens of the same organ tends to wilt, not exactly humbled by size, vigour, blatant blue veins ready to pop, but more as if, on the field of honour, I needed a little privacy, not being an exhibitionist. Besides, Julia naked or nearly so was an object as familiar as a tree and just as tempting.

Once I had been deported, I stopped writing about sex and bad behaviour. Is it true that once a murderer's locked away, he loses all homicidal impulse? You would have thought a Viddie, sent away for life, would have exploded with filth and rancour, letting it all dangle out like injudicious intestines. But no, I became decorous, although pathetic, imploring, cajoling. Please let me back in, I promise to be good. I will never compose *How To Come while Asleep*, or *The Use of Truncheons*, or *Fellatio with Vinegar*. None of that greasy folderol, prime packet of the old days. I have become, o my lord, an expert on decorum and bliss, joy and tact, the decent fellow they all hoped I would never lapse into.

Just as there is a law of diminishing returns, there is a law of increasing ones. If, like Viddie, you get exiled, sent off to the middle of nowhere, you get a greater share of *Outre Tombe* on your death – more room to float about in, more shades to quarrel with. There must be a logic to all this, requiring those

never exiled to remain in much the same spot while ne'er-do-
wells such as I drift querulously about, to make up for all the
non-entity I had to put up with when I was shipped off to
Romania. So: there must be a compassionate cosmic Overseer
somewhere, interfering and leaning on the scales of justice.
Barren life equals fertile aftermath.

There I go, making sense of the world, even the underworld,
the afterlife. There must be thousands here I'd like to meet, but
I never do, whereas I run into Rab all the time. So perhaps we
are grouped according to lifelong interests, with the ultimate in
pleasure accorded those who were executed for whatever
reason. It is they who get the social, comradely plums, when it is
too late *not* to keep their noses clean. Those beheaded, I'm told,
wobble when they walk, while those hanged or garrotted walk
in stiff, erect anapaests as if the police are watching. I, I slouch,
like Rab; we who have not kept our noses clean hover and
slink, sometimes going hand in hand so as not to overbalance
when we crouch.

Take Cicero, for instance, who died the year I was born, 43
BC. Surely, under the compensatory auspices of *Outre Tombe*
(permanent nightfall on the Romanian coast), he and I might
have met and talked. Perhaps one day we will, the stylist and the
tease. There is no way of applying, there is nobody to consult:
we just waft about, confined to a small clique of friends and
rivals (Catullus, Baudelaire, on the fringes), all carefully evalu-
ated, perhaps by that old censor Dante, for our quotient *lascif*.
The horniest get to know the fewest women, whereas
homophiles are not restricted. Or perhaps they work it
according to noses, in which case I – Naso – lose hands down, a
quite acceptable face marred by an enormous long, drooping,
scything tuber. Cut off his nose and he's quite an Adonis, they
used to say of me. Imagine that landslide of septum, that
waggonload of vomer, invading and disrupting your life, even

when, as they did, they whisper Big Nose, big below. As I was. Perhaps I should have switched the one for the other, breathing between my balls, coming above my mouth. I ask Rab, but he just goes away laughing *Fey sucker voodoo ah*, as if I knew French. Out here you can make no revisionist alterations: you're stuck with what you had.

So, to take my mind off such punishment, I turn to – wouldn't you know it? – the Germans, who dismiss the Julia business and say I was exiled for flubbing a public speech in the imperial presence, bowing to the audience without curtsying to the Emperor first. I, the eighth of eleven speakers hymning this new stadium (who cares?), could see only the hide-thick make-up over Augustus' pallor as he signalled me to begin, and I stepped up to the microphones, all shiny as pacemakers. I was as bored as Augustus, which was no doubt why I failed to crook the knee and honour him. That woke him up when, without preamble, I began with 'Citizens of Rome . . .' I electrified the senators and generals as well, the self-styled gentry. What is the fool doing? Where is he going? They all knew. Since Augustus and I were both fed up, why not behave like him? Did *he* bow to *me*, to poetry? Not a bit of it. So why bow to him? The Greeks called this hubris, but I call it opinionated bemusement.

So the right-minded moved in on me, the company clique complaining that I not only derided the wholesome but also lacked kindness to my fellow-men. And I scanted the Emperor. As German explanations go, it isn't bad, but like the Julia episode it's obvious, too easy. Did I prostitute myself with Julia *and* her daughter? Yes. Did I omit to salute the Emperor? Yes. My own view, though, is that I was sent packing for being unfaithful to poetry, for not writing the wholesome stuff the Emperor wanted; as the Boss, he owned all that was thought, said or done. To put it in Soviet terms, I had refused to come up with tractor poems, paeans to hydroelectric stations, to the founders of the party, to the rustic rabble and the proles of Rome. I was a snob, too much of one for the strait-laced Emperor, so he fudged up the political plot, as I call it, run by Agrippa Postumus.

So: not sex, not gaffe, not plot.

But failing to toe the line, penalised for being myself, a dangerous libertine who got the republic a bad name. To me, the whole retaliation is somehow circular, the Emperor knowing that, if exiled, I would write far below my best, and therefore exiling me for a future lapse. What a society in which they fault you for the mistakes you are *going* to make. Such mind-reading belongs in a Muslim bazaar, surely. I went to Tomis, there began to whine, and they said, See, we knew what you would do once you got there, so off you went. To the absurdity of nature, add the absurdity of men. All I can manage now is a maudlin complaint, a vacuous appeal, a lame-brained summary of my life. No more toad-stranglers, no more thunderbolts, just a few little scribbles as if from the temperate land of the *haiku:*

> Should I, the heron,
> Die from boiling,
> May it be in
> Clear water.

Poor stuff, *hein?* A castration has taken place, even though each day I try to get back into my old freewheeling ways; I have sunk to trying to please the Emperor, whose title I never fail to capitalise. I toe the line, as required, and bleat. I envy the pure-bred eloquence of certain courtiers, but am closer to the NCO in charge of the execution squad who, marching through the newly unlocked door of the condemned man's cell, asks punctiliously about the quality of the last breakfast and smacks his lips in studied envy of the other's lot. Now, *there* is *one* nervous breakdown I won't be having, either's. Rab has been at me again, babbling about 'mass wisteria' (he the linguist while I know only my own language and some rustic dialects). I sometimes feel like one of those rib prints in the sky, shredded white on celestial blue, when clouds appear to be going in the opposite direction to the ground wind. I miss boorish men with apologetic wives. What a mess of memories only at long last petering out: unrelenting Tiberius, the citizens of Tomis at last forgiving my charges of barbarism, telling my wife what demeanour to adopt in the halls of power, austere matrons and ribald princesses, intercessions by eminent patrons (or not), slipping the addresses of friends into my poems, Dalmatia and Pannonia, rinsed skies after heavy rain from the south, the endlessly protracted journey to Tomis, the goddess Dea Dia, love poems (none after AD I), firing up my *Metamorphoses* only to singe it a bit, ice enduring from one winter to the next, Greeks in trousers against the chill, wars meant to be talked about rather than declared, forty thousand survivors abandoned on the left bank of the Rhine, condemnation of wigs made from aliens' hair, being agile and mobile, the Concani who drank the blood of horses – Scythian or Spanish if they existed at all, the Romanian hedonist, a slightly overweight woman, who let her dog sort out and forward her mail, or so she said. These I miss, but there is nothing I do *not* miss. Once having met de Nerval and Rilke, I long to see them again in this *ronde* of shadows, but they do not come my way except under cover of pitch darkness. Where they come from, where I go to, I have no idea, I in a state of constant, erudite flotation, less a man than a condign figment, ever chattering to myself. What else, then?

The confusion about the two Julias.

Seeing forbidden arts performed in my own home.

Julia, *mère:* villa torn down, baby butchered, ashes spurned.

Mock funerals for detested rulers.

Women whose widowhood is in doubt.

Nocivity. Iracundia. Clementia.

Septuagenarian despots. Clever to begin with, I soon turned tactless. Banished, like Gibbon; an expert on Black Sea fish. Libraries from which my poems have been removed and burned by rotting aristos, diseased grammarians, hirsute bankers, freedmen, whores, haughty prophets. I pliant but far from feeble: alert, humane, humorous, industrious and stylish, never a drinker, always a slave to my art. I bleat on and on.

III

And so would you, marooned here in the paradise of dysentery and bubonic plague, all those diseases we suffered from and never had a name for. When I complained, the message came back: A mere pinprick, Ovid, considering all you've put us through. 'Well,' I eventually answered, 'there are pins and there are pricks. Let's hear it for the pricks.' An image from later reading has begun to afflict me – another of those Russian things. A commissar stands at a street window with a young troublemaker and they look out at the people hurrying by. Now, how does it go?

'What,' the commissar asks, 'is the difference between all those people going past and you?'

'I am inside and they are not. I have the inside track,' says this brash young Turk.

'No,' he hears. 'You, my young friend, are among the condemned. They are the accused.'

Perhaps not much of a difference after all. I was among the condemned to begin with, then they fudged up an indictment to round things off. I can't bear to think of it, it being the last consequential thing in my life. What do they say about me in Rome nowadays? *Veni, Viddie, Vinci.* They might well. This is a loser speaking, forever trying to come up with one last poem worthy of its predecessors, but the machinery is dead and rusted, the sense of rhythm dried up, the eye blurred.

I try, devising a poem to a dead wife (why not?), or even a live one in exile too. Such altruism. But all that comes is one of those strategic moans, addressed no doubt to some plausible emperor, beginning as follows (follow the process as it unfurls):

> *Please make the huge red hibiscus*
> *my dinner plate all grubby again*
> *while I, black bird-limed statue*
> *in a Romanian square, hunch on a giant plinth*
> *bearing contemptible insignia —*

I rest, thunderstruck by puny afflatus, then resume at the speed of a snail:

> *while a hesitant boy*
> *crosses the road. I beg for a tent to cover me,*
> *a quotation from piratic winds wobbling*
> *in the uproar above my skull.*

Now I begin to shudder and weep as the sap oozes from me and away:

> *I was unsafe to know*
> *so let me once more wind a tapeworm round*
> *my throat, in homage to treason.*

It ends there, possibly the last. In my head I have recast it a million times. It comes out burnished, barren, flimsy, nothing to write home about. At least it tells you about my favourite flower, and what I would do with it.

Took my time getting here. Stopped off everywhere like a man destined for the block. It is like being expelled from school, sent down from university. Wrote to all my friends as if, all their lives, they had been salivating for news from the Black Sea. Behold Agrippa Postumus also in exile, on the island of Planasia. After a while we both stopped pleading. Julia mother of Julia died on her island too. I'll never make sixty, nor would want to. Oh, just once again, to celebrate the festival of Fors Fortuna – carnival on the river, much drinking, as even now in Trastevere, the entire next day devoted to hangovers. I must pluck up the courage to write of Arabia, scarlet ocean and aromatic pastures. Anywhere desolate for this delinquent. As if it were Africa. I rest on Gibbon's *Decline and Fall*. How apt. My poems, he writes, 'exhibit a picture of the human mind under very singular circumstances; and they contain many curious observations, which no Roman, except Ovid, could have an opportunity of making'. Just think how many years that has soothed me, ever-drifting shade that I am, peevish, salacious, vivid, a tease and gabby.

A Bestiary of My Heart

Victoria Nelson

Dangerous animals

My purpose is to tell of bodies transformed into shapes of a different kind. When I was a little girl, animals were my enemies. Sharks shredded me. Grizzlies rent me. Tigers sprang out of the dead grass. Rattlesnakes bit and bit me.

All that I got used to, strange to say. I thought it was the way things were. I thought it was the way things always would be. But it wasn't. Other things happened. It's all different now.

The empty lot

All that was you, Father. You shredded my flesh. You rent me stem to stern. You sprang at me out of the dead grass. You bit and bit me. Here's what I did back.

Summer of my twelfth year, strolling in the empty weed-filled lot below the house, I bend down to pick a daisy. A rattlesnake coiled around the stem rears up to strike. I step back. The field erupts. Rattlesnakes, hundreds of them in boiling motion. By force of will I rise off the ground. I hover ten feet above the hissing snakes that carpet the hard dirt. If I lose my concentration for even a moment, I'll fall, be bitten to death.

So I must hang suspended like this the rest of my life.

Sharkbait

Same set-up with the sharks and the deer. Here's a sunny day, stags and does swimming in the warm waters of the Gulf Stream. The invisible shark attacks. No one can see him, but we know him by the marks he leaves. Slaughter, slaughter. Bright gouts of blood marble the deep green water. Bleeding carcasses litter the beach.

I go fishing for the shark. From up in the stratosphere where I've put myself I snag the creature. With my fish-hook made from a human leg bone, I reel him in. Then I fall, I fall thousands of feet to meet my catch. Land the shark, understand, the moment I hit water.

The next time I fish for the shark, he swallows the hook and tows me miles and miles through an underwater tunnel into the light.

The third time the shark comes, he's completely different. This time he has human eyes.

The new shark leaps over the bowsprit on to the deck of our fishing scow. 'This means trouble,' I tell my learned female friend. 'We'll need to move fast to get out of the way.'

We don't move fast. Slowly, slowly, we back up a step or two. The little white shark flip-flops on the varnished boards of the deck. Small but solid, he looks at us with impossibly pretty eyes.

I say again, 'We'll have to move fast.'

Slowly, slowly, we walk backwards through the cabin to the stern. Below us the water roils. Up leaps the shark over the railings. He lands squirming at our feet.

'This shark is dangerous,' I tell my friend. The shark looks at us. We look at him. His eyes have lids and lashes.

We move to another boat. And another. Shutting cabin doors, putting up barricades.

I say, 'Dangerous.'

Panther-parrot

Compared to snakes and sharks, cats are a piece of cake. Even big ones.

Night falls on the Indian subcontinent. A group of us ride camels through the countryside. Gratefully I climb off my mount, a practical way to travel but oh so slow and uncomfortable. I get separated from the others and now I'm alone in the jungle.

A sabre-tooth cat blacker than the shadows stalks me through the trees. But I'm no longer afraid. So it melts into a small growling dun-coloured bobcat running towards me. I hold my ground. I snarl back just as fiercely.

Really, I give quite a good snarl.

Things happen fast now. My snarling turns the bobcat into a little monkey who leaps up and perches on my shoulder. The monkey becomes a parrot chattering gaily in my ear. In all that gibberish I make out scraps of words, real words it has learned by heart from humans. Words in a language I still don't understand.

Black leather cat

I take the lesson. Better to be a scary animal than to meet one. And this is just as true of cities as the Indian jungle.

The other night, for instance. A young blonde woman complained to me her boyfriend was treating her badly. So I put on my black leather coat and trousers. I put on my black leather cat head with its vinyl whiskers. I picked up my black leather rod.

Now I was a black leather cat. And I taught that fellow a thing or two.

The cat hospital

But cats have their problems, too. Two men and a woman in white coats sit at a long table stitching up cut-open cats, a surgical assembly line. At the end of the table the woman clamps an oxygen mask on the striped orange muzzle of an enormous tiger.

To this cat hospital I bring my two domestic kittens. One is orange and one is black. Both are covered in blood and faeces. A doctor tells me they have *hydroangio-encephalitis* – that is, brain and heart rabies – because they were bitten by a rat. (Snake, I think, but close enough.) I know they are being cared for here in the cat hospital. But will my poor pussies ever get well?

My grown cat swims across the estuary and dives into a heap of rubbish. He catches a rat. Kills it. Large armadillos lumber through my living room. They are after the big grey rat who just jumped out of my old Shakespeare book, the rat I don't see creeping along the sofa, about to bite my neck from behind.

All rats are not bad. I know of a few that turned into kittens. But they were ugly kittens.

Between my cat and the armadillos, many rats are slain.

Now the bodies are starting to smell. I say to my father: It's not my job. You must bury the dead rats yourself.

Beasts of the air

Two days of the year my coastal town is full of monarch butterflies. One autumn day the monarchs pass through going south, one spring day they pass through coming back. My cat scoops them out of the air by the pawful, brings the delicate-winged bodies into the house for me to admire. I drop the ragged orange and black scraps off the second-storey porch. Some scraps fall straight to the ground and lie there. Other scraps flutter away: they do not die, but they are changed.

My father and I look at an abandoned beehive in the orchard behind the house. The queen bee is precious, someone says. Just then a huge bee flies out of the crumpled hive. I try to cover her with an empty plastic prescription bottle, but she escapes. Then I catch her by the wings in the next room. I call to my father, over and over. She must have a hive, I say. My father won't help me. I have to find her the new hive right away, before I hurt her pinched wings.

A young man with long white hair shows me a magic tree with red bees buzzing in it, plump red bees with black stripes on their bodies. Where's the hive? Over there, nestled out of sight in the leafy branches.

Beheaded

Back in that empty lot again. This time I'm standing on the ground in hip-boots of thickest rubber. I have a hoe, the family hoe. The rattlesnakes coil and strike, knocking their blunt heads against my boots. One by one I chop off their heads. This is a long and tedious task. Hundreds of snakes live in the field and I must kill them all. Chop, chop, like scything wheat, the cross-section of their rattlesnake necks always the same – a bony circle of spinal cord with a soft doughnut of snake flesh wrapped around it.

Finally I'm through. All but a few snakes are dead. To hell with getting every last one, I've made my point. I slop a little petrol on the dry straw grass where the bodies lie. Toss a match. KA-BOOM!

Boa-Boa

But some got away. Don't they always? Now big multicoloured snakes are sliding restlessly across the floor of my tiny room. Why won't anybody kill them?

Deep in the woods lies a cave. In this cave lives a giant snake. The snake draws me like a magnet. I wait at the entrance, reverently. A shape moves out of the darkness. The swollen, reared-up head wears a golden crown. Bow down before King Cobra.

Four men play poker at a kitchen table. The host owns a boa constrictor that has disappeared. The curtains heave at the window. The forgotten boa, bored and hungry, has crawled up the sill, slipped, caught his tooth in the long burlap curtain. He's dangling like a living cord-pull and he's really mad. But they're all too drunk to unlatch him.

My female friend has a cat and a boa constrictor in her house that I must care for. I feed the cat, forget about the boa constrictor. Then I find him in her cupboard, hanging snaggle-toothed next to her scarves. He drops to the floor. Now he's a gorgeous emerald-green lizard. He has legs. What if he crawled in the bed? I shut the cupboard door fast, but the lock is broken.

A man – it seems he is my lover, I know nothing about this – this man releases boa constrictors into every stream in the county. Too late to stop him, the damage is done. The snakes fill the streams to the brim. Water spills over and floods the countryside. All my labours for nothing – the snakes are coming and we are all being swept out to sea. But this time the great wall of water breaks the vicious circle and makes it a spiral.

Ring of light

My friend, have you heard the music of the spheres? In the Gulf Stream waters directly off that beach of carnage the beasts swim round and round in the mystic ring and I swim with them. Snakes, leopards, elephants, monkeys, sharks. Even a man on his motorcycle – the seawater doesn't hurt the engine, it restores it. Gulls, sparrows, hummingbirds circle and dive through wheeling clouds of horseflies and wasps. The ocean sparkles as the spheres sound one majestic chord: *harmonium*! In the split-second before the ring breaks and we revert to warring elements, I chant a prayer. The blood washes off my body. Praise to the life in all of us.

Report on the Eradication and Resurgence of Metamorphic Illness in the West, 1880–1998

Catherine Axelrad

At the beginning of the twentieth century, scientific advances and the triumph of rationalism finally led to the eradication of metamorphic illness, which had plagued mankind since antiquity. In the old days, the gods openly performed these sudden acts of transformation – no less spectacular than indefensible – which were enacted not for the public good, but for the instant gratification of desires as amoral as they were purely egotistic. Then, after the werewolves of the Middle Ages and the experiments of Perrault and Grimm in the seventeenth and eighteenth centuries, a new era was ushered in. Now the proud-hearted man, accompanied by his female companion walking just as proudly at his side, no longer had to call upon occult forces to freely express his desires, for these had as their sole objective the common good. And with the help of a brand-new therapeutic method, which subsequently went on to produce its proofs, the last surviving specimens of the old obscurantist world were treated on an apparently magic couch, the functioning of which, in reality, rested on the principle of microbial vaccination, simultaneously developed in France by Louis Pasteur. Thanks to these scientific discoveries, fittingly disseminated in the schools by a pedagogic method founded on principles of elementary hygiene, AME (ancient metamorphic epidemic) was at last conquered. In Europe, during the twentieth century, one encounters so few cases that it is scarcely possible to speak of an epidemic at all. Nevertheless, medical surveillance can never afford to relax, and these rare cases have been studied as attentively as possible; the present report aims to recall briefly their characteristics and consequences.

Four cases of AME command our attention. All four broke out in Europe, but at times and places so diverse as to make it very difficult to understand how the disease spread. It is certainly possible that the origin of the disease lay in the psychological make-up of the four, or rather five, individuals concerned, yet it is nonetheless extremely difficult, where these undoubtedly strong but all the same very different personalities are concerned, to uncover any common points with certainty.

We should first of all note an isolated case of AME which occurred in 1880 in Great Britain. Kept secret for as long as was possible, for fear that an epidemic might break out once again, the case of Mrs Tebrick was only studied forty years after it occurred by the Anglo-Saxon specialist Garnett – and the information contained in his report must obviously be treated with caution. Moreover, we are here dealing with a second-hand report, the case of Mrs T. having been brought to light by her husband, who only passed on to the specialist information which was deemed indispensable to his research. The report nevertheless calls upon a dozen eye-witnesses, though none of them seems capable of furnishing a convincing explanation of the causes of the attack. The transformation of Mrs T. into a fox having taken place during the very first days of the new year, the specialist tries to establish a connection between this annual shift and the attack of AME. Although this theory is largely unsubstantiated, the report remains of the greatest interest, and it is most deplorable that today it should be absolutely impossible to get hold of a copy in France.

In the twentieth century, strictly speaking, the first case of AME broke out in central Europe. The illness struck a man still in his youth, aged about thirty, living just before the First World War in the bosom of a nuclear family, made up of a hard paternal nucleus, a soft maternal proton and a feminine free electron, who was able to double in volume as a result of her brother's AME.

The subject, Samsa, whom we will here call GS, hadn't shown any unusual symptoms up until then which might have led one to suspect a primary infection. Neither, it would seem, had he expressed the least desire to become ameic. It is likely that the question interested him very little, indeed not at all. Having received only a fairly rudimentary level of education, it is possible that he had never even heard of the great epidemics of antiquity. Of sound health, despite a certain pulmonary frailty, he had almost never consulted a doctor. The wider family, too, shows no indication of a disposition towards AME, despite a tendency towards asthma on the maternal side.

The report devoted to the case of GS unveils a troubled sleep during the night preceding the transformation, unquiet dreams, the contents of which remain unknown, and a stubborn refusal on the part of the subject, during the first few hours following the attack of AME, to accept his new state. Less violent during the four months which followed, this refusal still remained sufficiently strong to affect the good-humoured and even-tempered disposition which GS had displayed up until then. Unable to cope with the attack, the subject seems to have let himself sink – in a spectacular and somewhat exaggerated manner – into a depressive anorexia which led to a rapid death.

The report devoted to his case presents little of interest: the writer brazenly refuses to tackle the case of GS within the framework of a global study of AME. More concerned with the purely spectacular than with the matter of science, he launches into a lengthy description of the subject's post-metamorphic state, and, worse still, goes on to devote endless irrelevant pages to the manner in which the subject's immediate family managed to adjust to the situation. Given the rudimentary level of analysis, it is not surprising that the writer – whose name science has not thought fit to preserve – doesn't venture even a single hypothesis on the origin of the attack of AME. It must be noted, however, that his report explicitly refers – by the very specific title which he has given it – to the great epidemics of antiquity. Obviously too affected by the case of GS to be able to study it with the necessary detachment, the writer has made use of singular language to discourse about the case, which allows us today to venture the following hypothesis: the transformation of the subject Samsa into a monstrous insect clearly represented, in 1915, an isolated attack of AME.

The upheavals created by the First World War not being of a kind to favour a return of the epidemic, it is some twenty years later, in France, at a time when it seemed to have been definitively put in check, that AME breaks out once again. This time it concerns a family case, two young children having been simultaneously subject to an attack of AME, and this case is sufficiently disturbing to attract the attention of the great French child specialist, Professor Aymé, who will dedicate a long report to it entitled *The Donkey and the Horse*. Here again, the reader will note the discreet reference to *The Golden Ass* of Professor Apuleius. However, the great interest of the case studied, apart from its familial nature, is that it takes place in a rural environment. It concerns two young girls from a peasant background, named Delphine and Marinette, who one night suffer a double transformation. The specialist having reconstructed the history of the attack of AME, it is henceforth possible to distinguish its different phases.

The subject, here plural, raises the possibility of a transformation before going to sleep. In the case of D/M, the first expresses the desire to become a horse while the second, she says, would prefer to become a little grey donkey with long ears. The symptoms observed on waking bear a marked resemblance to those noted in the case of Samsa twenty years before: bafflement, disbelief, despair. But this time we are in the presence of subjects both young and courageous, accustomed to life in the open air, who rather than shutting themselves up in a room to ponder their misfortune, do their best to adapt to their new conditions of existence. It should be noted that they are greatly encouraged here by the familial environment: while aware that these animals are none other than his own ameic children, the father sets them to work in such a way as to make profitable their presence at the farm. The severe physical punishments he inflicts on them when they display clumsiness are in reality part of a treatment which will enable AME to be conquered for the very first time. With typical peasant modesty, the father displays no pleasure when one morning he finds his children nesting in the straw of the stable. Above all, the report emphasises the disappointment experienced on discovering the loss of the two beasts of burden, and it unfortunately omits to examine the rationale of the process which allowed the reversal of AME. Yet this doesn't alter the fact that this victory represents a triumphant step in the eradication of the disease. The specialist later included his report in a collection of zoological observations devoted to a certain *Chat Perché*, whose sales still reach great heights, above all at end-of-year festivities.

The present study concerning itself only with transformations due to AME, we will leave out those caused by the Second World War. Moreover, these involve transformations more metaphoric than real, subjects acting *like* animals (which itself remains to be proven) in no case being identifiable with subjects having actually suffered an attack of AME. In France, after the victory of 1935 related by Professor Aymé, the disappearance of metamorphic illness seems final. Admittedly, since the fifties, with the development of film, AME is frequently represented on screen. The transformation of a man into a fly, for example, is one of those subjects tackled on several occasions by the movies. But it should be stressed that, contrary to those cases studied above, these transformations are of a purely fantastic nature and have no basis whatsoever in scientific observation. In fact, up until 1997, the eradication of AME had all the appearance of being complete, to the extent that the films dealing with the subject were in reality simply the refuge of a collective imagination in search of powerful sensations. In these circumstances, the announcement of a new case was scarcely going to catch the public's attention.

Once more, as in the cases studied by Garnett and Aymé, it concerns a female subject, whom we will call MD. A French-woman still in the flush of youth, from a privileged socio-cultural background, metamorphoses into a sow. The startling nature of the transformation is accentuated by the attitude of the subject. While the above victims of AME, being aware of the scandalous nature of their attack, endeavoured to vanish from memory, and confided the story of their experience to the ears of a specialist alone, the young woman in question refuses the help of science and advertises her monstrosity with a truly provocative audacity. Under the title *Sow What?* she relates in great detail, with the help of currently fashionable autobiographical procedures, the differ-ent stages of a classic case of AME, and seems to revel in her new state to the extent of refusing all medical treatment.

The consequences of this last case are many, and it is not impossible that they will prove to be of an as yet immeasurable gravity. Just as AME seemed to be conquered, suddenly it breaks out again in Europe, more precisely in a country where the health service and social-security provision have not yet been destroyed, and should accordingly facilitate the active prevention of attacks of this type. Moreover, in contrast to the previous cases, scarcely talked about during the lifetime of the subjects, and then with such discretion, the dramatic case of MD has had unusual repercussions. The power of the media has a lot to answer for here, as well as advertising executives and commercial interests. Profiting from this unexpected notoriety, accessory manufacturers of all kinds have decided to jump on the bandwagon. For two years now the market has been flooded with their merchandise: Samsa ties bearing the effigy of a cockroach, reversible headscarves with Mrs Tebrick on one side, and the handsome fox described by Professor Garnett on the other, rubber donkeys and horses for babies' baths, and porcelain plates decorated in the centre with a pretty pink sow.

These sociological developments would be without impor-tance if they did not contribute to the banalisation of AME, of which the sometimes mortal, often dangerous and always difficult-to-live-with character is carefully passed over in silence. At the moment of writing, a certain number of cases have just been brought to light in Great Britain, and one would have to be singularly blind not to see a connection between this resurgence of the epidemic and the latest case which has arisen in France. It is high time that governments got together to set up a common prevention programme; in fact, it is far from certain that our society could survive a new epidemic, one which would allow all and sundry, whenever they felt like it, to escape from their social circumstances by the use of procedures which stretch to the very limits accepted notions of honesty. The present report has no other object than to alert the authorities to the current problem, so as to maximise the chances of effective prevention of AME in the developed world.

Notes on contributors

Margaret Atwood is the author of more than twenty-five books of poetry, fiction and non-fiction, and her work has been translated into more than thirty languages. Her most recent novel, *Alias Grace*, was published in 1996. She lives in Toronto, Canada.

Catherine Axelrad was born in France in 1956. She has published four novels, including *L'homme au car VW blanc de ma jeunesse* (1988) and *La Varsovienne* (1990), which has been translated into English by Sacha Rabinovitch as *Warszawianka* (1994). She lives and works in Paris.

Rosalind Belben was born in Dorset in 1941. She is the author of several highly acclaimed novels, including *The Limit* (1974), *Dreaming of Dead People* (1979) and *Is Beauty Good* (1989).

A.S. Byatt taught at the Central School of Art before becoming a full-time writer. Her novel *Possession* won the Booker Prize and the *Irish Times*/Aer Lingus International Fiction Prize in 1990. She was appointed a CBE in 1990 and DBE in 1999.

Patricia Duncker teaches writing in the Department of English at the University of Wales, Aberystwyth. Her first novel, *Hallucinating Foucault* (1996), won the Dillons First

Fiction award and the McKitterick Prize. It has been translated into seven languages. She has also published a collection of short fiction, *Monsieur Shoushana's Lemon Trees* (1997). 'Sophia Walters Shaw' is one of a sequence, *Seven Tales of Sex and Death*, which examine the dark side of sexuality and power. Her most recent novel, *James Miranda Barry*, tells the story of the nineteenth-century colonial doctor, who was, among other things, a transvestite and a crack shot.

M.J. Fitzgerald was born in the United States and is a distinguished translator as well as a writer of fiction. Among her translations is Roberto Pazzi's prize-winning novel, *Searching for the Emperor*. 'Antiquity's Lust' is from a cycle of stories exploring themes from Ovid, on which she is currently at work. She lives in Minneapolis.

Paul Griffiths was born in Bridgend, Glamorgan, in 1947. He studied biochemistry at Oxford, and has worked since the 1970s as a music critic. Among his fictional writings are three novels – *Myself and Marco Polo*, *The Lay of Sir Tristram* and *a pale hope I* – and several librettos, including *The Jewel Box* (music by Mozart) and *What Next?* (Elliot Carter).

Gabriel Josipovici was born in Nice in 1940 and lived in Egypt from 1945 to 1956. He read English at Oxford, and is now Professor of English in the School of European Studies at the University of Sussex. His novels include *Contre-Jour* (1986), *The Big Glass* (1991), *Moo Pak* (1993) and *Now* (1998). Among his many critical works are *The Book of God* (1988), a study of the Bible, and the collection of essays *Text and Voice* (1993).

Nicole Ward Jouve was born in Provence, and has lived most of her adult life in the UK. Among her many books of fiction and criticism are *White Woman Speaks with Forked Tongue* (1991), a study of criticism as autobiography; *The Streetcleaner* (1986), a study of the Yorkshire Ripper case; and a novel in French, *L'Entremise*. Her most recent book is *Female Genesis: Creativity, Self and Gender* (1998). She is Professor of Literature and Women's Studies at the University of York. She is currently working on a family history.

Roger Moss was born in Cheltenham in 1951 and grew up in Croydon. He studied at Sussex University, and since 1977 has taught in the Literature Department at Essex University. Among his publications are two novels, *The Game of the Pink Pagoda* (1986), and *The Miraculous Birth, Secret Life and Lamentable Death of Mr Chinn* (1989). Since 1995, he has divided his time between the UK and Mauritius, where he is visiting Fellow in English at the university.

Suniti Namjoshi was born in India in 1941. Her first book of fiction, *Feminist Fables*, was published by Sheba Feminist Publishers in 1981; her second, *The Conversations of Cow*, by the Women's Press in 1985. Her most recent book is *Building Babel*. She lives in Devon.

Victoria Nelson was born in the United States and is an author of fiction and non-fiction. Her collection of essays on the supernatural grotesque, *The Secret Life of Puppets*, is forthcoming. She lives in California.

Cees Nooteboom was born in The Hague in 1933. He is a poet, the author of seven novels and ten travel books. His first international success was the Pegasus Prize for *Rituals*. More recently, for *A Berlin Notebook*, he was awarded the German Order of Merit. His other works, including *In the Dutch*

Mountains and *The Following Story*, have been translated into many languages.

Joyce Carol Oates is the author of many books including, most recently, the novel *Man Crazy* (1998), and contributes frequently to the *Times Literary Supplement*. She is Professor of Humanities at Princeton University.

Michèle Roberts is the author of eight highly acclaimed novels, including *Impossible Saints* (1997) and *Daughters of the House* (1992), which won the W.H. Smith Award and was short-listed for the Booker Prize. Half-English and half-French, she lives in London and Mayenne, France.

Ken Smith was born in 1938 in East Rudston, Yorkshire, the son of an itinerant farm labourer. He has worked in Britain and America as a teacher, barman, magazine editor, potato picker and BBC reader, and has been writer-in-residence at the University of Essex and Wormwood Scrubs. His selected poems, *The Poet Reclining*, is published by Bloodaxe. He lives in London.

Philip Terry was born in Belfast in 1962. He has lived in England and France, and currently teaches English at the University of Plymouth. A lipogrammatic novel, *The Book of Bachelors*, was recently published in the US as a special issue of *The Review of Contemporary Fiction*.

Marina Warner is a writer of criticism and fiction. She has published studies of myths and legends, in *Managing Monsters: Six Myths of Our Time* (BBC Reith Lectures, 1994) and *From the Beast to the Blonde: On Fairy Tales and their Tellers* (1994). *The Lost Father* was short-listed for the Booker Prize; her most recent novel is *Indigo*. A book about ogres and figures of fear, *No Go the Bogeyman: Scaring, Lulling and Making Mock* was published in 1998. The story 'Leto's Flight' is taken from a new novel, *The Leto Bundle*, on which she is currently hard at work.

Paul West is the author of some seventeen novels, most recently *Love's Mansion*, which won the Lannan Fiction Prize, and *Terrestrials*. His other honours include an award in literature from the American Academy and Institute of Arts and Letters. The government of France recently made him a Chevalier of the Order of Arts and Letters. He was educated at Oxford and Columbia Universities and now divides his time between New York and Palm Beach.

Acknowledgements

The following stories were specially commissioned for this collection, or appear here for the first time:

'The Elysium Lifestyle Mansions' © Margaret Atwood 2000
'Report on the Eradication and Resurgence of Metamorphic Illness in the West, 1880–1998' © Catherine Axelrad 2000, © this translation Philip Terry 2000
'Disjecta Membra' © Rosalind Belben 2000
'Arachne' © A.S. Byatt 2000
'Sophia Walters Shaw' © Patricia Duncker 2000
'Antiquity's Lust' © M.J. Fitzgerald 2000
'Leda' © Paul Griffiths 2000
'Heart's Wings' © Gabriel Josipovici 2000
'Narcissus and Echo' © Nicole Ward Jouve 2000
'*Hick, Hack, Hock*' © Roger Moss 2000
'Eurydice's Answer' © Suniti Namjoshi 2000
'A Bestiary of My Heart' © Victoria Nelson 2000
'The Sons of Angus MacElster' © Joyce Carol Oates 2000
'Hypsipyle to Jason' © Michèle Roberts 2000
'The Shell Game' © Ken Smith 2000
'Void' © Philip Terry 2000
'Leto's Flight' © Marina Warner 2000
'Nightfall on the Romanian Coast' © Paul West 2000

'Lessons', by Cees Nooteboom, is reprinted from *The Following*

Story, translated by Ina Rilke, © Cees Nooteboom 1991, © in the English translation Harvill 1993. Reproduced by permission of the author and The Harvill Press.

Thanks to all the contributors, especially Paul Griffiths, Gabriel Josipovici, Roger Moss and Victoria Nelson, and, for supportive and entertaining correspondence, A.S. Byatt and Marina Warner.

I would like to thank also friends and colleagues at the University of Plymouth for their invaluable support, in particular Jeff Collins, Robert Gee, Tony Lopez, Alan Munton, Susan Purdie and Anna Trussler.

I am indebted to the Ronald Duncan Trust (established to disseminate the work of the late Ronald Duncan and to promote new writing) for financial support. Special thanks to Briony Lawson.

Finally, I would like to acknowledge the constant support of friends and family: Ann Davey, Sarah Kember, Rose Scoular, Molly and Arthur Terry.

P.T.